THE

FARM GIRL'S

OPERA

JONATHAN LOVEJOY

For Andrea

*J*oy and gladness shall be found therein—
Thanksgiving, and the voice of Melody...

Isaiah 51:3

CREATION

1

After it is done, he'll decide when to take his own life.

Back in the heat of summer he had already planned it. The deed was all but decided until one afternoon, Vera Evans approached him after work, impressing on him how glad she was he had come to their farm. And how glad she was to see him every day. Anguished, she had pulled him into the house and given him a yellow layer cake with chocolate icing. She told him to take it home to his wife.

"I really want her to have this now, Chris, and you tell me how she likes it, okay?"

The cake was thrown in the kitchen garbage can.

He had sat in the living room in the dark, listening to my radio playing from in the bedroom. I can't do it, he had thought. He survived the long Sunday, and was back at work earlier than ever Monday morning. At lunch time, his heart leapt when he saw Vera walking to his truck.

There is always that vague fearfulness before a reunion, that it'll fall short of expectations. But they had to restrain themselves. Smiling. Laughing. Looking like they wanted to take a day trip together to be alone, to walk and talk privately. And not once for the rest of that day did he think about the little gray house. Or of its thin, sick prisoner.

Maybe Vera Evans had kept us both alive.

But that was months ago.

He steps out of the truck into the late December afternoon. The weather is just cold enough to foreshadow the coming winter. The sky is as clear as glass, and the sun burns like a ball of fire at the bottom of it. The world above him is already a deeper blue. After sunset, the west will tinge pale orange from end to end.

He is an executioner. Charged with carrying out this evil. But even the condemned get a last meal. And perhaps a last glimpse of the sunset.

The house looks uninhabitable. At sundown its hard to imagine a living soul would dare try to spend a night here. The closer he gets to it, the colder the world seems, and the more terrified he becomes.

The Fear of Death.

It is universal. Except to those who have gone 'round the bend, to where the insane gather to whisper promises of another world. But when the pain of living is long and heavy, death reaches out, extending an icy hand even to the normal and well adjusted. Their delicate balance may become overwhelmed, until they begin to wonder about the Unknown Journey.

And there are those who have been a victim from the beginning, who once craved life and the joy of living, but have reached the end of the proverbial rope. To them, the long road is a dead end, leading only to a fearful place. The only place they can go. The place where they belong. It pulls them, it draws them like a magnet. And then the terror is two fold: there is the fear of living another day—

And the greater fear of death itself. One they are willing to confront because it is singular, and will end in due time.

Christopher Adam Peele walks in terror. Towards the only escape from the pain of living. Towards the evil in the gray house, which had sought to destroy us from the start, and has brought us to the end of our long, dark journey.

His breath quickens with every step. The cold he feels is as much from the evaporating sweat as from the energy he tries to deny.

Its just a house…

He knows, he *feels,* that there might be an unspoken, undealt with Truth about his own existence—

That *he* is alive, because *I* am alive.

He fumbles with the front door until it is unlocked and opened. The dreary space feels like a chamber of horrors, with its ancient wooden floors and aged walls, gray with a century of misery.

Footsteps…

One pair, heavy and clunky, slicing through the walls with force and power. The other, light and fearful, drifting pitiful weakness into the cold air. The air in the house is poisonous. It has the sickly sweet odor of death. Usually he goes straight to the kitchen to rest. To sometimes cook and eat dinner and read the newspaper. He'll think about his Lady, and how he wishes things could be different. Every once in a while—and he hates himself for this—he will imagine, or even *desire,* that John Evans was out of the picture. What he feels for Vera is deeper than infatuation. She has kept him alive.

But this, he had decided, was the prisoner's final sunset.

In fearfulness, Chris unlocks the bedroom door—

And there she is, waiting for him.

Oh, the curse of humanity.

2

My cheeks are drawn into my ghostly face. My big, pleading eyes seem too large for my tiny head, and they are darkened, from a year of erratic sleep and malnutrition. My clothes hang off me as if they were made for a different person. The voluptuous shape is gone. Even the gigantic bosoms are diminished. I am a small, bony hipped version of myself, like one who has endured a bout with a long, painful illness. A wispy, white waif of exhausted, extreme melody.

But oddly enough, I think I look better.

"Can I have something to eat?"

A whirlwind comes from that whispery voice. The cold, razor wind. Acid guilt, slashing and burning him.

Come out here, he says.

I don't know what to do. Is it a trick?

Its okay, he says. Come on.

Not once in *twelve months* have I stepped out of the bedroom and its adjacent bathroom. After only a few weeks I had given up hope. Deciding I would live as long as I could, until my body went to sleep for the last time. But I kept waking up. Condemned to survive. To endure the pain of living.

But maybe, there is compassion.

And mercy.

"I didn't try to get out, Chris. I swear to God and Jesus I didn't."

I know, he says. Come out here.

I step into the living room as if it were rigged with hidden traps. I'm as nervous as ever, but I keep walking. We march that last, long mile through the kitchen. Then he shows me to the door, and we walk onto the back porch.

The world is exactly as I remember. It is cold enough to be uncomfortable, and the trees are ugly and gray. Dead leaves are everywhere, and there are ungathered pecans scattered over the yard. The coop is still there, but I can't see the chickens.

I don't remember the tree being that enormous. The thing scares me when I look at it. Past the Flowering Tree, at the end of the big backyard rests the empty field, beyond which is still the small woods.

In a violet sky, the sun shines like an orange disk. Like some weird, cosmic door to another universe. Chris ushers me off the porch, motioning towards the orange sun, which is millions of miles away, and still close enough to touch the horizon. I feel so strange being outside. Dreamlike. I had existed in a small room for four, lonely seasons, but it is as though I've stepped out of one winter, slept in pain and hunger, and stepped back into the same winter I had come from.

Last December seems like yesterday, and like ten years ago.

Above the evening, Venus rules celestial beauty. The world is vast, sharp, and clear as crystal. It is a place with the lonely, dusty smell of approaching winter--filled with deep, rich colors and crisp, fresh country air. There are even a few birds still out and about. How I wish it were summer! When the wind is warm on my face, and the air is filled with sounds from the woods and the grass, and the birds are so plentiful that they keep me from being lonely!

Oh, Heavenly Father

Protect me from the nights in winter.

I think about another winter on the cold, hard bedroom floor. I'm suddenly very sad and afraid. I want to turn and look at my husband, but I don't want him to see the emotion. I fold my arms, staring at the orange ball in the sky, and the tiny white one. Watching them both become quivery. I tuck my lips in and take long, quiet breaths through my nose. But the tears come anyway. I am content, though, that he hasn't seen me crying. And neither do I see the look on his face I have feared…

The tears are falling anyhow, so I blink to clear my vision. When I do, it triggers my ability…

From within my mood pours sound that only I can hear. Heavy, somber chords of slow orchestral flow. Inspired by my sad freedom, the pre-winter chill, and the beauty of the first sunset I have seen in over a year. I notice that the inspiration is extreme. A piece more mature and profound than any of my previous melodies. A single andante. A *Lamentation,* for Violin and Orchestra.

I've been scribbling trifles all year. But *this*.

I watch.

I listen—

Then the sun is gone.

3

*W*hat do you want to eat?

There is a pleasant, mildly astonished look on my face. *Maybe its finally over*, I think, sitting at the kitchen table, staring pitifully at an unopened package in the refrigerator.

"Can I have the ham?"

Would you rather I go buy something?

"The ham is fine. It's what I want."

Macaroni with Vermont sharp white would be to my liking. But the ham will have to do. He opens the package for me, and I devour the slices one by one. He retrieves my favorite beverage and sits it on the table…

Orange juice

I eat and drink so fast that I choke a little, and begin to cough.

Choke—

An epiphany!

The thought gives him a chill. Already he can picture it. He leaves me at the table and skulks into the bathroom. He closes the door, standing in the dark. Trembling. Shaking like a cold addict needing a fix and a blanket.

I don't want to do it, he says. Please, help me not to do it…

There is an old saying that goes '*My prayers hit the ceiling last night.*' His are slamming into the bathroom ceiling and bouncing around the room like a crazy-ball. If there *is* a God, Chris knows He hasn't heard a single word. He feels abandoned. And the pain is too great.

He can't do it anymore. He can't go on living.

But *I* am going to die first.

My footsteps appear in the living room…then the bedroom…then at the bathroom door.

I step up to him without fear, putting my spindly arms around his waist.

mm t keyu.

"I didn't hear you." My voice is low. Almost whispery.

"I'm going to *kill* you."

The types of fear are many, and uniquely distinguished. My speech is taken. I can only blink, while gazing. This time the words ring truthful and are laced with sorrow. I can only look and stare and search, trying to find something, anything that tells me this is only another fearful, empty promise. But his eyes are more merciless than I have ever seen them.

I open my mouth.

But there are no words.

Fill the tub, he says. Until I tell you to stop.

Reluctantly, I turn the faucet on. Pleas for mercy are stuck in my throat. Something won't allow me to speak.

The stopper isn't in. And he hasn't said anything about it—

He simply reaches down and puts it in himself.

My vision starts to blur again. But tears are without meaning…

I watch the bathtub slowly fill with water.

Where is my salvation? My deliverance?

Perhaps, it has taken form.

Boldly I put my arms around him, whispering, pleading with my eyes. With my soul.

"I don't want to die Chris please I don't want to die…"

Turn it off, he says.

I whimper while reaching down, turning off the water.

He takes a firm hold of my neck. It is thin.

"Chris I'm scared. I want to stay…I'm scared, Chris…"

He eases me backward—and downward…

"I don't want you to do it…please don't do it…"

In a sudden burst of strength, he dunks me backward, splashing me hard into the water. I thrash wildly, grabbing and clawing for help, splashing water all over the floor.

He feels my weakness. I have no more strength than a child. My hands tremble, grabbing at his face, pulling hard on his shirt…

My neck is fragile. Wet hair touches his arm…

I stop moving. But my hands…my hands are pulling… until one of his buttons pops loose—

The splashing starts again. I claw his arm. And then he hears me, underneath the water…

A scream!

I am dead.

Drowned. He remembers the wet. Sickening plop my body made when he dropped it to the floor. He can remember the bones in my body, poking against him, and the trembling weakness in my muscles. He remembers that his sinuses were hurting, and everything had looked bluish green. And he knows the rest of his plan is already shot to pieces. No way is he going to kill himself.

That is the hardest part of killing.

The country nights are so dark. The trees are black, skeletal silhouettes. The quiet is oppressive, like being inside a vacuum. Chris is shivering. The water makes it feel colder than it really is.

He remembers the water. There had been water everywhere. The tub had never looked that big before. The water had a beautiful, greenish hue. Oddly enough, the thought of it makes him thirsty.

Vera...

The thought of his own death is suddenly too terrible. Because of what he suspects. Because of what happens to condemned souls when bodies die.

He looks out the truck window, into the eerie glow from the black house. And what he sees makes him draw in a breath...

A *dark shape* wanders aimlessly towards the window, turns, and moves slowly into the kitchen.

That compulsion hits. The need to take a closer look. He gets out of the truck, never taking his eyes off the otherworldly light from the window. He hurries across the yard, hopping onto the porch and peering in through the window.

Across the dusty living room floor is a trail of watery footprints.

He opens the door like a madman, pretending to confront this oddity with courage. Like one does when taking the fool's step into a dark room late at night...

He suppresses the panic and wisely, or *unwisely,* chooses not to follow the water trail into the kitchen. He instead follows his bewildered gaze through the bedroom prison to the bathroom floor.

But there is only water.

And now, the soft, shuffling footsteps of a *water spirit*—

The shuffling moves from the kitchen, towards the living room. He sees a shadow appear, and then…

A pale, thin black-eyed thing with long, wet strands of black hair turns the corner and glides towards him.

It opens its mouth, its eyes bulge, it reaches unusually long fingers out for his throat.

He makes a quick, pitiful wailing noise, as the silver ice slides his blood. This is the only fear that matches the fear of Death…

He backs involuntarily into the bathroom and slams the door. The shuffling footsteps continue. They get closer, until they stop outside the door…

Soft scratching, and knocking sounds.

A watery spirit.

"Christopher…" A raspy, gurgly sound. He is going to Hell *tonight*…

"It's me honey," I say softly. "You don't have to be afraid. I'm alright." My voice is weak….

But it is me.

He opens the door, and I hug him as if *he* needs to be comforted. He hugs my dripping, soaking wet body—as though I had been on a long journey, but had come back to him.

I love you.

What manner of woman?

By what miracle!

The drowning water is released—and I am released from my winter's prison.

Tonight I don't have to sleep on the floor.

Sleep…

It finally came. Taking us both away from this nightmare. But Chris is taken into another one.

The images he endures are so vivid, so Hellishly real—

"Elizabeth! *Elizabeth, please help me!*"

I awake to a human alarm. Chris is screaming, flailing and thrashing around like a madman. I am afraid at first, cowering in terror. It is a loud, high pitched scream. It's like he can see, like he can *feel*, everything from that dream world he was just in.

I gather what little strength I have, fighting through the flailing arms until I have him around the neck, whispering loudly in his ear.

"It's me baby, I'm here. It's me, Chris. Elizabeth is here, honey. It's me…"

My voice is the remedy—his screaming finally calms into something like loud whimpering. I continue the soft reassurances—whispering, kissing and rubbing his face and hair. Before too long, his eyes return to sanity, and he is able to see me in the dark house.

I rest his head on my chest. With my hands and my hair, I wipe his sweaty face. He stares up at me in the dark, bewildered, and in cosmic disbelief and gratitude. For a long time, I softly kiss every inch of his face, while gently massaging his chest, shoulders and arms.

Because you hurt Elizabeth—

The words send a painful reminder through his leg muscles. He tenses and twitches against an acid burning in his right leg, that is *spreading*, to his entire lower body. As severe as the pain is, it's only a reminder. A shadow of what just happened to him a few minutes ago.

Pain. Every muscle. Every bone is reminded.

It makes him hold me tighter. My voice, my skin, my hair, everything about me seems cool and soothing to his body.

He is more than an abuser. He had tortured, and then became a murderer—

But now he understands that he never knew what fear, pain and suffering were.

He sees me as his guardian angel. His protector. He rests quietly while I hum one of my softest, purest inspirations in the dark. Afterwards I hum the melody from an old hymn I remember from childhood:

Jesus, keep me near the Cross
There, a precious Fountain
Free to all, a healing Stream
Flows from Calvary's Mountain.

In the Cross, in the Cross
Be my Glory ever.
Til my raptured soul shall find Rest—
Beyond the River.

As he drifts back to sleep, I feel a total peace. Maybe this time my prayers are answered.

It is something that I know.

Because you hurt Elizabeth.

The reason was clear. It echoed through him, until they were the only words his mind could hear. And each time I was there when he woke up, to pull him out of that horrible place. A guilty place? Maybe. But the guilt had taken life and form in his dreams. For six, Hellishly vivid nights in a row he barely slept a wink. He hardly ate or spoke, and hardly left my side.

He is lucky. The week of Christmas brings no work to the Evans' farm. Vera hasn't seen him in this condition, and for that, he's grateful. A couple of weeks ago, she had invited him for Christmas dinner. He was glad that he lied, telling her I would be too sick. Vera had wondered how anyone could be so sickly.

But maybe it hadn't been such a lie after all.

Sometimes it strikes him funny, that Vera doesn't even know his wife's name.

"Where are you goin'?"

"Do you want a tree?" he asks, putting his boots on.

"A Christmas tree?" *To chop up and throw in the fireplace when you get angry?*

"Yeah."

"Do you even feel like going out today?"

He finishes sliding into his boots, then goes to the closet for his blue and black flannel.

"I've been in here long enough. I might as well buy a tree while I'm out."

"But its Christmas Eve."

No answer.

"A Christmas Tree..."

What is the world comin' to?

"How long will you be gone?"

"Hmm?"

"How long will you be gone?"

"At least a couple of hours. I'm just gonna take my time, breathe a little fresh air. Don't worry, I'm coming back. I promise."

I watch him brush his wavy brown hair. Truthfully, it hardly needs it. I touch him on his arm. "Does your head still hurt?"

"A little. Why don't you come with me?"

"No thank you." I say it emphatically.

Chris slips into his denim jacket. He picks up his keys and cuts a pitiful, guilty glance.

"I'll be back in a couple of hours."

I follow him to the living room door. After opening it he stops, and kisses me firmly on the lips.

"Come back soon. Chris?"

"Yeah?"

"Get lots of white lights, and as many red and green as you can."

"Okay."

He shakes his head and steps into the yard. Lights. I know if he has to drive to ten stores, he'll find me those red and green lights. I watch him drive down the long dirt road. I watch him until he is gone.

Christmas Eve. Good luck finding a tree. And lights.

Its been a year since I've watched him drive anywhere. Last Christmas Eve and Christmas day, I was in the closet. Howling from pain and hunger, until he finally had mercy and let me out. He had untied me, fed me and helped me bathe.

It is midmorning. I am hungry again. In only a week I've put on five pounds. I go back in the kitchen to make myself a grilled cheese sandwich. Or two.

That's right. Fill 'em back up, piggy.

Laughter. A woman's quiet, sinister voice. But I don't care.

I am hungry.

And what of my mother? Barbara Jean [Coletti]?

Did she steal quietly away into the night, to love and happiness in the arms of a stranger? Was she swept away in a romantic whirlwind of champagne and diamonds, living as a wealthy, beautiful woman of leisure, with a luxurious villa in Passy, strolling the streets of Paris?

Maybe.

Or maybe those same horrific nightmares, in some variation or another, had come to visit her one night, when she had decided to kill her twenty one year old daughter. Maybe they had terrified her so completely that she had run out of the house, quietly into the night, trying to sneak away from the horrors that she thought were real. Sneaking away, into the eternal safety of the thick, black woods.

Maybe.

Chris has broken his promise. He is gone for more than two hours. And for every minute past that point I have worried. But after a while the truck comes revving into the yard, and I'm on the porch waiting for him. He's surely outdone himself. Laying proudly in the back of that black truck is a seven foot Frasier Fir. Fragrant. Sturdy. World famous, I think, for its perfect shape and beauty. The so-called Cadillac of Christmas Trees.

It's going to take up the whole living room.

His heart leapt when he saw me. I'm still on the porch, staring at the tree like its about to jump out of the truck bed and chase me into the house. He gets out and smiles. For the first time in a long while, he feels pretty good.

I hurry to the truck, then gaze as he does most of the work. But I finally get a hold of one end, and we manage to get it into the house. The big tree leans tall in the corner while he goes back to gather the stand, the lights and the decorations. I stare as he slides the tree onto the metal spike, standing it upright.

It's a big tree for our tiny living room. But the farmer has done well. It easily passes for a perfect tree. A shape of remarkable symmetry.

"It's beautiful."

7

*T*he house is filled with the sweet, pleasant aroma from the Christmas tree, courtesy of the Great Appalachian Forest. New Frasiers are lifted from the southern Appalachians every year and shipped all over the country. A few of them even find their way into this eastern county to those lucky enough to know which scraggly lot might have some. Chris had driven past it many times this month. Three weeks ago, those trees were the last thing on his mind.

He is thinking about me as I prepare our Christmas Eve dinner. A large, tender turkey breast with gravy, my homemade stuffing (the one good thing my mother left me), country ham seasoned green beans, candied sweet potatoes and a pumpkin custard pie. Soft, buttered rolls are nearby, waiting to join our little cooking feast.

On the table is a thin, clear vase with a single red rose. There are cookies, bags of fruit, and chocolate candy of all kinds, including chocolate covered crème drops, which I refuse to taste, because I wouldn't be able to stop. And there is even a small bag of so-called Christmas candy—those multicolored things that taste so bad no person has ever eaten more than one per year.

Our little house is alive with Christmas. Even the radio is in the spirit of things. The selections have been extraordinary. For once. We're in another world. An unfamiliar place. There is no violence, fear, or sorrow. There's only a faint, distant sadness. A quiet, intangible longing for the end of the long journey.

We are lonely.

She feels a lot better, he thinks. She arranged those lights for hours. She said that green is *Creation*, red is *Redemption*, and white is *Salvation*.

I don't think my heart can take the strain of another dream, he thinks. And Dear Lord, my head hurts. And that noise in my ears…

A few minutes later, a cool hand touches his face, pulling him back from the edge of sleep. I smile and sit down on his lap, feeling lighter than I used to. Not as curvy.

"It won't be ready for about an hour", I say. "I love that tree, Chris. And the candy, too." I ate only one piece. A yellow piece that looked like sweet lemon perfection.

It tasted like Pine-Sol.

"Can't we turn the tree back on? It's almost dark outside."

"In a few minutes. Do me a favor, honey, go get me those aspirin. My head's killing me."

"Okay. How's your hearing?"

I walk to the bathroom, retrieving a tiny red and white bottle of headache pills.

"The same. The noise is still there. It's so loud honey. Its driving me crazy."

"I'm sure it'll be gone in a few days." I give him three of the pills and a small glass of water. He takes all three in succession.

"What about the tree, Chris?" I am like a child. He wishes he could feel better for me. But truthfully, he feels like a sick man.

Suddenly, he remembers something…

"Wait right here. I've got something in the truck. Don't plug the tree in yet."

"Alright." I start my kitten walk again, behind him to the door.

"No, you stay in here. Go in the kitchen. I'll be right back."

The door closes gently in my face. I obey him and go to the kitchen. I can hardly believe it, but there is no apprehension or fear in my heart. There is only a strange, dreamy feeling of hopeful anticipation. A stir of happiness. An echo of joy itself.

He soon returns. I hurry into the living room to see what Chris Kringle has done. To get a look at what new kind of gift I'm getting from my husband. He sits the last of the rather large boxes down on the floor. On the sides are pictures of curious contraptions. Sleek and modern, full of buttons. Words about a three disc sub-phonic something or another, guarded by two imposing boxes bigger than a small child. Mozart, one. Rossini, the other.

"Oh, and here you go."

He hands me the plastic bag, and I slide the contents out. I cannot believe my eyes. My body has a sudden flash of memory, a spark of exhilaration. The thrill I'll get from the diamond earrings tomorrow morning is nothing compared to this.

"I remembered you mentioned it a couple of times," he says. "You kept saying how you wished it would come back on the radio."

I haven't taken my eyes off of what came out of that bag. The bag is now empty, and laying desolate on the floor.

"That's why it took me so long to get back," he says. "I had to drive all the way to Rocky Mount to find 'em. There were two recordings of that Opera, so I bought 'em both. Oh and I got you one with *overtures*, too. By that same composer, see?"

No matter how small, the right present is a rare and special thing.

A perfect gift.

He knows me, and knows I can't say a word until the shock and emotion has passed. I lay my present aside, and give my husband a long, quiet hug.

"Let's get those lights," he says. We rush around the little house, turning off the lights. The house is nearly black inside. Through the window, the sky still has plenty of violet to offer on this Christmas Eve.

He takes hold of the power chord and plugs it in the wall...

We stand together. Quietly.

The green, red and white lights come together in fine tradition, revealing the perfect shape of the Christmas tree. The shiny decorations and branches reflect the light, so that the tree is softly lit from top to bottom. The three colors blend into a single power-- that cuts through the darkness of our world like a sword.

And when we both look at the star, we are filled with a sense of peace. And love for one another.

"*B*e glad you never had children, Vera. Especially a daughter. The drama in that girl's life…she's not even going to marry that medical student now. And she's been in classes for one semester, and already she's met a professor from another school…"

They are in the garishly decorated kitchen. In private. And then, Amazing Grace Harrison herself walks in. A Nordstrom's mannequin in cable knit cashmere—very thin, very attractive, and very blonde. A hobgoblin of Harwich Acres.

Like mother, like daughter.

"Is everything alright, Mother?"

"Yes dear, everything's fine." A kiss. "Oh, Kate, I was just telling Vera how well you did this semester."

"Are you still in classical studies, Kate?" Vera asks.

"Yes. I think I might like to teach."

"College was a great time. Vera its too bad you didn't get a chance to go."

"I always regretted it. I think I would have loved to have studied art, or fashion…"

"Kate and I both minored in fashion," says Brenda. "But you couldn't have gone to college anyway, honey. You got married in high school."

"I never did get a chance to finish."

"Well, you've done fine, haven't you? John's cornfields are all over the place…"

Vera knows how Brenda feels about farmers. But still, she is trapped. She is just the sexy-pretty, upper middle class lapdog Brenda needs. Keeps her ego nice and fat.

"Kate, how are your piano lessons coming?" her mother asks.

"Well, if I could find more time to practice. It's a lot harder than it looks."

"Maybe you can play a Christmas song for us," Brenda says.

"Kate, are you still going overseas this summer?"

"I wouldn't miss it for the world."

"I always knew you'd be successful," says Vera. "You were always so busy."

Busy getting pregnant

"Vera, get me the butter," orders Brenda. The Lady obeys like a whipped house girl.

"Is Adrian going to Paris with you?" she asks.

Kate begins to whisper, and walks rudely into the pantry. Brenda follows her in without a word to her guest. Their whispering is loud.

At the dinner table later that evening, they are both brutal to their guest. They erect an invisible cage around her, waiting until the fifty thousand other people are in their own little conversations.

"Are you feeling alright, Honey," asks Brenda. "We were worried about you. Your eyes look so dark and tired."

"Well, to be honest, I…"

"Farmer's wives do have to get up early don't they," Kate says. Vera can see that Kate wants to laugh.

"Yes. We do."

"I've got to hand it to you and John," says Brenda. "A lot of farmers around here have gone bankrupt. It's only going to get tougher for you."

"Mother, you haven't said a word about my dress."

"It's the prettiest one you've ever worn. Don't you think so, Vera?"

"It's lovely. But all of her dresses are."

This is true, if designer popularity determines the loveliness of a dress. It doesn't.

"They're expensive though," says Kate.

"I've always liked that dress you're wearing, Vera. Kate was telling me that she liked it the last time she saw it."

The Lady smiles.

An electric twinge flashed every nerve in her body. They had just dropped a bomb on her favorite dress. Crème--with a subtle, midnight blue flower pattern, matching her navy pumps, which shares with her Klein crystal timepiece the designer name she loves. And the truth is, they hadn't seen the dress since last Autumn, over a year ago. With the fancy, overspiced food gnawing at her stomach and the phony, overbearing hostess clawing at her nerves, Vera begins to wonder how much more she can take. Brenda even mentions the piano again, and has the gall to ask Vera if she'd ever played before…

It went on like that for the rest of the Christmas Night. Until she felt like she had stepped face first into a thorny bouquet of holly leaves. When she finally got the courage to think up an excuse to leave, they had both acted like her departure was their sweetest sorrow.

"Vera don't leave yet. We're just getting started…"

Compared to Vera's grain farming husband, Conrad Harrison's pathetic attempts at a fortune had already failed. John Evans' bankbook had to be lifted with a crane it was so heavy. But not even Vera had known that bankruptcy papers had been filed to protect old Conrad's diminishing assets. A failed business man, now commuting to work at an office every morning over two hours away.

If Brenda was secretly jealous, what did it matter? She was supposed to have been Vera's best friend. But Vera noticed that sometimes she treats her like a dog. It happens whenever Brenda feels threatened. That's when she will reach a ghostly hand into Vera's empty womb and torment her. Then she will drag up Miss Prissy Puffed Orpington, miss preppy-pretty blonde haired, Tri Delta pledging, Aspen slope skiing, Vermont inn staying, Swiss Colony cheesecake munching inch of make up caked on, type-A personality freak of nature, and throw it all in Vera's face. And tonight she had brought Miss Prissy in on it. At one point, Vera had actually gotten angry with herself, because they had again succeeded in making her want to cry.

Brenda had been Vera's so called best friend. Vera had confided in her for years about things she'd never even told her husband. But dear God, oh dear God in Heaven… she had *never* mentioned that angel eyed farmhand. Nor that ghostly, raven haired angel in her dreams.

Sometimes there is no where to go. No one to turn to.

"You're not fallin' out on me are you?" John asks.

"I'm just restin'."

Good old John. Her real best friend.

"Ole Conrad and Brenda outdid it this year, didn't they?"

Vera is suddenly nauseated.

"That food was disgusting. Who serves shrimp cocktail at a Christmas dinner? I hardly ate anything and it still gave me a stomach ache."

If I hear another word about Conrad and Brenda Harrison…

"So that's what's wrong," he says. Pitifully.

"I'm fine, sweetie. Really. I'm just done with this day, that's all. I'll be glad when we get home."

After a while the car finished its dark, back roads journey. They leave Oldsmobile luxury behind, starting up the long walkway to the back steps. She is glad to finally be home.

Vera's heart was heavy as she stared at the thousands of bright winter stars. She thought fondly of the angel eyed young man, hoping that he and his wife were safe… and filled with joy of the Christmas season.

9

*P*eace and Joy.

"Pace e Gioia…"

Count Almaviva, disguised as a music teacher, repeats this to Don Bartolo over and over, to trick his way into his home. Why? Love, of course. For a few precious moments with the lovely Rosina. But the duplicitous Don Bartolo is her fierce guardian, and plans to marry her himself.

Perhaps, love will prevail.

This is the present course in the farm girl's opera. But I am fast asleep while the disc plays. The music activates my imagination, and I find myself in the red and gold opera house. Watching the lover's comedy unfold. The dream has come once before, but I missed the action last time, because I never took my eyes off the conductor and the musicians. As amazing as the singers are, I learned after only one hearing:

That *a truly great operatic performance revolves around the orchestra…*

Chris' shopping hands were on fire that Christmas. He had gathered recordings by one Galliera and one Varviso. The two classics were sitting there neglected. Waiting. I bided my time, until the need to listen overwhelmed me. Then I finally undertook that epic mission—as Olympian as any of the Twelve Labours themselves—

Removing the plastic from the compact discs!

But I managed it. When Varviso's orchestra slid into the *Piano pianissimo*—pitched upward just so—when it was first introduced to my ears, I put my hand over my mouth, shaking my head in disbelief…

Harmonies from that strange world, where music has shape and color. A *devil* of a composition…so far beyond mere talent that it made me laugh. But when I read in the notes that the score had been written in two weeks, I said to myself *"that sounds about right."*

Impossible. Unless that lightning inspiration were to hit my mind, like it has every so often. My notebooks contain a few of these. Brilliant, fascinating neoclassical gems. In every shape. And every color.

April 4ᵗʰ

"The idea that much of Rossini's grandest music begs <u>transcription</u> plagues me both night and day—this

sacrilege being mainly in the form of single, three movement pieces for solo instruments with full orchestral accompaniment..."

April 9th

"Rossini possesses all the talent of a great composer, but none of the pretense. The result is music that is always fun to listen to. But I cannot deny that the fabric of it is woven from the same genius passed from Vivaldi to Mozart, perhaps even superior to Bach and Beethoven, but lacking the discipline of extreme self criticism, or the benefit of German technical mastery..."

I never attended the sixth grade. But so many times, I think my own inspiration has been complete enough, that it might baffle every composer, conductor and musicologist in the world.

A *Fire Sonata* for Strings. An *Italian Overture* in Blood. A *Winter Concerto* for Piano and Orchestra. A *Lamentation* for Violin and Orchestra.

Carmen Angelina Coletti.

Julliard, weep.

I wake up, well rested from my opera nap. I yawn and stretch, then stroll outside to tend my chickens. Something I always save til the early afternoon. Something to do.

Inside this little house, I have survived a decade of winters. I hope this is the first spring of a new life.

"Here, chick, chick," I say, tossing the feed to the ground. "There you go."

Three months. For two of them, my nerves were on a razor's edge. Once I had even lost my composure, and began to cry from phantom terrors. When he touched me I had yipped like a pinched puppy, then cried in his arms. For eight weeks after it ended, I stood stiff and ready whenever he was in the house. As if we were always on the edge of violence.

I know that he's stopped. He hasn't even threatened me. It's as though he's too afraid and guilty to touch me.

So why then am I so uneasy?

At night he takes walks down the dirt road. He never used to do that. He asks me to sit in his lap and read Scriptures to him. He doesn't let me out of his sight. I can't even go to the bathroom without him standing at the door waiting for me. Listening. If I open my mouth to speak, he's there to catch the first word. He acts like he's afraid of me. Like he's scared to death. Is he sorry, or is he guilty? He never used to come home at lunch. But he's been home for lunch twenty seven times in the three months since Christmas.

My winter aches and pains are gone. No more open sores, or cold, hungry nights on the floor. And my jittery, neurasthenic nerves have subsided. Some.

I watch the chickens scratch and peck at the corn. I remember how they used to jab and pick on the speckled one, until I got them trained not to. It took a long time. Lots of brooms to their little heads. Lots of water. Several light shoves with my feet. But they don't seem to do it anymore.

Miraculously, none of them died last year. For some reason, Chris kept feeding them when I was away.

I finish feeding my pets, then put the feed bucket back in its place. They have been such good company. Every one of the poor things was smaller when I first came out to feed them this winter. But they were alive.

The weather is too chilled to be comfortable. Even in April, these Carolina mornings still shock with an icy fingertip.

Back inside, the lovely Rosina's music lesson is over. Her and the Count's destinies are tumbling steadily along. Soon there will be a violent storm. Set to chords of manic ingenuity. Sent to complicate matters a bit.

It's time to start dinner. I have to peel and slice the potatoes, and prepare the fresh picked beans. So I gather the potatoes, sit down at the table and start peeling.

There is no relief from the worry. Sometimes, I allow myself to think the one thought, the one question that haunts the back of my mind all day, every day, and up into the night.

How long will it last?

10

A back country road is risky anyway.

But in the springtime…

The old tractor in front of him had probably never seen the top side of twenty miles per hour in its life. The rickety old tiller hangs down behind it, spreading rusty claws across the entire width of the road. A few inches lower and there would be a noisy shower of sparks. The tractor barely moves to let the oncoming cars pass. Chris regrets his decision to hang back, until the dusty thing finds a field to turn into. After the fifth century, it finds another road to hog. It turns away, hauling its old passenger to who knows where. The old man on the tractor couldn't have cared less for the black truck and its young driver, who had been following behind him for so long.

Chris takes a leisurely detour to the old country store not too far from the house. Gathering seedless white grapes and a bag of so-called red ones, which aren't red at all, but are black. He pays for them quickly and strolls back out to his truck, sorry that he didn't have more conversation for the old man behind the counter. The old man should have talked more. Chris would have been glad to listen. It had ended with one of those painful silences that often happens when two unusually friendly people meet, but are soon terrified of offending one another because there's simply nothing to say.

Some had said he was *too* polite. Some had called him conceited. In high school, he had been so quiet and reclusive that he was almost completely ignored. Almost. The handsome jocks and all the busy blue ribboners respected him, because of his build and his looks. What could they say? Most of them were butt ugly compared to the boy. And he had stopped keeping track of how many girls had invited him to this or that. Not a single invitation had he accepted.

Sometimes, an aggressive girl would pinch him hard enough to make him jump. And then she would glare at him, daring him to act offended. Every now and then, he would get one of those quiet, challenging looks from a jealous, second rate jock. And the nerdy kids were just plain uncomfortable around him. Never sure how to act around someone so quiet, whose face made them ashamed to look at their own reflections in the mirror.

And the teachers. One in particular. She said something to him.

In private.

But it was only one of the reasons high school didn't cut it for him. By then, he had been on his own, and working a job anyway.

For four years after that he was alone. Until that morning, when he had decided to wait near the church, to see what manner of people would walk out.

When a mother emerged in Beauty.

With a daughter in Humility.

When he gets to the house, he wonders why I don't come outside to greet him. But as he approaches the front door, he hears that a twelve minute Swiss Odyssey has begun. He knows I can't hear a thing, except for the sounds flowing from my little stereo with the big speakers. My private Opera House.

He decides to leave me alone with my overture.

He takes a seat on the steps, and listens to the cellos *suggest the calm of a peaceful soul, while echoing a distant longing and indefinable sadness of spirit*. He understands the timpani's announcement of the coming storm, and the arrival of the crescendo that starts small and builds to *a violent climax—a deluge of cataclysmic power and destruction*. He then listens to the *purity and complete inspiration of the pastoral melody, as it tells of nature's profound beauty and the serenity of solitude*. Then he rides with the *Light Calvary of the Gods, who sweep down to Earth, charging mightily across the countryside upon horses of epic vengeance and revolution*.

Serenity. Fury. Beauty.

Victory.

"Well, hey there," I say, flashing a smile. "Is everything alright?"

"Everything's fine. We just finished early today."

Then, a kiss. Nervous, tender. Ripe with tension.

"The food smells good," he says.

"What's this?"

"Grapes."

Gladly, I carry the bag into the kitchen. I intend to wash them, until I taste one of the plump, juicy white grapes. It tastes so natural, so sweet, that it is a shame to spoil that earthy taste with water. They taste like I just picked them off the vine myself. They remind me of the juicy, red mulberries I would pick and eat in the woods when I was a little girl.

He follows me into the kitchen like a house kitten. We sit together at the table, and I go to town on the white grapes.

"We'll be plantin' in a couple of weeks," he says.

"Are you gonna do this field yourself?"

I stuff a grape into my mouth.

"I'll ask John to let me do it. I'll drive the planter over here the day before. I don't know why he ever bought this field. It seems too small."

John Evans has too many cornfields, for miles in and around Martin County. In June, summer winds move over the leaves, sending waves rolling the length and breadth of them. Like an ocean.

"I'm glad he bought it," I say. "If he hadn't, you might never have met him." I am shoving grapes into my mouth, one right after the other.

Just like a child, he thinks. He watches me eat the grapes, and can't help but notice that my eyes are no longer tinted with fear.

My skin is kissed with the fairest hint of color, from days spent in the sunlight. The Italian heritage is apparent. My long hair is still raven black, shiny and full bodied. And my large, dark eyes are clear, seeming to sparkle with life. I hope he notices that my white teeth are very straight, giving me a smile that I have never truly hated. Sometimes I notice the way he looks at me. To him, I hope my appearance has blossomed. To me, it has not.

"I'm gonna watch you plant the whole field," I say. "Every bit of it."

You probably will, he thinks.

Suddenly, the stove sizzles a warning. The pot has boiled over.

"It's a good thing I started dinner early. But it'll still be a while. Here, eat some more grapes."

He obeys me.

"What kinda meat are you cookin'?" he says.

"What do you want?"

"You know I always want pork chops."

"What about sausage?"

"Oh," he says, almost choking on a grape. "Go right ahead then. Whatever you want to cook is fine."

"No, I'll cook chops. It's no trouble. They cook twice as fast anyway."

"Are you sure?" he asks.

"I'm positive."

I take out the block of frozen tenderloin chops. He follows me over to the sink, worried that he is getting on my nerves.

He is.

"It's *alright*, honey. It'll only take a little while to thaw them out. It's no bother."

What is his problem?

I stop fiddling with the meal, then look at my husband. The look that slices through the tension. Ripping right into a person.

I see in his eyes an echo of the fear I have always known.

"Are you afraid, Chris?"

No answer.

"You love me, don't you?"

"Yes," he answers, shaking his head.

"Then, talk to me. And tell me why you're so scared."

If he speaks, he might cry. That may be one reason he is so quiet all the time.

"This is the longest its ever been. It's been over three months. It has to be over. That's the only explanation, honey. It's all behind us."

"Sometimes, I *do* get scared," he says.

"Of what?"

"Sometimes I'm afraid that I'll hurt you again."

"But you don't want to hurt me anymore, do you?"

"No, I don't, Elizabeth. I swear to God I don't."

"Then you *won't*. You have to believe that, Chris. *I* do. I don't want you to be afraid anymore. Sometimes it feels like you're afraid of *me*."

A long pause.

"Chris, *look* at me…Chris, how can you possibly be scared of me? I haven't given you a reason to be afraid. I've never threatened you. I've never threatened to leave you, and get you into trouble. Honey, help me understand how you can be scared of somebody like *me?*"

"But I'm not."

"Then stop *acting* like it. I want us live in peace, Chris. I'm sick to death of fear and being afraid all the time. For one reason or another I've been scared to death every day since I was a little girl. I want us to get beyond it, and to try to be happy."

He breathes a deep sigh.

"Even when we were first married, before we came here, there was always so much sadness underneath it all. I don't want that anymore."

I pause…

"Do you know that I've never really been happy before? I don't think I even know what it feels like. This is the closest I've ever been. But I can't be, if I know you're miserable from guilt and fear."

"But how can I not be?"

"Chris, don't be scared anymore. I'll never give you a reason to be afraid. And I know you'll never hurt me again."

We hug one another. A warm, loving embrace.

"I don't hold any of it against you. I never have. I know you don't believe me, Chris, but I never blamed you. I was never angry with you. I couldn't be."

We hold each other for a long time. Trying to comfort one another.

"You know something?"

"What?" he says.

"My mother. My mother never cared about me. She never did. And I've never known anyone else long enough for them to care if I lived or died. You're the only person who ever loved me."

11

*T*he ground yielded its promise for another year. The landscape is colored in every shade of green and every color of the rainbow. In June, we are happy. There are long walks, sunsets, and long kisses under the moon and the stars. And for the first time as we can remember, there is no true sadness nor pain and suffering. The faint, distant longing has less power, and loneliness is kept at bay. The house shadows are held captive, made ineffective by the mercy of Fate and the strength of true love.

Tonight we stand outside. Gazing into the face of eternity, at the thousands of stars across a darkened sky. I turn away from the darkness, looking into my husband's eyes, to see if the stars are reflected in them. And we are both amazed, because no matter how completely we search, we can find no traces of guilt, sorrow, or fear.

"I didn't think it was possible. These are the best days I've ever had."

I look back at the Heavens. Gazing through the universe, into ages long gone.

"I think that people have to suffer to earn grace. The more grace we're given, the greater the suffering."

"Maybe you're right," he says. "Lord knows you—"

"I don't even know what that means. Probably nothing. I say some dumb things, don't I?"

I feel him smile within himself, while he hugs me tight.

"I feel sorry for people. I think that to be born is to be cursed, and to live is to suffer. Chris?"

"Yes?"

"Please don't go to work tomorrow."

"How come?"

"It seems like you're gone longer every day."

"Well, I usually am in the summer."

"I can't help it. Just this one time."

"I can't just not show up. I've never done that before."

"You can go to a phone and call 'em, can't you?"

"Okay," he says. "But on one condition."

"What?"

"If you'll come with me."

"Well…"

"It's nighttime, honey, there won't be anyone around but us. It's just a public phone, a few miles away. It'll give you a chance to see the stars behind these woods that you been missing."

"I seen 'em." My best Carolina gal talk. "I ain't missin' nothin'."

"You gonna come with me?"

"Where'd you say we were going?"

"Just to a phone, a few miles up the road. The thing's isolated, Elizabeth, there's nobody around it."

I am wary about breaking the Primary Rule of Hermitism. But it's a fair trade. If he is willing to miss work, then I'll go for a ride.

"Okay. I'll go."

"Alright then, let's do it." He has a big smile on his handsome face. His blue eyes twinkle as if we just finished packing for Honolulu.

"Don't even go back inside," he says. "Just stay here, while I get the keys." He can't believe it... Elizabeth Peele is going to leave the blessed yard.

An old school recluse. Breaking the rule.

"I'll be right back."

I watch him as he bounds onto the porch and in the house. I take the leisurely walk past the giant tree, towards the black truck in the front yard. The starry sky makes me remember a night from my childhood on my mother's farm, when I stood alone in the open field.

I thought You had abandoned me.

I haven't seen him in such high spirits in ten years. Since before we rented this old house. I have to admit it—I love the isolation. I need it. But I can hardly take pride in that house. From the beginning, it has never felt like a real home. But it's familiar. Safe. And he is here with me, and not hurting me anymore. Maybe that's all that really matters.

I glance back at the sky. To the infinity of distant, barren worlds.

Maybe we'll go far away. To a place we've never been…

"Elizabeth!" He is in the back yard, looking for me. "Where are you?"

"Over here."

He follows my voice through the thick country night, until he finds me.

"I want to get in on your side."

From the driver's side, I slide in first. The truck seems like another realm. Cold, hard, unfamiliar. I watch him do something or another with the jingly keys, and a monster rumbles underneath my feet and all around my poor body, and we begin our nearly historic trip down the long dirt road. I like being with him. But truthfully, the further away we get from the house, the more uneasy I become. But I will fight hard, with all the emotional strength I have gathered, and pretend it is the easiest thing I have ever done.

"This'll be a lot of fun."

"Who was that on the phone?"

"That was Chris," John says. Watching her, to see her reaction. And he isn't disappointed. She stops in her tracks like she has seen a ghost.

Why in God's name didn't I get the phone

"Is anything the matter?"

"He's not comin' in tomorrow. Somethin' about him and his wife takin' a little vacation."

Vera tries not to let it happen. But the silver-green ice gets in her lungs anyway, and nearly takes her breath.

"H…How long will he be gone?"

"Day after t'morrow."

"Well, that's good", she says. Her silken white gown bears a rose pink flower pattern, matching her pink satin robe. John rests in their big cave of a living room with the TV on.

"You're not comin' to bed now, are you?"

"Can't honey."

"John, do you have to go? Why can't you take care of this mess on the phone?"

"They won't budge on the phone," he says. "I need to go up there and grab one of 'em by the collar."

"What if they won't listen?"

"I don't think we'll be any worse off. Come the fall, you'll be the richest woman in this county."

"Well, I'm goin' to bed," she says. "Don't stay up too late."

John watches her walk elegantly out of the living room. Her lovely robe flows behind her, catching and reflecting the light. Like a curtain of silk.

"This is your good morning breeze," says the beautiful voice at the window. The angel vanishes, and what follows is the most perfect breeze imaginable, which blows gently through the window, until she opens her eyes into a world of joy and peace.

The cool of the evening fell as the morning dew, shimmering every blade of grass, and the leaves of every tree. The day warms slowly in the sunlight, until there is only comfort for me and my husband. We wake up together after a long, glorious sleep, and spend the morning embraced in passion. I gently massage him, working every muscle into sublime, tingling relaxation. We have the smallest bit of fruit for breakfast, so we can better enjoy a truly *Elizabethan* lunch, which we eat outside, in the shade of the Great Flowering Tree.

In the late afternoon we take a leisurely walk, strolling together down the long, country road, listening to the birds, and the wind whispering through the trees. For the first time in years—*seven years*—I gather the mail from our mailbox at the end of the road—and just like every day, there is a newspaper, and the colorful advertisements I love to read.

He speaks to me every now and then about the farm. About the big silver grain bins and the harvest they hold. We talk about whether or not we would ever want our own farm. He mentions his love for the fields, especially in late spring before the corn gets too high. "An ocean of green," he always says.

I talk incessantly about the Crown Prince of Melody, chattering on about how in twenty years of listening to the radio I have heard scarcely more than *William Tell* and *The Barber of Seville* (*The Thieving Magpie* notwithstanding, as was a rendezvous with *Tancredi* a decade ago—which nearly gave me a heart attack, reducing me to tears and changing my writing style forever, and *Il Signor Bruschino* which left me in a giddy, laughing fit.) I am still taken aback that such music exists in the first place, *music that sparkles with such joy and beauty…bright, shimmering rhythms and brilliant melodies, as if they sprang from an inexhaustible well of inspiration...the full flowering of Mozart's Genius. Music that comes alive when played with skill. Ensnaring the soul with happiness, exhilaration and delight...*

To him, it is just Bugs Bunny. And The Lone Ranger.

And every now and then, I make him regret asking about my avocation. I begin to speak too much about dotted rhythms and broken chords, runs, leaps and trills, sharps and flats, and the ugliness of twelve tone composition. I'll slip into chattering about principles of harmony and texture, the importance of inspired melody, the necessity of learning to play Mozart, Beethoven's monumental grasp of theory, the difficulties in performing Rossini's music, and the dangers replete in Bach's sound on the modern keyboard. And once, I accidentally said the word *counterpoint.* Trouble.

"But some of that stuff in your notebook doesn't look like music," he says. "It looks like little shapes."

"That was one of my old notebooks. I haven't written that way in years."

"How can you tell one thing from the other?"

"It's easier than it looks. But I never really forget anything I've written down."

"How many pieces have you written?"

"Too many."

"And you say the music just, appears? You *see* it?"

"Sometimes I only see an object, like a diamond crystal, and I'll hear the music from it. The first thing I ever wrote down was for the *harp*, when I was a little girl, and that's the way it came to me. But other times, I can see the music itself..."

Chris listens to Synesthesian Theory.

Dimly.

"…every note, every chord has its own unique color. These are shaped by the various instruments. The best melodies and harmonies give off the most beautiful shapes and colors you can imagine. Besides Mozart, Rossini and Vivaldi are the only other two I've seen that—"

"You missed your calling," he says, shaking his head. "Lord knows, you missed something or another."

Or something.

But I'm not Carmen Angelina Coletti, world famous pianist and bel canto musicologist. Specialist in composing 19th century style Italian overtures and piano concertos.

I'm just Elizabeth Peele.

"Birds don't really sing. They *talk*. And a lot of it sounds pretty scary. Its hateful and violent."

The longer Chris listens, the more he is inclined to agree.

I glance upward, beyond the road, toward the crown of the giant *Carya* in back of our house. A great southern pecan tree. One that has seen the birth, and growing pains of a new world.

"You think those tree people are coming out this year? To poke around and take pictures, and slam on our door for an hour?"

"If they do come, we'll invite 'em inside for dinner." he says, with a wry smile, his cheeks dimpling just so.

We share one brief moment. Complacent. Comfortable in our lonerism.

"Its guarding us. Watching over us."

"If it falls, we're dead."

"Stop," I say, pulling on his arm. "Do you enjoy living out here, alone with me?"

"It's probably the only thing that ever mattered to me."

"I know we should move from here. But I just don't have the strength. I feel tired inside, Chris, and I don't want to go out into the world. Maybe if we tried hard enough, we could make a home out of that house."

"I don't want to. I can't."

"Well, why don't we just move away? Why do we stay here?"

"Maybe were just afraid," he says.

"Of what?"

A sudden breeze blows my hair over my eyes. I brush it away.

"I'll bet if we had children, we wouldn't be so lonely. I'll bet we wouldn't be afraid to leave then."

"Do you really want to leave?" he asks.

I look around, gazing at devil trees and bushes, listening to demon birds screech unmentionable horrors…

Then I see the giant tree, and remember the beauty of the approaching twilight, and another night in isolation under the glorious star canopy.

12

*T*he farmer's wife is in her beautiful kitchen, ready for guilty pleasure. In country golden hair braid and blue collar shirt tucked in, she stands at the sink, cutting the green stems from red, ripe strawberries. Their sweet smell is familiar. With her husband out of town, she has been alone in the house all day.

A voice echoes in the Lady's mind. A voice from the evening.

Vera knows the woman's voice, and her shy, fearful manner. She knows the scent of her hair, which is often sweet, like *strawberries*. And sometimes her face is dirty, and her hair is unkempt, smelling strongly of burned wood and kerosene. This beauty tries to be happy. She smiles from behind dark eyes of sorrow. But at times the inner pain is too great, and she won't talk. She only cries. Vera holds her, and is tormented by her loneliness. And sometimes the clouds will gather, and a terrible storm whirls over them. When the storm rises, she can't find her. She hides from the rain, and the thunder. Everywhere Vera goes, she glances at the faces of young, dark haired women. Not hoping, but simply wondering.

As I lay grieving at Death's Door
She came to me under Cloak of Night
As I lay breathing in the Bosom of Pain
She came to me in Fires of a Dream...

"Ms. Evans?"

The back door opens suddenly, startling her.

"Oh, it's you" she says, politely. "You scared me."

"How you been doin'?"

"I'm fine, Joe. How about yourself? Is everything alright up there?" She wipes her red-stained hands. Courteously.

"Just droppin' by," he says. "Quittin' time you know."

She has no desire to visit with Joe Little. So she doesn't.

"You need a ride home?"

"Naw. My car's parked up the road."

"Well then, what can I do for you?" A dangerous, loaded gun of a question if there ever was one.

"You can tell me where you been keepin' yourself all this time. We missed you up there."

"Oh," she says, a little flattered. "Well, I've had so much to do. I just haven't had the time. Besides, you boys didn't need me busy bodying up there anymore. But it's good to be missed every now and then."

She almost relaxes, even though she knows better. Even while the pleasant, respectful look on his face darkens into a calm, bold look of intention. In these clothes, Vera suddenly feels nude in front of him.

"I missed you a lot," he says, glancing at her cleavage.

A chill...

"I'd better get back to this dessert," she says. "Be sure and tell Louise I said hey."

The young man walks boldly over to where she stood.

"I'm in no hurry," he says. "Just go on with what you were doin.' "

"Well, alright. But I'll bet your grandmother's already wondering where you are." She turns to the sink, picking up the small, sharp knife.

"When's old John gettin' back?"

"He'll be back soon. Maybe tomorrow morning."

"Tomorrow, huh?"

"He might be back earlier," she says. "He does that sometimes to surprise me. He might be on his way right now."

Joe decides to stop talking, and begins to watch her. In quiet, lustful disbelief, he watches her refined beauty and fully curved figure. Her fitted jeans display full, womanly hips, quite remarkable in their shapeliness. Above the firm, curved waist, her bosom is rounded and heavy. How can it be, that a face and body so exemplifies what a person lusts for?

What a person craves?

Damn

"Joseph?"

"Oh," he says, "Yeah?"

"Shouldn't you be gettin' home?"

"You're probably right."

But he steps up behind her, resting his hands against the sink on either side, blocking her in.

"Joe, what do you think you're doing?"

"I just want to talk that's all."

"This isn't my idea of proper talkin,'" she says. "I'm married, Joe, and I'm a lot older than you are."

"Honey, that makes it all *better.*"

Another chill...

"If you take your arms from around me," she says, "and leave now, I promise I'll forget this whole thing. It'll be like it never happened."

"Alright. I'm goin'. On one condition."

She stays quiet. Waiting.

"You've got to reach back," he says, "and kiss me like you *mean* it."

The comment sickens her, and makes her furious. She drops the knife in the water, and slams her body back against his, making him stumble backward a little.

The look on his face is pure exhilaration.

"Get out of here," she says.

Joe steps up again, putting both hands on her waist, and she turns around and shoves him as hard as she can. *Very* hard.

"I can't *believe* you just put your hands on me," she hisses. Joe's look is less tolerant.

"You send out strong signals, though, don't you?"

"I haven't given you any sig…" She takes a deep breath, and regains her composure… "Joe, you're not even worth my time. I want you to get out of this house, and pray to God I forget you came in here."

A quick, evil pause…

"Just pretend I'm the one with the *blue eyes,* honey." He grabs her violently, and kisses her hard on the neck. A deep, sucking kiss.

She breaks free, slapping him viciously in the face, hard enough to make him see blue lightning. And her hands were wet, which made it worse. He stands there, touching his face, staring as if she had just dug her own grave. He makes a quick move, and she sucks in a breath of fear…

Then, the door opens…

And everything just stops.

"You can go outside if you want, Vera." Chris says.

She is frozen.

"Its… it's alright, Chris. Joe was just leaving."

Vera sees the pale in his eyes go blank. They seem to change, until they burn with a cold, blue flame. Chris walks towards Joe Little, and Joe braces himself, all the while reaching towards his hip pocket. He is like a fearful younger brother, who knows that his demonically tempered older brother has had enough.

Vera steps between them.

"Joseph was just asking me a question about something, Chris. He stopped by to ask me when John was coming back, didn't you, Joseph?" She touches Chris' arm tenderly, staring at him with a pleading expression.

Then she steps over to Joe.

"We'll finish talking later," she says, ushering him to the door. "John'll talk to you when he gets back, okay?"

Vera touches Joe's arm, and he cuts her an angry, bewildered look, as though he feels betrayed. "I'll see you later, alright?" she says, smiling, while he hauls his humiliated hide out the door. Vera closes it behind him, sighing deeply. She opens her eyes, and looks across the big kitchen at Chris Peele.

"Are you alright?" he says.

"I'm fine."

They can only stare. They are like two separated by a great river, who want to go to one another, but don't know how.

But it is only a kitchen.

"John'll be back in a few days."

"That's good," he says. "It's not the same around here without him."

She is held immobile, in a kind of breathless shock.

Electric.

"I'd better get home," he sighs.

"Okay. You have a good evening."

They are saying goodbye, but *she* is the one standing by the door. He finally begins to walk towards her, with his eyes down. Respect and Politeness. To an extreme. He is about to float past her, when she decides to jump in, and swim for dear life.

"Chris?"

He stops in his tracks.

"Thank you," she says. "Thank you so much."

His eyes bore a Cerulean sky.

"If... if you ever need anything from me, anything at all, *please* don't hesitate to ask."

"Okay."

"You can come directly to *me*, and ask for anything, and I *swear* I'll do what I can to help you."

He nods.

"Promise that you'll come to me if you need me."

"I promise," he says. "I…"

"What is it?"

Dear God, what is it?

"I missed you."

The words are a guilty whisper…

They slide into Vera's body, and down her spine.

"Well, I've… I missed you too, Chris. I really did."

Their eyes lock. For a long time they stand, frozen in the moment, afraid to move, afraid to speak.

Finally, she steps forward, full against his body.

Their arms slide smoothly around each other, until they are locked tightly together. Vera pulls in long, trembling breaths, trying hard to control her emotions. Chris feels her body tremble, feeling her chest rise and fall against his. They hold each other close, breathing together, bound by a feeling they can neither resist nor understand. Vera's body begins to ache, and she has to grab onto him and massage his back firmly, whispering *o my God* to herself over and over. The scent of fresh strawberries is strong.

"Would you like to stay?" Her voice quivers.

"Yes, I would."

Struggling for a breath, she holds on for dear life, until her aching, her quiet river of tears is done. She presses a long, sensuous kiss on his cheek, close to his lips. He squeezes her tighter, nearly lifting her up while closing his eyes, enjoying the feel and shape of her warm body, and her soft lips against his skin.

After a long time, they let go and stand close. Holding each other's hand as he moves slowly toward the door, until their hold slips quietly away.

And then he was gone.

13

"*G*et the Hell off my property, you son of a *bitch*!"

John stands firm over top of Joe, who is sprawled flat on the ground.

"If I see you again," John says. "I'm gon' kill you."

Joe gets up, with a mouth full of blood. He spits on the ground and steps away to gather his wits. Then he starts back to the middle aged farmer…

Until Chris steps up beside John.

"It's 'tween me and him," Joe grumbles.

"Joe Little," says John, huffing, "You got 'bout two seconds left, before I break you into seven different…"

John loses it and tries to get to him again. But Chris grabs him, pulling him backward.

"Let me go, Peele, so I can get my hand 'round that bastard's throat!"

"It's over John," Chris says. "Don't bother with it."

The farmer keeps struggling, realizing he can't break free of Chris' grip. He finally stops making a fool of himself and stands still, panting.

"You don't know how lucky you are he stopped you," Joe says.

"Chris, I'm goin' to the house," John sighs, out of breath. "And I'm comin' back with a loaded shotgun."

John staggers away towards the farmhouse. But he suddenly whirls around, teeth gleaming that angry grimace.

"I always knew you were *nothin'*" he says. "You came from nothin', and you're always gon' be nothin'. "

The words slice Joe's anger, laying his soul bare. As John storms away, Joe looks ashamedly at Chris, waiting for trouble. But Chris only stares at the ground, his face bearing a somber expression.

"I wouldn't be here when he gets back, Joe."

They exchange an awkward glance.

"I'm outta here," Joe says. "I don't need this shit no more."

He ambles away, towards the white mustang he had finally saved up enough money to get. Before long he was inside, spinning a shower of gravel in the air as he drove away.

Chris had wanted to say something. But what could he have said? Good luck, Joe? Nice knowin' you? Don't worry, it'll all work out for you soon, Joe?

Chris allows himself the appropriate farewell for Joe Little.

Goodbye.

Maybe I shouldn't have told him…

The hour is late, and Vera starts to wonder where her men are. Dinner is ready, but John isn't around. Chris' truck is still parked. She switches on the kitchen TV, and sits at the table to watch.

But what Joe did… what if Chris hadn't been here?

Thank God I stopped John from taking that gun.

Sometimes, I worry about him.

About us.

The local news distracts her attention—the sickest, most violent and sex crazed show on television. She listens to the grisly, perverted details, when her heart leaps at the sound of Chris' truck starting. She almost leapt herself, to the dining room window. But she closes her eyes, and waits for her husband.

A few minutes later, he comes in the door.

"Afternoon stranger," she says. She stands up, marching boldly over to him, and gives him a hearty, bosomy hug.

"Goodness," she says. "Look at all this dust. Did you go in one of the bins?" John kisses her, and they sit down at the big kitchen table.

"I was in one of 'em alright. Just out of it a few minutes ago."

"You're thinking about Joe, aren't you?"

"Joe's the last thing I'm thinkin' about right now, Vera."

"What's the matter?"

"You know how the grain sticks sometimes," he said, "and you have to get in there and work it loose…"

His tone was pensive. Melancholy.

"Vera, in twenty years I musta done it a thousand times."

She stares with pity, and total understanding.

"Well, honey, this time I slipped and fell, right on my back. I don't even have to tell you what happened next."

Vera's mind pictures it. The grain pouring down on him, swallowing him until he's buried alive. Unable to move. Suffocating. Trying to call out to her.

"You know Chris is always the last one to leave," he says. "He must have heard the grain slip because…"

John pauses, as if he suddenly remembers being trapped. Being buried.

"I heard him callin' me. But I couldn't answer him. I couldn't move. I couldn't breathe. I couldn't see anything. Vera I thought I was gonna *die*. Next thing I know, I'm wakin' up on the ground with him sittin' beside me. Vera, he… he wanted me to forgive *him*, for not gettin' to me fast enough. I just sat there, coughin' up dust and lookin' like a damned fool. He sat with me for a while, 'til I was ready to walk, then we came down the road together. I begged him to stay with us, Vera. But you know how he is."

She knew. Vera stands up, coaxing John to his feet. She gives him a long, quiet hug. But her thoughts, her longings drift beyond her husband.

So far, and so blissfully beyond.

14

Carmen's mother looks at her. Calmly. She closes the door, then slaps her daughter hard enough to bloody her nose. Barbara Coletti undoes two buttons on her own dress.

"You don't know how long I've waited," her mother says. "Do you want to fight me? Get your goddamned clothes off and let's <u>finish</u> it, then!"

She pauses, while her daughter stares in terror.

"No? I thought not. Don't you <u>ever</u> snatch your arm away from me again as long you live..."

I am shocked awake very late in the morning, frightened by something I haven't thought about in years. The room is warm and bright. Exactly as it had been in the dream.

I'm well rested. And hungry. In my white cotton summer nightgown, I slide out of bed and stroll to the kitchen to fix breakfast. My body is fully curved again from months of good, regular eating.

I smelled perfume on his shirt the other day.

I hope he's not mad at me, because I said I didn't want to move.

I'll move today, if he wants me to.

I shuffle around my little kitchen, gathering a small pot and three eggs to boil.

I'm clinging him to death. But I can't help it. It's been so long since any of it happened.

Since winter.

As I prepare my breakfast, I have a flash of memory. And it scares me. For a moment, my eyes widen into my characteristic expression. I want to retreat to the bedroom, turn on the radio and write in my little notebook all day. Staying quietly inside. Not making a peep when he gets home.

But I decide to wait.

I cook my breakfast, and eat it through the sudden loss of appetite. The hours begin to tick away, as I go about my daily routine. Cleaning, washing clothes, preparing dinner, feeding the chickens, even writing a few bars of poetic musings, memories and melodies in my Rose Diaries.

Waiting.

Dream memories are veiled by the passage of time. And fear motivation is unstable ground.

It's been six months since he's had the guilty nightmares…

And the ground has crumbled away.

"We're so happy to have with us today the winner of the International Young Artist Piano Competition…"

Late afternoon. I rest at my bedroom radio, in the old, comfort-cushioned arm chair. My lasagne recipe, cheeses blended by Heaven's Kitchen, languishes prepared on the stove.

Elitism. It might be the death of Melody.

Such is the grandest music among us.

Poets.

Such are the wildest thoughts among us.

Composers.

My mind drifts away from the prodigy's piano.

To my notebook.

> *Melodies resound the Great Music Hall*
> *Above the river valley of Nowhere's Land*
> *Harmonies pour down a crystal waterfall*
> *To nourish the Valley of Cerulean Sand—*

Heaven's might beams from a darkened sky
Above the Players of Orchestra's Light
As their dreams wish where mountain eagles fly
Souls are redeemed by this otherworldly sight—

Whispering peace in the fields of plenty
By the river valley of a distant land—
To this new world I have traveled alone
To walk these Shores of Azurean Sand.

The country girl listens to the young piano phenom. Fumbling clumsily, chromatically along.

How I wish they would play simple, beautiful music! Let the piano sing its voice! Allow the fingers to flow across the keys, to draw sounds from them as if by magic. Give no place to gray, cloudy music. Music that has no life.

No melody.

Through the bare window, I see a world imbued with a pale, reddish glow. Gladly, I turn off the radio and stroll into the back yard.

I have seen many sunsets. And they have all been lovely.

Goodness gracious...

Over the west, hanging low in a hazy sky, is the reddest sun I have ever seen in my life. It looks like a gigantic red disk. Clouds have gathered— scattered across the sky like a thin blanket, streaked with rust and blood.

Probably dust in the air, making it so red.

The sight is so amazing that I listen. I focus. I concentrate, to see if there is a melody.

But none came.

It'll be another good night for Chris and me.

We're meant to be happy.

The red sun contrasts beautifully with the field. The corn is high, and grows the deepest shade of green.

We'll leave this place, and get our own farm. And then we'll start our own family. We'll have a little girl, and we'll be kind to her. Maria, her name will be. I'll learn to play music, and I'll teach it to her. Every night when she's older, we'll play music for Chris. And he'll love it. He'll love us.

He'll love me.

The call of an angry blackbird shakes me awake from my daydream. I step off the porch, into the back yard.

God shows himself in nature...

The true essence of nature is perfect order. Flawless designs. Clockwork precision. I believe that in the Earth itself, in the sun, in the moon, and in the stars, God reveals himself to the hearts and minds of men.

Have I been destined to suffer? Or is it part of a chaotic mess—random causes and effects? Where does the will of man end, and the Will of God begin?

I've known You since I was a little girl. So I must have done something to deserve it. Something specific. You wouldn't have let my mother do those things to me, if I didn't deserve it.

But why? What did I do?

I always tried. I tried so hard.

Heavenly Father—

Please forgive me, for all the things that I've done.

I notice the sun creeping lower. Closer towards the evening. The stars are hidden by the strange, crimson violet.

A few minutes later, the red sun disappears from the sky.

15

*T*he sun had set an hour ago. Already, the window frames a dark summer evening. In the bedroom, I listen to the country night sounds, and watch the shadows on the wall.

I have endured the heart of battle. There is strength in my body. I will swallow the silly fears, and go boldly to my husband. To comfort him, and to *be* comforted. I am strong, bold, and ready.

But from the deepest longing—

I wonder what color my rose will be.

When I hear the truck, I ignore my nerves, and go out to meet him. The truck pulls into the yard, and I run bouncing to the driver's side, kissing him on the cheek. A moaning, loving kiss.

"Hey, baby."

"Hey there," he replies.

I glance around the inside of the truck.

Looking for a rose.

A beautiful rose.

"Come on out, so I can hug you."

I open the door, and we embrace. Clinging for dear life. I kiss him deeply, breathing with him, stroking his hair. I hold nothing from him, pouring myself into him, until my heart begins to beat faster, and my chest begins to heave against his...

But he suddenly pulls away.

"You missed me a lot, didn't you?"

"Mmm *hmm,*" My eyes are hypnotic.

"Let's go inside."

"Alright. Hey, what's that in the truckbed? Under the tarp there?"

"Just some stuff I had to pick up for the farm," he says. "I'll take it in on Monday."

"Why not tomorrow?"

"I'm stayin' home this weekend."

"Thank *goodness.*"

We glide close together, up the porch, and into the house. I suddenly think to myself what a small, dingy, depressing little dwelling it is.

"No picnics tomorrow, though," he says.

"Why not?"

"Farmer's rain. Long and heavy."

"Oh yeah. I heard about it. But if you want to go somewhere in the truck tomorrow, just ask me. You wanna get ice cream tonight?"

"Maybe," he says. "I'm too tired right now, though."

"Well, are you hungry? Lasagne's been ready for an hour."

"Maybe later."

He tosses his keys and wallet on the dresser, along with the black pocket knife he had intended to throw away. He unbuttons his light blue heavy shirt, and plops down in the comfortable bedroom chair. He looks spent. Uneasy.

"Is everything alright? Chris?"

He seems startled.

"Are you alright?"

"Just tired. I think I need a nap."

"You want me to massage you?"

"No thanks. I'm just gonna rest here."

"Okay."

I have to talk to him.

I have to.

"Chris?"

"Hmm?"

"Can I talk to you?"

"Sure." His eyes are closed. He is resting his head.

"Can I sit in your lap?"

He motions to me, and I park my hips full into his lap.

Shapely, I am. Fully developed.

I gaze quietly, until I have his attention. Easily done.

"We have to leave here."

"Someday."

"No, Chris. I mean it. We have to move away from here. I don't know what'll happen to us, to *me*, if we stay in this house. You can understand that can't you? After what we've been through here? Chris, I've been thinking about it, and… it's this *house*. I know it is. I know there's something about this place. These walls. The floors. The windows. Everything. Can't you feel it? It's so dreary and depressing. We're miserable here. If you said we could, I'd move right now. I'd move *tonight*, if you said we could."

Please say we'll move tonight…

"Chris, I… I'm afraid to stay here any longer."

"Okay," he says. "I'll start looking for another place in a few days."

"A few days," I repeat softly. I look around the bedroom, at the outdated, ridged wooden walls, the brown ceiling with the exposed light bulb and string click- switch dangling, the ancient wood floors with dark stains from ages ago, the old bathroom door with the jagged hole, and the stupid, box-closet space in the corner.

The house is an anachronism.

A relic.

"Can we go somewhere tonight? Maybe just to take a drive, to get out of here for a while?"

"That might be fun. Let me rest a while first."

I kiss him on the forehead… and on the eyelids… his jaw…

It relaxes him. It relaxes him too much—

And he falls asleep.

I eat dinner alone. Chris is snoring away, and I don't have the heart to disturb him. My dishes are done and put away now. I'm wanting for his company. I sit at the edge of the bed in disappointment, watching him sleep.

Tomorrow, we'll go looking for another place to stay.

Our time here is over.

I decide to take a bath. Maybe wash my hair and listen to a disc. So I turn the bathtub water on, then go to check my little music collection.

My two favorite composers are my bread and butter. My rhythm and my melody. But I need something with more depth tonight. Something to relax me. I flip through the albums, past the overtures, operas and concertos, until I run across a certain collection of symphonies. Then, one in particular.

As it rings true of my own composition, my composers are the purest melodists who ever lived. Maybe the two most gifted of all time. Their music is brilliant. It sparkles spontaneity and effortless invention. Lord, forgive my boldness in the bars of music!

But perhaps we were *never* as profoundly inspired as Beethoven, when he composed his Pastoral Symphony.

I turn the music on, softly enough to not disturb my farm prince. I smile a little, as the scene by the brook awakens pleasant feelings in my country soul.

My husband misses quite a show as I shake, twist and jiggle out of all my clothes. I place my shampoo and my soap neatly by the tub and turn off the water. My breasts feel heavier than ever as they swing and pull gently against me. A symphony in F. My mother's bosom. Only not as gigantic.

The water seems too warm when I step in. But I deal with it while I slide down into the tub, watching the water rise around me. I lean back in the big, old-fashioned bathtub, resting while I think about the old house, the giant tree, the red sun, and the long, dirt road.

I relax and draw upon my gift. Expanding the Great Symphony in my mind's cathedral.

A noisy hairdryer. Doors opened and closed too loudly. Big, long sighs. A plastic cup dropped on the kitchen floor. None of it is enough to wake him up. And now I am upset…

Because I have stubbed my little toe on a kitchen chair. I sit at the table, rubbing my bare toe, and thinking about how long it had taken the pain to come. It is the most pain I have felt in a long time.

I step into things a lot. Nothing is safe around me half the time. My clumsy feet always find a way to kick something. But usually, I'm in a pair of shoes. I've just gotten used to the idea of walking around barefoot. There's been no reason for me to worry about hurting my feet. Or my toes.

I am suddenly distracted by the wind, whooshing loudly through the trees. The breeze comes in quickly, seeming to blow away all of the warm, humid air at once. I step onto the porch, noticing that the clouds have already started to gather and thicken. The air is strong with the unmistakable, dusty scent of rain.

Closing my eyes, I breathe deeply, as the wind blows my long, black hair and white nightgown. It is a cool, comfortable wind. I listen, to see if there is a warning. But there is only a breeze. A cool, summer wind, foretelling the coming rain. I step off the porch, strolling leisurely towards the tree. The sound of the approaching storm whispers loudly. But I am bold in the face of it.

There is a faint, white glowing underneath the Flowering Tree. It is a Woman, in her white gown, facing the wind without fear, with a spirit in full bloom. The childish fears are being carried away. Maybe she is feeling something new, something she has never felt before. Not joy. Not peace. Not happiness or pride…

Confidence.

Inner boasting about the future.

The wind howls across the darkened land. Across tobacco country, and the Great Field of Plenty—

Cooling the tears of a lonely woman.

A strand of her hair blows to her face. The Lady brushes it free, and she remembers. She remembers the power. The energy of an embrace.

Standing at the edge of the storm, she prays he will be safe and protected.

And loved.

16

*I*n the third hour after midnight—

Dread grips me in my sleep. Overwhelming terror. And though I am dead to the world, I am fully aware. I lay frozen on my back, unable to see the thing that holds me captive in fear.

I hear the screen door open, slamming with loud assurance. Then the sound of shuffling, movement in the living room. I'm terrified for myself and my husband, struggling to breathe so I can call his name.

And then it appears…

Heavy, determined footsteps of inhuman strength and power. Thumping loudly towards the bedroom.

A fear, a *terror,* hits me like a shock. The scream won't come, to chase away the sleep. Each footstep is louder. Closer.

I have to wake up *now.*

I can't give in to the helplessness, so I keep trying to scream. The footsteps end abruptly, just at the doorway…

Then I feel the demon enter the room, and I believe, I *know,* it is here to suffocate me until I'm dead. I am helpless to act…

Even when I feel the mattress go down beside me. I watch the bed drop under the full weight of the invisible thing in the room with me.

I feel it moving, moving slowly and deliberately on top of me. Instantly it is harder to breathe. I feel like I'm being crushed. With all my strength, I struggle to wake up from the dream. Then suddenly…

I can't breathe.

I can't breathe, and I can't see. The dream fades into a haze, then blackness. I don't know if I am awake, asleep, or dead. A craving for air makes me panic, renewing my strength, and I slowly regain the ability to move.

With a final, deliberate burst of strength, I pull myself out of darkness, and I'm wide awake. I see the source of my terror…

I am staring it directly in its pale, blue eyes—

He is on top of me, pinning my body under the sheet, holding my nose and mouth tightly shut.

I manage to free one of my arms, pushing him hard in the face, pushing my thumb into his eye. It works just enough. He has to let go of my mouth and grab my arm. The breath rushes in, and I gasp loudly for the life that is being taken…

And I *scream.*

He quickly pins my flailing arm, while I shriek the loudest scream in Creation. Only one of his hands is free now—it will be harder to cut off my breath. But with just one hand, just before I scream again to God and Christ at the top of my lungs, he clamps my nose and lips tightly shut.

I can barely even squirm. His grip is like steel. And I catch one last glimpse of his expression…

His eyes are blank, and without mercy.

I grow weaker. My lungs burn, and I can taste blood. Everything merges into a purplish fog. My mind will hold no concept, except for God, and my mother…

And then…

Nothing.

For months, it had built up inside him.

He crisscrosses the thin, strong ropes across my chest and stomach. He watches me breathe, and every time I exhale he pulls the ropes tighter, until I'm hardly able to breathe at all. He ties my legs together from top to bottom. My arms are pulled back as far as they will go, and are bound tightly.

He hurries back through the house, out to the truck. The last item had been resting unused behind the equipment barn, at the Evan's farm.

The world has a strange, grey glow from the gathering clouds, and the wind has begun to rise with intensity. The temperature has fallen a great deal. There is a definite chill in the air. He carries on through the cool, gray wind, until he has dragged the long tool box into the back yard, past the giant tree, down towards the edge of the cornfield.

I awake to a cool, gentle breeze.

I have shed a lot of tears in my life, most from physical pain. The fear and sorrow, I had dealt with. But tonight, as I realize what is happening, the tears begin to flow immediately.

There is *no* redemption from the Fear of Death.

As the cool wind dries the sweat and tears from my face, I begin to shiver. I can see the tall effigies in the cornfield, blowing wildly, and I see the huge, dark shape of the pecan tree. My bloody sky is now dark, with a grayish hue in the low hanging clouds. The wind blows unmercifully into my face, making it harder to catch a breath.

A precious *breath*…

I can't move a muscle, and what my breath is doing can hardly be called breathing. It is more like choked little gasps. I feel like the accursed asthma victim being crushed by something heavy on her chest, or being squeezed to death, as if wrapped tightly in the coils of a large serpent. My heart seems flattened—I feel each thump against the inside of my chest. Each spot where the ropes cut into my skin is trapping blood, making it squeeze to get through. Every beat sends new pain through my body…

And through the tears, I see the dark figure drifting towards me.

My blood is changing. Being slowly replaced with something thick and cold, that makes me cry and tremble.

"Christopher?"

I can barely draw a good breath.

"We can go inside now, Chris. And we can leave, honey. We can leave this place…"

The words choke in the back of my throat. I am afraid to speak again. Maybe, this is just another attempt to scare me. Maybe he'll leave me in the rain, and come back for me.

My watery gaze is transfixed by the shadow. It seems to watch me, waiting for the terror to take hold.

And then, something happens…

I don't know if it is exhaustion or what. But I experience a strange calming effect. Some of the terror subsides. Soothed away by unearthly sadness. I am flooded with sorrow and regret—regretful that I won't live to see the happiness given to some. And sorrowful that my love and devotion has brought only Hellish pain, and the misery of loss and betrayal.

I am overcome with great pity for him, one so profound that I can hardly bear it. My only desire is to save him. To rescue him from the pain in his own life, and to protect him from whatever harm that might come to him. I perceive an extreme, intangible tugging inside. For a moment I am unaware, and my view is fixed on a better place. A place which comforts me, and keeps me in times of sorrow.

He steps quietly to where I am laying. I am remarkably calm. Almost peaceful. He imagines me lying on my back in the dark box, screaming as I slowly lose my mind.

A sudden, quick flash of memory. A phantom reminder. The sound in his ears, the faint, acid burning in his leg.

The *nightmares.*

"Not this time…" I hear him say.

He takes hold of the ropes at my feet, and begins to drag me towards the box. As I call his name, he looks around fearfully, like he is suddenly being watched.

"Chris! *Christopher!*"

He hears it in my voice. My terror has returned enough to match his own.

They were both afraid, the two of them.

"Chris, help me! Please, help me! Chris you're the only one who can help me!" I sound out of breath, like I've been running. "Chris, don't leave me here! Please, honey, please!"

As he places me inside the box, he notices the incredible look on my face. A mixture of fear and sorrow that goes beyond anything he has ever seen.

"I don't want to stay in here! Chris, *please* don't make me stay in here!..."

There is pity. Enough to cause him pain.

But no mercy.

My arms are bound underneath me, raising me up enough to tilt my head back uncomfortably. The ropes against my body dig into me, cutting off my circulation. My fingers and toes are already past tingling and are starting to hurt.

"Chris, I can't breathe. Help me to breathe. *Please…"*

I stare in horror, as he turns his back on me.

"Come back! Chris, please don't leave me here!"

He does come back.

He is carrying the lid.

The fear in my body suddenly flows out through my voice…

Then the gray world is darkened, as the lid is placed onto the box.

Pitch blackness…

The box seems to vibrate with quick, loud screams. Constant screaming. A river of them, flowing out of my mouth. It sounds like I can suddenly breathe better. There is power, tremendous force and energy, as though I am being eaten alive. He is amazed by it all. Every muffled scream is shot like an arrow from the tiny, dark space, and right into his chest.

Inside the box, I try to calm down. I stop screaming, and I sob, calling my husband's name. But the sound is trapped in the darkness with me. It seems to me like he can't hear, like the box is sound proofed.

And airtight.

There is no sound above me. I stop crying, and listen.

Rocks and dirt hit the lid. My mind becomes a theater of images. A sea of vivid regret. Through my own screams, I listen. I listen for another pile of dirt on the lid. A grainy thump.

A grainy *thumping* sound…

He has to get away. Away from the wind. Her screams. His betrayal. A quick glance at the dark clouds reaffirms his doom, along with her desperate, breathless calls for help. In nervous haste, he hurries across the yard, away from his disobedience. He feels like a projection of nightmares.

Inside, he rushes to the kitchen sink. Nauseated. Sickened by what he has done. For a long time he stands there, breathing deeply. All he can hear is the loud wind, and the memory of her pitiful screaming.

Vera …

He retrieves a plastic cup, filling it with cold water. He gazes out the kitchen window as he turns the cup to his lips. The reflection of his own eyes in the window almost scares him to death, until he remembers that his eyes really *are* that pale.

After the drink, he calms down. A little.

Dawn approaches from somewhere behind the thick clouds. The blackness is thinning out. If he is going to do it, he'd better do it soon. The temperature is dropping, and the wind blows fiercely.

It will be a long, cold summer rain.

He wanders back outside, standing still in the breeze. An unseasonably cold wind blows from the clouds.

Chris stares fearfully across the back yard. Towards the darkened field.

The box has a sweet, sickening pine smell, which only worsens what is a splitting headache. My eyes are dry—scratchy as I blink in the dark. My throat is so sore, I can barely swallow. Every cell in my body cries out for water.

But I endure, as I am accustomed to.

I want to breathe. Just one deep breath. Just one. But the ropes are so tight around my chest and stomach. The quick, poisonous little breaths will have to do. If I try to take a deep breath, and it doesn't work—

My beating heart. Pumping slowly. The blood moves with every beat. Pushing, straining through the vessels. Numbness would be a blessing. Every inch of skin tingles and itches. Every muscle is agony. Only my hands and feet are painless. I wonder if they are dead from lack of blood flow. My whole body throbs in time with my heartbeat. Every beat still pushes razors through my brain. A blinding headache, bad enough to give me nausea. And my neck muscles are not spared. They have a severe, knotting cramp, that makes me move my head to try to ease it. My left shoulder feels like a knife is inside, slicing back and forth without mercy. And my poor back. An invisible, loathsome creature is upon it. A creature whose purpose is to torture human back muscles. A Hellish claw, dug in deep, twisting without compassion. All of this works together on my mind, spinning it into a hazy dizziness, a dizzying haze of thoughts, images and emotions. But most overwhelming is the sadness—a depression of profound depth and severity. The weight of Death itself begins to envelop me, pressing down on my body and spirit, until there is a sense of inner weeping and unfathomable misery.

And what of Death, and Elizabeth Peele?

They had reconciled. The natural dread of death is vanishing. I nearly welcome the impending loss of consciousness. The pain has become too great. I am breathing without air. The only sounds are quick little wheezings from my throat, and the splashing of blood pumping through my head. My body is on fire. The need for cool, fresh air and water is infinite. And now there are short, involuntary little cries of helplessness. The darkness itself begins to swirl around me. Exhaustion has taken my will, and there is nothing to do but wait. Wait through the poisonous burning in my lungs, which seems to spread, even to my brain.

And what of God, and Elizabeth Peele?

I feel abandoned by Him. I truly regret the day I was born, believing I was created only to suffer, and then to die. In my coffin, I display what may be my greatest gift. An epic fearlessness, the courage of the battlefield, the ability to love and persevere as I face Death, through Hellish suffering and torturous pain.

And of my husband, there is only a severe longing. The rarest love, that defies logic and reason. I have fulfilled my duty, which was to endure. Loving him with all of my heart. Even unto death.

Oh my

The darkness expands. My mind swoons about, sliding to infinity, whirling pain into icy cold. The grave provides no comfort, and death will not console me. Then at last, the Veil is illuminated by Faith, and a voice cries out from within—

Our Father, who art in Heaven

Hallowed be Thy name

Thy kingdom come

Thy will be done…

And with that, I slip away from the pain of my many, many sorrows.

17

The glow of dawn is absorbed into the thick rain clouds, bathing everything in an eerie, gray light. The first drops of rain then fell onto the coffin, and onto the roof of the dark house. Signs of power thunder softly. The rain on the old tin roof is light, but still makes him jumpy while he paces the kitchen floor. Sweat glistens, trembling him as if he were in a deep freezer.

He stops the useless pacing and seeks refuge at the kitchen table. Hiding in his madman pose—with his dirty face leaning into his dirty hands. Rubbing and pulling on his hair.

A deep breath helps him face the facts.

It's those dreams…

If he lives to be a hundred, he'll never forget them. And he'll never forget the way she had been there to save him. The way she had comforted him, giving him hope. She had been like an angel, having power over the dark images, and the terror they caused. He remembers how each time, the darkness took shape and form, until the real world was around him again.

He remembers the angel that delivered him.

From the distance, the thunder is louder. Stronger. The rain is falling harder above him.

He lets the tears run down his face and fall to the table. Through terror and intense, burning pain, he stands up and walks out to the porch, gazing across the yard to the wooden box. Wondering what he has done and how in the world he could have possibly done it.

But it isn't only fear and guilt this time.

The rain pounds the porch roof above him. Chris looks again across the yard, and is almost afraid to go. He doesn't want to see it. He doesn't want to see her body inside that box…

Just then came the storm's first serious proclamation—in a quick, bright bolt of lightning. Thunder blasts, and at once he runs across the yard as if obeying an order. He braves intense dread, a strong awareness of his own mortality, and a profound regret for what he has done.

Quickly he opens the lid, tossing it away. In the smell of pinewood is blended the odor of her urine, and the sickly sweet aroma of her shampoo. He is struck by the grotesqueness of it all and tries not to look. But he catches a glimpse of her face, which makes him stop for a second and stare. Her expression is indefinably peaceful. But to his relief, to his infinite, cosmic relief…

My face is *warm.*

It fires new strength. New determination. He had thought my heart had failed. He is about to pick me up, when something happens…

Call it fatigue. Wet ground. Haste. Whatever. But a sudden, strong gust of wind blows into him, and he loses his footing as completely as anyone ever has. He then falls, he *flies* backwards—slamming into the ground, hitting his head so hard that he sees a flash as bright as silver lightning. In this second, he can swear he feels something, something infinitely stronger, pinning his shoulders. He draws a breath of panic, and is about to start wailing. But instantly he can move again, scuffling to his feet.

He shakes his confused, aching head. As quickly as he can, he picks me up and takes me into the house. Away from the storm. And the grave.

The skies uncurl. Across the windswept Earth unfurls this rainful mourning. Inside, he lays my wet body on the bedroom floor. With his pocket knife, he cuts and pulls away the surface ropes. The ropes underneath, against my body, are wrapped so tight he can hardly get his own hand underneath them. But he finds a place to cut, and does it quickly.

He then freed me from the rope cocoon, picked me up from the floor, and laid me onto the bed. The tight ropes leave deep, red marks on my arms and legs. My hair is soaking wet, and my face, legs and feet are dirty.

But I am alive. He feels my heart beating softly. But my face is deathly pale…

In that moment, he hears the sound of a dreary, husky voice, seeming to flow up from the floor and the walls around him. Every fear he's ever known comes together, prickling his skin, spinning him about, wide-eyed and shivery. He whimpers, peering through a haze, looking for the ghostly origin of the sound…

He glimpses the pale, bruised figure of his unconscious wife. Through blurred vision, he sees that my mouth has opened, as my lungs draw the loudest, most protracted breath imaginable.

I saw Death far away from me
Power lifted the cold winds
When leaves of color drift and swirl
Its touch is removed from my soul

Heaven is revealed in the clouds
Striking fire in the hearts of men
Resurrection from the Fear of Ages
Rest from dark and painful years

Haunted by these mournful spirits
Only sadness, no Curse of Gray
Paradise for another time
Another eternity.

I am sleeping soundly. Taking deep, regular breaths. Chris had watched me close for an hour before he could leave my side. He removed my wet, mud stained nightgown and cleaned the dirt from my skin. He wiped carefully the scraped, bruised skin that marked where the ropes had been. With a towel, he dried my hair the best he could, then slipped me into a clean, dry nightgown.

It's time to clean up the mess. The pile of muddy ropes is making him sick. He quickly grabs every rope, taking the short trip through the kitchen and out into the rain. The storm looks, it feels, like the leading edge of incredible power.

Chris sloshes his way through the pouring guilt, through the wet, weeping world. He makes it to the box without getting struck by lightning, which he had fully expected. The box, the shovel, the ground itself, are nothing more than faded shadows of horror.

Without hesitation, he throws in the bundle of rope, which makes a wet plopping sound when it hits inside. He picks up the lid, and can't resist the urge to place it on correctly, to give the ropes a proper burial.

Anything to ease the guilt. It claws into him with black, razor talons. He wastes no time picking up the shovel, setting fast to work in the pouring rain. The gravedigger, trying to bury his past in the ground.

Guilty fear. A wrongdoer's poison.

It courses through his veins, as he strikes the earth like a madman.

"Hello, John?"

"*Speaking.*"

"It's me, Chris."

"*Hey, son. What can I do for you? It's... It's Chris, Viv. I don't know, let me find out. Just let me get a word in, will you? I'll ask him, if you'll wait a minute... hey, Chris? You still there?*"

"Yeah."

"*Sorry about that. What can I do for you?*"

"John, I'm gonna have to take a few days off."

"*A few days?*"

"It's my wife. She's coming down with something, and she's gonna need a lot of rest. And she doesn't want me to leave her."

"*Is she gon' be alright?*"

"She'll be up and around in no time. I think she's just exhausted. She wants me here with her, to take care of her for a while."

A brief pause.

"*How long will you be gone?*"

"If you don't mind, I—" Chris stops. For some reason, he can't continue without getting choked up.

"*Well, it doesn't really matter. I tell you what, just take the whole week off, and don't worry about anything. It's gon' be rainin' for a couple of weeks anyway.*"

"I appreciate that, John. I really do."

"It's no problem. Call me back in a few days, and let me know if your wife's any better."

"I will. And thank you."

"If there's anything you need, just call me, okay?"

"Okay. Take care…" (And tell Vera I said hi).

Chris hangs up, and can't help but think about her. He had prayed she would answer the phone, though he had no idea what he would've said to her.

He hurries out of the rain, back to his black truck. He can hardly stand to be in this miserable weather.

Away from me.

The rains fall with steady assurance, each drop giving full account on the world below. The wind swirls and waves across the summer cropfields, making them like oceans in a violent storm. The clouds are thick and dark, absorbing into grey all the light of color. The light of joy and hope.

A summer rainstorm. One of controlled fury, with harsh rains of protracted, melancholy endurance.

Inside the house, Chris is in the comfortable old arm chair, listening to the raindrops attack the tin roof above him. The sound can be either soothing or unnerving, depending on the mood.

Expeditiously, he had stripped off his muddy clothes and thrown them all away, except for the boots. The belt was cut into little pieces. He then took a good, long bath, gladly washing the filth and stench off his body.

He wishes he could understand it all. The years of it. But he does know it is the last time. The desire to hurt me is gone. He remembers my premonition, the way I had begged him to move. Can betrayal ever really be forgiven? How long will it be, before he is struck down? How long.

Chris stands up from the chair, stepping lightly over to the window. He leans against the window frame, watching the water splash hard against the glass. The wind blows harder, driving the rain into the house in short, quick bursts.

Margaret Peele…

The source of those pale, blue eyes of his. A woman he can't bear to think about. For years, memories of her prompted the rage—at least in part. But today, thoughts of her only crush him.

His heart is broken.

After a while, signs of new life come to the little room. He turns and sees that I've begun to move. I moan softly, as though emerging from a long, restful sleep. He rushes to my side and sits quietly on the bed.

"Elizabeth." His voice is low. Almost whispery.

I open my dark eyes and begin to look around. But my expression is unclouded. I seem at total peace, unraveled by any apparent concern.

Chris lays close beside me, and we hold each other tight. He closes his eyes and listens as the rains fall in weeping. In lamentation for past sorrows.

Far into the night, the wind blew the rains across the eastern countryside. From the Peele house, over the Evans field…and beyond.

19

The house was built in 1910.

Under a comet.

Comets are harbingers of nothing. They foretell nothing.

Natural phenomena. Lonely travelers through the universe, on an endless journey around the sun. So rare and special that they cause foreboding. Misplaced fears and superstitions.

Someday, one may pass close enough, so it can be seen for what it is—

A glowing nucleus of cold, uncaring power and cataclysm.

If it were close enough, it would fill the sky both day and night. A sight to cause worldwide terror, panic, and weeping. Showing our cosmic insignificance. Illuminating a hopeless condition.

Revealing the truth.

But Fate holds them at a distance. Icy, hazy curiosities in a dark'ned sky—

Harbingers of nothing.

Like all houses, this one has a history.

The first to live in her tiny house was a farmer.

A *sexual sadist*—

And his wife.

The woman suffered for many years. Abuses too horrible to be discussed. She was granted mercy by fate, when her husband's sadism was fully realized.

Her final lesson ended when her throat was cut, and her blood was spilled on the bedroom floor.

The house was built in 1910.

Under a comet.

20

Two beats per measure… like a clock.

I wake up on Sunday morning, clutched in the arms of my sleeping husband, listening to the rhythm of his heartbeat. I want to drift again and let my mind take over. I want to hear what is going to happen. What sounds will come—

But the nausea in the pit of my stomach won't allow it. It makes me remember that icy January morning so many years ago. It always does. At that time, I lived in mortal terror of getting pregnant again. But when it happened, the stress of worry took care of it for me. Mercifully.

No babies… no children

The storm gives a brilliant, frightening account. From the north sky begins a river of blue lightning, which spreads into a network of energy. What follows is the voice of doom and eschatology. Fury unleashed—the nature of catastrophic power. I sit up quickly and look at my husband, who only stirs the slightest bit. The house shakes, while thunder rolls like a thousand cannons over the farmland.

Like the sky split in two

My hand rests over my heart, and I take deep breaths. Maybe, it's time to get up. I rub my husband's arm gently, then stand up…

But the room spins around. Something invisible seems to push me back onto the bed.

Aside from my headache, all of my muscles are sore. My shoulder feels like something inside is sliced halfway through. But I want to get up. So I push through the spinning and the soreness, change into my midnight blue fabric, then take my old radio to the kitchen table and plug it in. A souvenir of my time.

The only thing I can think about is orange juice. A craving so strong I wish I *was* an orange. I click on my radio, then pour a glass of my favorite beverage and sit down at the table.

"…but did you notice the drop in dynamic level? Kind of to a furtive pianissimo. At least that's what it sounds like to me (smug laughter). There's that eerie sense of stasis you feel when the harmonic changes reduce to a simple, tonic-dominant oscillation…"

What?

I think I'll flip around, to see if there's anything else in the radio wasteland…

Quickly, I turn it off. And listen to the rain instead.

The raindrops are loud on the tin roof. It makes me think of a barn. The house is cold. Filled with emptiness. I take another sip, allowing my gaze to fall on the little window beside the back door.

Even as I rub the knotted pain in my shoulder, and look at the bruises on my arm, I can't fathom it. I rub my temples, then run my hand through my hair…

And pull out the tiniest piece of a dead leaf.

I feel like a ghost. Like I could stand up, and walk right through the wall into the bedroom.

But I am flesh and blood.

And this is real.

Immediately, instantaneously I go to the bathroom, and spend the next few minutes brushing my hair like there is no tomorrow. But I can't wash it yet. I have no desire to be submerged in water. Not today. After I finish, I plait a thick braid down the length of it and go back to the kitchen. Back to my orange juice.

Dear Lord…

Please send someone to love me

To protect me from evil…

Amen.

For most of my life, there's been a profound, distant sadness to my expression. The past few months has done a lot to remove it, but events have summoned it again. My face— my *eyes*—again bear the pain of a lonely, tormented condition. I am helpless as the depressive spirit creeps up behind me, and reaches into my mind and body.

A flash of light bursts through the window. Thunder breaks from the clouds again. Not as loudly as before, but the house still shakes. When I look at the big window over the sink, I see the glass coated by driving rainfall, blocking my view of the gray, grieving world.

Suddenly, the noisy bedsprings creak, enough to make me think he is getting up. But then, silence.

I'm not hungry, but he might be. Neither of us has eaten since—

I give my arm a good pinch, and shake myself hard.

Yes. I am awake.

Still in quiet disbelief, the Lonely gets up to fix breakfast. But the room betrays me and tilts, knocking me and my Indian braid back into my chair. Then the room spins about, daring me to get up again. I have to sit still another five minutes or so, until I feel better. Finally, I'm able to get up and start breakfast. The standard fare—little breakfast links. My favorites. And there is a box of frozen waffles we haven't opened yet. Maybe I'll cook eggs, and a pot of grits.

There aren't any eggs. And those chickens haven't laid in ages…

I hear footsteps, shuffling in the bedroom.

"Chris?"

No answer.

"Chris, honey?"

I go to look in the bedroom. But he is fast asleep.

I'm uneasy. Dreadfully so. Every tiny hair on my neck stands on end. Fearfully, I step back in the kitchen, click on the radio, and continue fixing our breakfast. Before long, the sausage is cooking on the stove.

The storm blows fiercely. The kind of rainstorm that drenches at once, running a person back inside and making him sorry he went out.

The stove's heat is more inviting. And I notice the air around me…

I turn away from the stove, glaring at the ceiling. Gazing beyond it.

"Don't you do this to me", I whisper—a hurt, anguished hiss. "I don't *deserve* it. I'm scared and I want you to help me. I'm *tired* of being scared of every shadow."

But grief has come to claim me, along with the burden of recollection. My throat develops that lump inside. The warning that a flood of tears is building up. I turn back to my breakfast, but the stove becomes clouded in my vision. My face has that ugly, contorted look of anguish and inner pain. As I whine and struggle against the sadness wave, I make a curious and interesting portrait—an unadorned brunette in my Indian braid and country dress, at a cooking stove, in a gray shack in the middle of nowhere, whining from emotional exhaustion

I turn the stove to a lower setting and sit down, clutching myself as tightly as I can—

And the wave of grief hits. Doubling me over, causing me to howl softly in physical pain. For a long time, I mourn and cry under a burden of remembrance. Mixed with the noise of the pouring rain is the sound of lamentation, as I weep for myself, and a lifetime of undeserved pain and suffering. What I feel runs deep—so much deeper than the scars, and the healed abominations. All of it takes me captive, until my mood is as bleak as the weather. I wail and howl for evil itself, to the heavens, and to the uncaring rain.

After a long while, I'm able to get up. The front of my dress is damp, where it has captured some of the tears. I need to go wash the itching off my face, and out of my nose and eyes. So I walk slowly through the house, through the odd, unseasonable cold into the bathroom. When I flip on the light, I jump, and nearly scream when I see it…

"Chris…"

I want to wake him up.

But it was just a shadow.

Something must have flown outside the window…

My skittish nerves annoy me. So I step confidently into the bathroom and wipe my face, looking in the mirror just long enough. Just long enough to see that my face is clean. But I don't stare into my reflection. Into its eyes. When I am done, I put away my washcloth, turn off the light and march nervously back to the kitchen. I retrieve my orange juice, noticing that the radio sermon is good company. The crying is finished, and now I am left empty. A cavern of sorrow.

The fogged up window at the sink draws my attention. I step over to it, and draw several curious shapes in one of the window panes. But I can't shake the strange feeling. Like being on the edge of a nightmare.

A long, brilliant flash flickers. A powerful glow, cast from miles away. The storm is huge—it takes a long time for the thunder to rumble over the house.

My nerves are in pieces.

And now—

The lights.

It's already dark enough inside. Even with the kitchen light burning. Anxiously, I glance around, but there's nothing to see. It's only the kitchen, my little breakfast, and the comforting voice on the radio.

Another brilliant flash. As bright as sunlight.

The lights twitch between life and death. The radio voice continues on.

Another flash.

The lights flicker…

Darkness.

The comforting, familiar hum of the refrigerator is gone, and the radio is silent. The rain is a deafening clamour on the roof.

The morning has progressed, but the storm has devoured the sunlight. Darkness permeates everything, appearing as though the sun has never risen.

I stand still and quiet, tucked away in the sink corner by the window. The refrigerator hides my view of the living room. I clutch my empty glass for dear life, listening to the last sounds of hope fade away…

The electric stove has died. The food's quiet sizzling is drowning in rainfall.

I remember the shadow.

I can't move. But my mind is sound and alert, making me stare wide-eyed into the darkened room before me.

The time has come. Time to look in the other room. To face the silly fears of nothing, so they'll go away. With what little courage I have left, I step forward. I lean forward. My lips are pressed together, and I don't dare breathe.

The living room comes into view…

I see pale, elongated *shadows,* weaving and twisting about. Ice runs through my blood. But I breathe a sigh of relief, realizing they are merely from the rain, cascading down the living room windows. But the fear won't die. I step backwards to my corner against the sink. My eyes are wide open.

Unnatural cold. The corner shadows are bigger.

The rain gives rise to another sound. From the chattering rain comes the faintest breath…

Every nerve in my body tingles. My skin prickles, like a thousand cold needles.

The seeds of an eternal scream are planted.

So I *close my eyes*.

The whispers grow. They have clarity and purpose. Soon, they are loud enough to hear over the rain, penetrating my mind. Craving what is left of my poor sanity.

I whimper…

I open my eyes…

A shriek bursts forth like a fountain. My glass cup falls. Pieces shatter. The whispers are louder than the rain…

"accursed woman…"

The hazy figure vanishes through the wall…

And the whispering fades.

21

*F*or a long time, it's been coming.

A talk.

Vera sits quietly at the kitchen table of her southern palace. Listening to the storm.

Waiting.

"Elizabeth, wake up."

I blink my eyes open.

"Are you okay?" he asks. "What happened?"

"I don't…"

My mind whirls. My whereabouts swirl about me.

"You shouldn't have been cooking anyway," he says. "If you were hungry, you should have told me."

"That's right. I forgot all about your breakfast. Come sit with me in the kitchen. I'll get it."

I'm so determined to get up that I almost succeed. But he gently ushers me back to the pillow.

"Don't you worry about that. You get some rest."

"Are you sure?"

"Of course," he says, touching my forehead gently.

"Did your breakfast get done?"

"I don't know," he says. "When did the power go out?"

"Just before you woke up."

"Is that why you screamed?"

"I guess so."

I have taken my place among the unfortunate. I've opened my eyes, and I have seen it. But who will ever know?

"I was dreaming," he says. "that it was snowing outside, and that it was as cold as winter in here. And then I heard the loudest *whispering*. Your scream woke me up, and it was so dark I thought it was the middle of the night. I got up to see if you were alright, and when I touched you…"

"What?" I ask, eyebrows raised.

"When I touched you, you fainted."

"I…I was just scared because the lights went off. You know how I am. I jump at every little shadow."

"I swear I wasn't gonna hurt you."

"I know. It wasn't that at all."

"It's still kind a dark in here," he says, glancing around the room. "That's probably because the power is out."

"You're right. It's probably because the power is out."

Darkness permeates the house. Like a gray twilight. Lightning flashes, and the thunder soon follows.

"This is a big one," he says. "A farmer's rain. Its gon' be around awhile."

"What'll we do when its gets dark?"

"We'll need some light. There's a kerosene lamp in the shed."

We are both uneasy, but especially Chris. I notice that he seems downright fearful.

"Well, I'm starved," he says. "You hungry?"

"A little."

I think he's beautiful…

"I'll go to the kitchen," he says. "I'll see if breakfast is done."

He gets up, and starts toward the kitchen.

"Chris? Will you eat in here with me?"

"Okay."

"Chris!"

He stops dead in his tracks, and hurries back to my side.

"What is it?"

"I forgot to tell you. You'd better put some shoes on."

"How come?"

My voice gathers a mysterious, faraway tone…

"When the lights went out, I dropped my glass on the kitchen floor…and it broke into a thousand pieces."

The peculiar storm churned with perpetual self regeneration. At times the rains fell gently to the ground, covering it with life giving mists of water. But then, there would be a noisy, violent deluge, drenching the countryside with heavy outpourings of unwarranted, undeserved fury.

We take refuge in the darkness of this storm, resting together in the bedroom. We sit calmly together, with Chris in the old, cushioned armchair, and me at the head of the bed. For a long time we rest in silence, hearing the rain clattering on the tin roof. We are both in a calm, restful state of shock, reflecting to ourselves on the horror that has been our marriage, and the horror of our whole lives.

I sit still. Clutching the soft pillow, staring blankly into my own thoughts and memories. We languish still and quiet, listening to the weather, examining our own emotions in peace. My thoughts carry me outside the house, through the rain and downward, to where the box is buried. Through the wet pine I go, revisiting the smell and claustrophobic darkness. It makes me take a deep, reassuring breath. I can almost hear the raindrops pounding the coffin lid, while I wait for the water to rise. The water will soon begin to pour inside the coffin with me, slowly creeping upward, finding its way to my lungs...

I shake myself, drawing another deep breath. Chris's look is pitiful. Filled with concern. Truthfully, I feel sorry for him, knowing he's burdened with guilt too heavy for anyone to bear. But there'll be plenty of time to comfort him later. To assure him that he's forgiven for everything.

You alright? he asks.

"Yes. I'm fine."

I think there is a dreamy, depressive color to my voice. He notices in my eyes a wistful, contemplative stare.

I'd better get that lamp before dark, he says. He gets up from the chair, and retrieves his black, hooded raincoat from the closet. There's an umbrella, but the cloth is pulled half away from its metal skeleton.

"I just remembered something," he says. "We got a formal dinner invitation not too long ago."

"With who?"

"My boss, and his wife. John and Vera Evans."

"Are you going?"

"I don't think so. But they're nice people, I like 'em a lot. I think you would too."

"Well, I hope you didn't invite 'em over here," I say, sounding more antisocial than I meant to. "I mean, this house and everything."

"You know I didn't invite 'em. But I'm startin' to get the feeling that—"

"That what?"

"Nothing. I was just thinking about some odd things that happened over there a while back."

"What things?"

"Nothin' important, I guess."

We're both quiet again. Staring aimlessly into the gray room.

"I'll be back sweetie." We have a good kiss, that lights us up like the sky during this lightning storm.

"Honey?"

"What?"

"Your feet."

"I'll just dry 'em off when I get back."

"What about the glass in the kitchen?"

"I swept it up," he says. "I'll be fine."

Through our algid, eidolic space, I follow him to the back door. A loud, infinity of rainfall greets us. It seems to pour from an eternal source, unbounded by time. Beholden to no earthly rules of logic or duration.

The rain pelts the coat as he hurries across the lawn, sloshing through the puddles to the tiny shed, just behind the chicken yard. Inside the shed, the hatchet gives him a chill when he sees it. He grabs the old fashioned oil lamp and kerosene can, and splashes back through the rain towards the house. When he steps onto the porch, there I am, holding the screen door open for him with a towel in my hand.

I take the lamp from him, placing it on the kitchen table. He sits the can on the floor against the wall, then closes out the rain.

That rain is cold, he says.

I drape his raincoat over a chair to dry. Kneeling down with the towel, I begin to dry his legs and feet. As he looks down at me, his heart is crushed under a powerful remorse, love and compassion.

"You'll catch a chill. Come put a shirt on over that t-shirt."

He goes obediently, and gladly with me. After helping him into his blue and black flannel, we sit down on the bed together. I breathe a deep sigh.

'That's my favorite shirt.'

How do you really feel, Elizabeth? he says.

A pause—

"Like I just woke up from a nightmare."

Ever since they got home from church today, John has been avoiding her. Cooped up in his stuffy office. Worrying his mind over matters of big grain, and big money. But it is time. He raises up from the big leather chair and blows a breath, rubbing his fingers backward through his sun-lightened dark hair. Anxiously, he leaves the cold office behind, moving slowly towards the kitchen.

He has never been so afraid of anything in his life. Except for the grain. When it swallowed him that day.

"Hey, Viv."

"Hey."

"Everything alright?"

"Mmm hmm."

"Reason I asked, is 'cause you look like you've had a lot on your mind lately. You been gettin' that look in your eyes."

"What look?"

"Like you forget where you are sometimes. Like you're a million miles away."

She smiles. A lovely, demure smile. Her pinned up hair is golden.

"Anything you need to talk about?"

"No," she says. "I'm just feelin' the weather. I'll be fine."

John wanders toward the counter. He notices the white roses in her crystal vase.

"Well, honey, there's somethin' *I* need to talk about," he says. "Somethin' that's been botherin' me a lot."

He gazes right into her eyes.

Oh my God

"Viv, we've had a lotta guys come and go on this farm. A lot of 'em have been good lookin', and a few of 'em were nice, even perfect gentlemen. Good people. The kind of fellas you like havin' around."

Her expression is fixed.

"You never gave me a reason to worry about this before, Viv."

She stares quietly.

"I want the truth."

"I…"

"Vera, you've to be kidding me," he sighs. "Dear God."

There is a long, epic silence in that kitchen.

"You're gonna sit there at that table, under this roof, and admit to me that you…Vera, cut this sh*t and *talk to me!*"

"I don't know why, John," she says, through tears. "I don't know why it happened."

"And that's supposed to make me feel better?" he says. " 'Cause you don't know *why?*"

"But I *don't*. All I know is that I can't stop thinking about him."

John grabs the crystal vase, stomps toward her and smashes it at her feet. She suppresses a scream as he lunges, brimming a jealous rage. For a brief instant, he imagines his strong hands at her beautiful throat. But her tears dampen the fires, and she gazes pitifully. Ashamedly.

"John, I—"

"I know what it is," he says, clumping back to the counter, running his fingers through his hair. "I mean, he practically saved you from being *raped* right here in this kitchen. And what he did for me. If he hadn't been there that day… I mean… things like this can affect people, Vera. Make 'em think that…"

John looks out the rainy window, and thinks about how insignificant his life had become.

The wealthy man turns toward her again, to bluish gray eyes. Betraying eyes, glistening. While fury threatens, deep hurt takes hold, marching him angrily down the long hallway, and their palace resounds with the loudest door slam Vera's ever heard. Even so, she feels relieved. At least part of this storm has come and gone.

White roses lay scattered among pieces of broken crystal. A drop of water tickles her leg. But she ignores it and stands up from the table, drifting to the patio door. Touching the hazy glass, the farmer's wife watches the lightning, and hears the thunder roll across the dreary earth.

22

"*lizabeth?*"

"Yes?"

"I have to ask you something."

I hold his hand tightly.

"I'd like to ask you if you could... if you could find it in your heart to forgive me, for all the things that I've done."

The memory of those long, dark years presses down upon us. The question itself sends a wave of disbelief through him, making him shake his head. He thinks of how ridiculous it is for him to still be alive anyway, asking his wife to forgive him for causing her more suffering than most people could ever imagine.

The tears of his regret gather, then begin to flow.

A decade of torture.

But I had never surrendered to blame, nor contempt. It had all been to me like a dark shadow. Acting through him, of its own volition. For me, there is nothing to forgive. But for his sake, I speak, and try to give him the absolution he so desperately needs.

"I never blamed you, or hated you for any of it. Chris, I love you."

He looks away from me, shaking his head in total disagreement.

"Look at me, Christopher."

"I can't."

"Do you love me?"

"You know I do," he says, with a pitiful, choked voice.

"Then look at me. I *love* you."

A quick pause..

"For everything that you've ever done to me. I forgive you."

He lowers his head again, powerless against the repentance wave. I stare in disbelief, watching quietly as my hopes began to take shape before my eyes.

"I'm sorry, Elizabeth," he whispers. "I am *so* sorry."

He begins to tremble, as the grief tears at his insides.

"Come here," I say.

At first, he leans on my shoulder, while I put my arm around him. But the trembling soon gives way to outright shaking, and he grabs my dress hard enough to pop a thread, sliding down to his knees.

"Please," he sobs. "Please forgive me..."

"I do. I do forgive you."

I can feel the strength in his body, as he clings to me.

"It's alright. Everything will be alright."

In that instant, his quiet sobbing transforms into a sorrowful, pathetic wail. I hold on to him, as he endures the horror of remorse, and the pain of genuine contrition.

But I feel no sadness. I am numb, and can only hold him in pity.

"I always loved you," he says. "I never wanted to hurt you, Elizabeth. I never wanted any of it to happen. I didn't…I didn't…"

He breaks down for several minutes, crying loudly in my arms.

After a while, he is calmer. Sniffling and breathing quietly.

"Please tell me why I did it. Please tell me."

"I don't know. I don't know why evil things happen. It was just meant for us."

And suddenly he is fearful, as if a phantom were creeping towards him.

"Those things I did," he says. "How could I have done it… I don't want to see it. Please don't make me see it anymore…"

But his mind takes him all the way back to the beginning. He slowly begins to remember everything.

And his pitiful howling resumes.

His contrition came in long and short bursts. Lasting the entire Sunday afternoon.

23

The rains fell across the entire landscape, saturating every forest and every field, swelling every brook and stream into a small river. John and Vera were tucked safely inside their southern palace, protected by their country fortress. They couldn't hear the rain pattering their expensive shingles, and they were well protected from the hand of cold suffering and misery.

But there are issues. There are always issues.

They haven't spoken in hours. The entire time, she had been in her bedroom, trying to understand.

A deep, cosmic love. So much stronger than passion or infatuation.

She's been crying in the room for most of the day. Loudly. And she didn't care if John heard her. She hoped he did. She wonders how much more of it she can handle, anyway.

She needs to know why. Why she loves Chris like—

Suddenly, she understood.

In some strange way, Chris Peele is like *family*. But with none of the petty foolishness and bitter angst that runs through blood ties. There is no blood connection. It is spiritual. Deeper than anything her and John Evans ever had.

Vera rises up from her comfortable bed and puts on her slippers. To quickly go look for her husband.

She knocks on the office door, surprised to find that he isn't inside. So she goes to a guest bedroom and finds him lying on the bed, watching the little color television set.

"Hey there."

"How do, stranger," he says, trying to pretend he hasn't noticed her. "You can turn that down. It was puttin' me to sleep anyway."

Vera turns it off, then sits on the guest bed, beside her husband.

"I've got somethin' to tell you."

Already, he knows it's something he doesn't want to hear.

"I just figured somethin' out," she says. "It's like a burden just lifted off my shoulders."

"I'm listenin'."

"The way I feel about Chris," she says. "It hasn't changed. I *do* love him. I have from the time I first met him. And for a long time, I thought it was romantic. And yes, I did wonder about him. For that part of it, I'm really sorry…

"But I'm *not* sorry for loving him."

No. She isn't sorry for that. In Vera's gray eyes is the hint of storms past, and pain buried deep inside her. A tempest born from John's betrayal, forged with the heat of her raging, passionate anger.

Her husband's own indiscretion—

Many years ago.

"Chris and I have a *connection*," she says. "It's been gettin' stronger, and I've been killin' myself trying to figure out why. Who knows, maybe I've just tricked myself into believin' it. But one thing about this whole mess is clear to me now…

"I love him as surely as if he were a part of my own family. I don't expect you to understand, or to even forgive me for the way I've acted…but he needs me, John. He hasn't said anything, but I can't shake the feeling that he really needs me. Maybe his wife is hurting him, I don't know. But he won't talk to me about it. There were times when I think he wanted to, but…

"I have to become a part of his life. And I don't know where this is goin', or even if he wants me around, but I have to find out. I don't expect you to understand, and if you want to throw me out, there's nothing I can do."

Vera lowers her head, and sighs deeply.

"But I have to go to him. I have to see what kind of pain he's in. And I know I'll never rest until I do."

She'd been prone to bouts of depression their entire marriage. There were even a few times when he thought he'd have to put her away. But he has never seen anything like this.

"You're right, I don't understand it," he says. "But I trust you, Viv. If he's touched you this much, then I know there's gotta be somethin' to it."

She leans over, and hugs him.

"I'm sorry for the way I've been."

"There's nothin' to be sorry about," he says. "He is kinda special. Sometimes I've felt like a father to him."

"I wondered that, myself. But I just never felt like a mother to him. I still don't."

"It's no wonder. You're not old enough to be his mother."

"If I was, it would have been a lot simpler," she says. "Would have saved us all a lotta trouble."

"There were a couple a times when Joe tried to start somethin' with him," John says, "and he would either just look at him, or walk away. I only saw him get mad at Joe once."

"What happened?"

"They say it's always the quiet ones."

"Hmm?"

"Oh nothin' ." "They didn't fight or anything. Joe's tough, but I bet you he woulda been sorry that day. You know somethin', Vera?"

He pauses.

"That boy saved my life. I'd be dead if it wasn't for him."

"John, you really do need somebody to help you run things."

Outside, the thunder sounds softly, as if echoed from another world. Their country empire seems a vast, oppressive thing. A monster, that sought to devour everything around it.

"He's been taking more and more time off, hasn't he?" Vera says.

"Yeah."

"Tomorrow," she says. "We'll go tomorrow."

"I'm scared to death, Elizabeth."

"You don't have to be. We don't have to be afraid anymore."

But I *am* afraid. Afraid of the world itself, and of our uncertain future. I fear every corner of our little house, and the shadows that move inside.

It's just the storm...

Storms are sometimes a welcomed diversion for me. A time of escape and reflection. But this one is dreadful. The air itself clings to otherworldliness. There is a foreboding that hangs over me like a darkly veiled canopy, keeping me from seeing clearly beyond this rainy day, or even the hour.

The wind whirls suddenly, pushing against the foundations of the gray shack, driving the rain harder into the walls and the roof.

And then...

A Hellishly loud *clamour* against the metal rooftop, which becomes a loud scraping, clawing sound. We jump, and I scream to the top of my lungs.

The gust of wind had snatched a dead branch from the giant tree, and flung it on top of our house. It had slammed into the tin roof, sliding down to the ground. Lying there, between our house and the woods is my phantom and Chris' nightmare demon. Mocking us both. Resting comfortably in the dreary storm.

"I'm sorry I screamed."

"It's alright," he says, his hand on his chest.

"Have you ever seen a spirit?"

"What do you mean?" he says.

"Ghosts. Do you believe in them?"

He listens to the clamour of rain, while glancing around the shadowy house.

"I think maybe I do."

I want to tell him about the shadow, and that gray thing in the kitchen.

"I don't believe that ghosts are dead people. I think that when a person dies, his spirit leaves the earth. So if you see one, you're not seeing a person."

"What are they then?" he asks.

"Demons. Or maybe even angels. But they're just spirits. Either good or evil."

"What about people who claim to talk to the dead?" he says. "The spirits know things, things that only the dead relative can know."

"They're being tricked. Compared to us, demon spirits are all knowing, and all powerful. People can't imagine how clever an evil spirit is. It can make a person believe anything. It only wants to deceive, and then destroy."

Chris thinks about his own behavior.

About the evil.

"Sometimes I wonder about this house."

"What's on your mind?" he says.

"Nothing."

"What is it?"

"Do you think places can be evil?"

We both pause, and take another good look around.

"How else could you have done it all, Chris? I don't know if any of that stuff was in you before we came here."

"All of it was my fault," he says. "I'm the one to blame.. not this ridiculous house."

"I'm only saying that maybe it was a *part* of why it all happened. Just think about the horrible things that went on in here."

"I don't want to."

"We're gonna have to. When was the first time you hurt me?"

"In the back yard. When I brought you here to see the house. It was at sunset, under the tree."

"You had never acted that way before. There had never been the slightest hint of it. And I had never snapped at you like that. It was terrible."

"I wonder who lived here before us," he says. "There were times when I walked in here, and I swear I could feel it pressing down on me. You don't know how many times I wanted to grab you by the hand and just run away from here, but I *couldn't*. I always got so tired and depressed I just didn't care."

Chris watches the lamp flame give life to the shadows. He shakes his head, staring with contempt at every archaic inch of the dingy shack.

"It's too bad your house got sold," he says. "We could've stayed there a long time."

I remember my old house. And the things my mother did to me.

In private.

"It could have ended differently for both of us," he says.

"My worst fears came true. For a long time, I was afraid that you were going to kill me."

"But I didn't. And it was a miracle. How did you endure it for so long, Elizabeth," he asks, looking at me. "How did you survive?"

"I don't know. Maybe prayer, and my music."

"But…"

"Go on."

"The bathtub. I could have sworn…I thought I had done it, Elizabeth. I th…"

The memory washes over me like a flood. I remember dying.

"I was looking for you. I didn't know where you were."

Amazement, then relief. In his memory, he had held me there for a long time.

Such a long time.

"What did your Momma do to you?" I ask.

The question nearly takes his breath away.

"Whether I deserved it or not," he says. "It went on until I was about thirteen years old."

"Did she hurt you badly? Did she torture you?"

He sighs, but cannot answer yet about the boiling water, the hot knife burns on his back, or the cigarette burns in his side. But I understand, especially when I think about my own mother—

Cruel, *twisted* things.

In the dark, flickering light, I notice his expression. It is quietly fearful, and very humble and meek. He seems to me like a lost soul, seeking refuge from the loneliness of his existence.

But I am still afraid.

"I know I deserve to die," he says. "I wanted you to hate me, and sneak away and get lost forever, so I could never find you and hurt you again."

"Really?"

"I swear to God," he says. "But I couldn't stop hurting you. It was like an addiction."

"I'll bet it was because of what your mother did. But I know part of it was my fault."

"Don't…"

"It's true. I could have left, but I didn't. I could have gotten help. I could have kept trying until I was brave enough to get away. But I never did. And I blamed it on love and fear. But if I had really wanted to, I could have gotten away."

"Could you?"

I understand the question. Knowing it has nothing to do with the year I spent locked in this bedroom, or threats of being tied to trees and nailed through the hands. Even now, I can hardly accept the reality that I am content to live in isolation and be treated like a dog. The seeds had been planted at birth, and had been nurtured by my mother's contempt, and my husband's cruelty. A natural shyness, that has grown to pathological dimensions…

But not a literal fear of open spaces. It is a terror of the world itself. A dread of leaving the confined, familiar space of the house and the yard. Like a prisoner who has grown to love her cell, and every chip and crack in the walls. Add to this a fear of social situations, a terror of public ridicule or humiliation. My mother had worked on me for years. So skillfully and completely, that my self-esteem was gone by the time I met my husband.

I was raised by my mother alone. Who took me out of school when I was 12. Starvation, imprisonments and beatings were standard. Was Barbara's husband dead, because her daughter was born? Had she suffered in poverty, alone, because her daughter was born? One Sunday afternoon when I was 19, twenty years of repressed obsession and blame spilled over, after Mother saw me return a young man's admiring gaze in church. When we got home, in the tradition of her own upbringing, she disrobed to her undergarment, then removed every stitch of my clothing, tying my ankles together with my bra. When it was done, the leather whip had stripped the blood, dripping from my back, and the wooden hairbrush had split the skin on my buttocks and thighs. The wooden handle was pushed deep into my backside, until it was veiled in blood. Barbara Jean then stood behind me, and twisted my nipples unmercifully, listening to me scream. Feeling me scream. She released them in a hard, biting pull, and took hold of my throat. With her other hand, she memorized all of my flesh, then fumbled with her own bra, until her own massive breasts had spilled out, pressed against my back like two white flesh pillows. On her nipples, the sensation was unbearable. Her movements became more determined. They became involuntary. Rhythmic. She whispered, *"no,"* denying what was happening inside her. But then, with more power than she could have imagined, two decades of repressed energy *exploded* into her body. She shook violently. There was a scream for the ages. A cry for mercy.

"Put your tongue in my mouth," Barbara whispered, tears streaming down her face.

I clumsily pushed my tongue into my mother's mouth. The woman began to suck my tongue—gently, slowly, up and down the length of it. Sucking the life. Sucking the life from her daughter's spirit.

All of my confidence. *All* of my joy and self esteem vanished into a vapour of hopelessness. Afterwards, I retreated whole heartedly, into a private world of darkness. Where there was only prayer.

And color.

24

"*J*ohn, I'm ready!"

Vera stands impatiently at her kitchen door. Waiting to go.

I'll bet she is the skinniest, bossiest, funniest faced little thing in Martin County

With all of her heart, Vera believes that whoever she is, she had him whipped to death, along with claws dug so deep in his poor back that he couldn't move without her permission.

Surely, she'll be a problem.

She won't let me help them. She'll make him leave the farm, and I'll never see him again.

Vera's mind feeds her images of a country witch, casting her spell over the angel. Doing unspeakable things to him in private. Holding him captive. Making him stay home for nothing, just to keep him close to her evil bosom.

Sometimes it struck Vera as curious, that she didn't even know the woman's name.

"John, will you hurry up?"

"Just go get in the car. I'll be there in a minute."

"Well what's keepin' you?"

"None of your business, Vera. Go on, now, I'll be there in a minute."

"I'm waitin' right here," she says.

After another minute or so, he comes out of the bedroom. He'd been getting his money right, deciding how much to take with him. How much he'd be willing to part with, if it came to that.

"John, do you have to wear that coat?"

"What's wrong with it?"

"Were going to somebody's *house*," she says. "You don't dress like that when we go to other people's houses, do you?"

"It's just Chris. It's not like he's somebody important."

"First of all, that denim coat is disgusting. It's filthy, and it smells like grain. And when it gets wet it'll just plain stink. And second, Chris is about the most important person you've ever met, in case you've forgotten already. And third…"

"All *right*. I'll change it."

"Nothin' fancy honey," she calls after him. "Just put on your blue waterproof jacket."

And I wish you would change those pants

Vera's own clothes are casual, but striking, from the royal blue dress with black print design, to the black Klein pumps and matching black leather purse, and she is covered in a full length raincoat of the darkest gray.

She leaves her farmer husband behind, and steps out into the rain, opening her umbrella—which is the exact color as her coat—taking the long walk down the concrete walkway to their silver luxury car. The silver Oldsmobile is a refuge, and still smells brand new inside. The gray interior is soft. Very comfortable. How she regrets that her favorite car is fading into history! She stares blankly at the frosted windshield. It is the middle of Summer, but the day is as cold as one in Autumn.

She's met hundreds of people. But Vera has to admit to herself that she is scared to death of meeting this woman.

The car door clicks and swings open, and John hurries inside from the rain. He is clearly bothered. He likes Chris a lot, and is grateful. But to him, he's just a good man and a great worker, who helps him keep his farmer's pockets full. John Evans has been one of the lucky few. A rich farmer is as rare as an honest politician, a straight lawyer, a virtuous minister, or an impartial judge.

Rare.

"Okay, Prissy. You satisfied?"

"Much better. You don't look so much like a farmer."

"Me lookin' like a farmer's done alright by you, hadn't it? I know how much that outfit costs. It's a sin to pay that much for a coat."

"God forgive me, then," she says, under her breath. "Why don't you send that truck back, and then we can talk."

"Amen."

They drive down the rain-soaked driveway, beginning the short trip to the old house by his southernmost field.

"You never did come take a look at that field."

"I haven't seen the last *two* fields you bought. John when you first met Chris, you didn't see her at all?"

"Nope. I don't think I would've known he was married if I hadn't asked him. I couldn't believe somebody actually lived in that old house. If Charlie had sold me all that land, I would've had that thing torn down. I think he kept it because of that tree."

"A tree?"

"You'll know what I'm talkin' about when you see it."

"Where would Chris have gone, if you had torn his house down?" she asks, trying to antagonize.

"He would've had plenty of time to move."

"Maybe you can sell Chris that field," she said. "You could work somethin' out with him."

"I thought about that. I might just talk to him about it."

"It would be the least we could do," she sighs.

"Sounds like you been makin' plans. When were you gonna tell me about 'em?"

"I just thought about it," she says. "You've got to admit, it makes sense."

"What if this doesn't work out, Viv?"

"What?"

"What if he and his wife don't want to be bothered with us. With you?"

The question cuts her with an icy blade.

"Do you really believe he wouldn't want me in his life?"

"The truth is, I'm not sure," he says. "I know he likes us, but he never jumped at a one of our invitations. Not a one."

"Do I have to remind you of the kind of a person he is?" she says.

"I know he's shy, but sometimes I think it's more than that. Maybe he just doesn't like to be bothered. If that's the case, we could be makin' a mistake."

"I don't think so."

Of course you don't, he thinks. Here I am in the rain, on a Monday morning driving to a good looking man's house because you're *obsessed* with him. I think you're going crazy. This whole thing is…

"Crazy," he whispers.

Vera heard him, and it hurt her feelings. Yes, it's madness, but she can't help it. It's something that has to be done.

They drive on in the heavy rain, past the miles of trees and summer crop fields, and even the occasional brick farmhouse, all of which are largely obscured from their view.

What if I really have gone crazy?

The closer she gets, the more terrified she becomes. Vera feels like an invader. An unwanted, uninvited guest. The small contempt she'd developed towards Chris' wife is gone. Replaced by fear.

All I have to do is put on my charity face. My angel of mercy face.

I shouldn't have thought badly about her.

She'll understand.

"Lonely out here, isn't it?" John asks.

Vera squints against the rain, hoping to catch a glimpse of the little cottage. They had turned down the muddy road, and the wheels are splashing in and out of the shallow mud holes, making the car rock gently back and forth.

"I was thinkin' about gettin' rid of this field anyway. It's too small to be doin' me much good."

Vera can't even hear him. How could she? Through the universe her mind had traveled, and all across the ages. Past her own origin, over her miserable days and years, unto this present day and time. She perceives a power—a crossing over—a traversing from the past to the present, into the far and distant future.

Nerves...just nerves

"There," she says, "is that..."

My God it can't be

"That's not it, is it?" she asks.

"It's the only house on this road."

"It...it must be the rain," Vera says. "It looks more like a *shed* than a house. It looks abandoned."

Vera is as anxious as ever. A frightful nervousness.

"There's his truck," she says bewilderedly. "*Darn* this rain—I can't see a thing. You'd think a hurricane was going through here."

"It hasn't rained like this in years," he says. "But it's good for the crop."

They are both nervous now, as he pulls the car into the front yard. After all, it isn't just Chris they have to worry about.

There is his wife.

Vera squints through the windshield, in shock at the pile of gray wood presuming to inhabit space in the shape of a house. She bites her thumbnail as John parks the car near the steps and turns off the engine.

"We pay him more than *that,* don't we?" she says. She is embarrassed for her angel, that he lives in a toolshed with windows and a sheet of tin for a roof. For a few minutes they both sit quietly, neither of them seeing the other staring at the little house. She can't resist the negative thoughts, so she lets them sink in, and run their course.

Accursed

"Is he in there?" Her voice is low. Almost whispery.

"Prob'ly."

"You ready to go in?"

"Let's go."

With the umbrella's help, they splash forward, surviving the short trip through the puddles to the front porch, which is barely sheltered from the driving rainfall.

Finally, Vera finds herself at Destiny's door. Afraid to knock, and terrified of what awaits her on the other side.

25

I open my eyes from the long, restful sleep, nearly convinced I hear a lonely knock at the door.

Is it a dream? Who would come here?

But the screen rattles again under the force of knocking. The sound clatters, reverberating through the house.

"*Chris!*" I hiss a loud whisper, shaking him until he moves. "Chris, wake up."

"Morning," he says. My hair is clean, and silky smooth. Those strawberries from my shampoo light a fire in him.

"Good morning."

"What's the matter?" he says.

"I heard a knock at the door."

"In this weather? You sure you weren't dreaming? This house'll play tricks with—"

There it is again. Louder, and more determined.

"Maybe it's somebody looking for food. Somebody came here asking for food once."

"Let's wait a second," he says. "If they knock again, we'll answer it."

A third, loud knocking. Full of desperation.

"You answer it."

"Alright. But we probably shouldn't answer it at all."

He slides out of bed, moving sleepily towards the door, regretting in his heart that he isn't going to work today. To maybe catch a glimpse of her.

To be near her.

Outside, the Lady listens carefully to the shuffling, the footsteps coming towards the door. She braces herself, overwhelmed by desire. As a benefactor.

"Who is it?"

"It's *me* Chris. It's *Vera.*"

The voice grips his soul. He is almost afraid to answer it. He doesn't want her seeing him in this house. In this shack.

"Um… just a minute. I'll be out in a second, okay?"

"Okay," she says. "But the rain is killing us out here."

"I'm just gonna put on a shirt and a pair of pants. I'll be right out."

O, woe is me! A hermit girl's worse nightmare.

Invaders.

"Chris!" I hiss again, through clenched teeth. My head peeks from behind the door. *"Christopher!"*

He hurries in, ignoring me, flying into a pair of jeans. "Toss me the blue shirt," he whispers.

"Who is that?"

"My boss and his wife."

"What are they doing here?"

"Get those towels from the kitchen," he says.

"No. They can see me through that window."

"Honey…"

I ignore him, digging around in the closet for something to put on. With long sleeves.

Chris gathers the towels himself, and throws them in the bedroom. The damp towels fly into my face, landing over my hair. I look like a towel rack.

"Get the door," I whisper, "and *close* this one. *Close the door!"*

He closes the bedroom door, takes a deep breath, and goes to answer the knock. The wealthy farmer's wife hears the doorknob rattle loudly. The old door swings open.

Standing there, separated from her by the screen, is the object of her obsession. His eyes are blue.

"Vera."

"We... we were about to run some errands," she says, voice trembling, "and we thought we'd stop by, to see if there was anything we could do."

Chris has to shake himself from a trance. Finally, his meekness comes forth, and he unlocks the screen door for his guests.

Vera steps into the house, sidestepping vain pretension. Not a single word is exchanged as she throws her arms around him. Chris closes his eyes, feeling their strange reunion power. John quietly closes the door, and doesn't speak.

Chris and Vera hug each other tightly, both of their faces showing the anguish of past sorrow.

"Hey, John," Chris says, barely looking at him.

"How you doin', son." Vera finally lets Chris go, and he extends his hand to John. An awkward handshake.

"How are you, Chris?" she asks, wiping her eyes.

"I'm okay."

"I never thought I'd hear myself say this, but you look terrible." She smiles through the tears, staring profoundly.

"I haven't been sleeping too well."

"Don't you worry about that, honey. I'm the best dream queen in this county. I've got pills that'll give you all the sleep you'll ever need."

She touches his hair, looking at him like she hasn't seen him in a year. John can only stand idly by with his arms folded, bewildered, but humbled by the sight of something he cannot fathom.

"Is your wife well enough to see anybody?"

"She's getting dressed. She'll be out any minute. I'm sorry it took me so long to get to the door. If I had known it was you…"

"We would've waited forever," she says. "It was nothing."

Chris suddenly remembers where they all are, and is mortified.

A house of shadows, she thinks.

I listen to the strange voices in the living room. Fearfully.

"Let me take your coats. Have a seat right here. I'll go see what's keeping her."

Chris goes into the bedroom, closing the door quickly behind him.

"Kinda cold in here, isn't it?" John's voice is low. Almost whispery.

"It's just the weather. It was chilly in our house this morning, remember?"

Vera takes a deep breath, and looks around the living room. They both do.

There are two windows, but both of them are as bare as a tree in autumn, with not a curtain in sight. There is a fireplace, that is as black as midnight inside. The soot runs from inside it, up the front, all the way up the wall. The bare floor is scratched and scarred, and the walls are stained with ages of smoke. A thick wire runs down from the center of the ceiling, with a bare light bulb at the bottom of it.

There isn't a single plant or flower, knick knack or decoration of any kind. There are no other chairs, and no end tables. A large black iron rod leans by the fireplace, and in the corner is the tiniest little bookshelf, with a few old newspapers and old hardback novels, and a stack of textbooks on music composition and theory. On the floor beside it is a stereo disc player with large, powerful speakers, and a collection of at least four dozen albums. Vera notices that one of them is an Italian opera she thinks she may have heard of.

And hanging over it all is the odor of kerosene and burned wood, mixed with the unmistakable smell of *poverty*. The sickly sweet smell of filth, hopelessness, and despair.

Vera wants to say something. But there are no words.

She sees John look over at her, but she can't look back. Vera focuses on the books and the music, trying to imagine the plain, pitiful, spindly little harpy with cat glasses and a smart attitude that is hiding in that bedroom. The house has a mournful, oppressive aura, exuding a spirit of melancholic sadness. The Lady sits quietly on the little couch, studying every detail of the so-called living room, listening intently to the quiet shuffling behind the door. She has a sudden shock, when she thinks she hears the whispering voice of a woman.

After another minute or so, the shuffling in the bedroom moves closer. Vera puts her purse on the little couch, and stands up quickly, tapping John on the leg. He stands up beside her, and they both wait.

The bedroom door opens, and they see that Chris is alone. But he reaches over to beyond their view, and takes the hand of his invisible companion.

He steps awkwardly out of the room first, and then, from behind him, moves his wife.

Vera's mouth opens, and her body becomes as cold as the nights in winter.

Every so often, the Flow of Time will cease to be…

And a moment is frozen, for a brief eternity.

From the gray world of Vera's dreams—

To her reality.

"John, Vera, this is my wife Elizabeth."

Vera sees my eyes widen, and I look like I want to run and hide. John says his Greeting—but Vera doesn't speak.

From this, came forth her undoing.

In her mind, I am the most beautiful woman she has ever seen. Features of extraordinary appeal, but which cannot mask the sadness, the longing, and a soul of tragic naiveté. To her, my eyes bear the most genuine humility imaginable, and my manner betrays an extreme shyness that makes me seem fearful and odd.

Vera is overcome with great pity, and a compassion that makes her heart ache.

"Hello, Elizabeth."

She sees me glance at Chris. Then my mouth trembles as if I tried to speak, but lost my nerve. So Vera just steps quietly towards me and hugs me. She closes her eyes, believing in the tangible proof of clairvoyant possibilities. She is hugging the angel of her recurring dreams. A living phantom of her years of hope and despair. But she is awake, in full awareness, breathing the scent of strawberries from my hair, and the faint smell of smoke from my clothes.

Vera hugs her dream daughter tightly, and fights the urge to burst into tears.

Luck decides to be kind, giving us light for the morning. But it has been flickering dangerously from the start. The men are in the living room, discussing Chris' new salary, and his new duties as man in charge. Already, John Evans' enterprising mind is on fire. The marshall, and his new deputy. Images of Evans-Peele Grain and Storage, and other such nonsense.

Vera and I are preparing the grandest breakfast the little kitchen can provide. For some reason, we are all starving.

She had restrained herself. Trying not to look any more awestruck than she already did. She didn't want to scare my poor self, who looked like I might jump out of my skin at anytime.

We are both fiddling about in the little kitchen, until Vera realizes it is too small to keep me from bumping into her at every turn. Without me knowing it, she gradually eases out of my way, and watches me prepare the breakfast myself.

"Honey, would you mind if I sat down for a minute?" she says. "I had a long weekend, and I'm still exhausted."

"I wouldn't mind at all. Please, go right ahead."

Vera takes her place at the table.

"Your dress is beautiful Mrs. Evans. I love those colors together."

"Thank you. And please, honey, call me Vera."

It's been a while since a compliment felt so genuine to her. I finally said two words without being asked a question. Vera wants to sit unnoticed, and watch me move around in my old, dark green, long sleeved blouse, and pleated gray peasant skirt that goes all the way down to my ankles. A frontier ghost. Whispered from 1910.

She wants to stay quiet and just watch me. Believing I could cause problems and get away with it, though I seem to have no knowledge of it. Vera wonders if it is some kind of a highly evolved cutesy, coy act. But she quickly realizes that my shyness borders the pathological, and she wonders if I believe that I am in any way attractive.

Vera wanted to stay quiet and just watch me. But as soon as she sat down, she could *feel* how uncomfortable I became.

"Your husband's as quiet as you are," she says. "I couldn't get him to tell me a thing about you. I don't know where you're from, if your parents live here, or anything."

"I grew up here. But my parents are dead."

Good, Vera thinks. An angrily satisfying thought. She watches me at the stove, measuring grits, pouring them into a pot of water.

"Eleven years," she says. "That's how long he said you've been married."

"Yes ma'am. It'll be twelve in November."

"I married John when I was a teenager. That was twenty years ago."

"Do you have any children?"

"I couldn't have any. We tried for years though. It just wasn't meant for us."

"I'm so sorry."

"No, its fine," she says. "I got over it a long time ago. I keep busy enough, and after a while, John and that farm was more than I could handle anyway."

Vera's gaze is everywhere. Studying my hair. My face. My strange, pioneer clothes. And when she isn't staring at me, she's looking at the kitchen, into every spot of rust and filth. I, Mrs. Peele, am suddenly overwhelmed with self consciousness.

"I'm s-sorry about the house. And my c-clothes."

The Lady stands up at once, stepping boldly towards me. I gaze in nervousness. Vera gently, firmly ushers me to the side, in the corner by the sink. Staring right into my eyes.

"You," Vera says, "are the most beautiful woman I've ever seen. And not just your face and your figure. Elizabeth, I didn't think I'd ever live to see it, but when I look at you...I see a soul of goodness. And I think you already know clothes and houses don't matter."

We look at each other in a powerful silence. Laced with awe and wonder.

The two of us sit at the table, waiting for the breakfast to cook. Country ham slices are in the skillet, and have just started to enliven the little house. Vera can hear her husband prattling about the price of grain, and how he didn't think he'd be getting any richer from now on. Vera had sworn that she wouldn't, but she found some instant coffee anyway, and had made herself the proverbial cup.

"Is it hot enough?"

"It's just right," she says, smiling.

"What about that milk?"

"It's fine. Don't you want some?"

"No thank you." *Definitely not.* I hate coffee, and care little for tea. But like in every kitchen, I have some.

I sit up straight at the table, and breathe a quick, deep sigh. Vera notices again how top-heavy I am, and it makes her wonder why I have no children.

"When are you and Chris gonna have your own family?"

"Oh… it just never seemed like the right time."

"I think you might have a housefull someday. Believe me, Elizabeth, you two owe it to the world. I can't imagine what your kids would be like."

She notices me rubbing my shoulder, and sometimes, my lower back.

"Are you in pain?"

"No, Ma'am."

Knowingly, she takes a sip of her coffee, which is very sweet. Too sweet, which is how she likes it.

Bright lightning flashes through the window, followed by a blast of thunder. I jump like someone pinched me.

"You're as jumpy as a house kitten."

The Lady is still dazed. My lack of confidence is fascinating to her. She looks at me like I'm an exotic bird in a small, dingy cage. Jittering in terror.

"I've always loved the name Elizabeth. It means *God's Promise*. When I was a little girl, that was my favorite name."

"Really?"

"Vera May is too country and plain. It reminds me of paper towels for some reason."

I smile, suppressing a tiny giggle.

"What's your middle name, honey?"

"Angelina Elizabeth *is* my middle name. My first name is *Carmen.*"

A word borrowed from the French applies. It translates as *already seen.* It engulfs the rich woman, transporting her backward—

"*Momma?*"

"*Hello, sweetheart. You didn't tell me your name last time. I don't know what to call you.*"

"*I'm sorry, Momma. My name is Carmen…*"

Vera loses hold of the cup, and it falls hard, splashing her coffee all over the table.

Our husbands are assured that only a cup has caused problems. The Lady makes quick work of the mess, and fixes herself another cup.

"I'm really sorry, Elizabeth. I don't know what happened."

But already, her expression has grown distant again.

"Mrs. Ev—Vera?"

"Hmmm?"

"Your coffee."

The cup leans dangerously. She puts it on the table and pushes it aside.

"Are you okay?"

"I don't know what's wrong. My mind is all over the place. I just remembered there's something important I have to do this morning."

"You don't have to go, do you?"

"Not yet. But soon. I just remembered it. I can't believe I'd already forgotten."

The house lights flicker again. Reminding us.

"I hope that food gets done," she says. "Check it for me, sweetie, I have to go to the bathroom."

I have a sudden shock of horror.

"That bathroom is *filthy*."

"I'm sure it's alright, sweetie."

"Wait just a second. I'll be right back."

Through the living room, through the bedroom, into the damp bathroom I hurry, yanking down the two half-wet towels, tossing them to the bottom of the closet. Then, I rush back to the kitchen.

"You can go in now. But it's still bad in there."

She smiles politely, touching my face. Then she goes into the bedroom and closes the door.

A prison

Vera is overwhelmed with a sense of misery. The claustrophobic feeling of being trapped. She looks around the little bedroom, at the old clock radio, with a little notebook and pencil lying beside it. A flower girl languishes in a portrait by the bare window. She notices the bed, with its ancient linen and low, sagging mattress. The comfortable chair looks like something someone had thrown away. And there is a moist, sickly stench, that smells like nothing she had ever smelled before.

Blood

She doesn't really have to go to the bathroom. She just has to be alone for a moment. None of us knew that she could have fainted dead away when she first saw me walk out of that bedroom. The Fine Lady steps into the bathroom, closes herself up in the dark and stands there. Listening.

Wondering.

Noisy rainfall.

It is so loud that she almost feels comfortable enough to cry where she stood. Earlier, she'd nearly made up an errand for the men, so she could be alone with me. To bawl her eyes out, and tell me she'd been dreaming about me for ten years. But how can she ever tell me such a thing?

The bathroom is the only room in the house with curtains. The thin, blue cloth filters the gray morning, coloring the room with a gloomy, phantasmal hue. Vera grabs the sink and steadies herself in the blue dark.

Carmen—

She notices a gray cloth on the door. Touching it, she can tell it is tacked over a large, jagged hole.

I was dreaming of the future.

How can I tell this to John? How can I convince him to do what I have to do?

A sudden, cold oppressiveness envelops her in the dark—she feels the hairs on her neck stand on end. Fearfully she flips on the light switch, and the bulb makes a loud *pop!* Dying in a bright blue flash. The woman screams, throws open the door and hurries out of the bathroom. The bedroom door flies open, and Chris and John rush in, followed by me.

"What happened?" John says.

"I'm alright," she insists. "The light blew out and scared me half to death, that's all."

"You sure?"

"Of *course*, I am. I told you the light blew out and scared me."

"Come in here and sit down."

"I'm going back in the kitchen—now let me go." She snatches her hand away while they both walk out of the bedroom, bickering a little, forgetting all about their hosts.

Chris and I look at each other, then stare at the bathroom.

Quietly, we follow our guests.

"John, there's something I've got to do this morning. It's important, and it's got to be done today."

"What are you goin' on about?"

"We'll talk about it on the way there."

"We're gonna stay and eat first aren't we?"

"Of course we are," she says.

At that moment, cataclysmic thunder cracks the sky. The lights go out immediately. The four of us stand still in the dark, in awe of the booming, apocalyptic sound.

27

It is a strange and powerful storm, appearing as the arm of a great hurricane passing overhead. Strong gales will swirl with frightening speed, then die down just as quickly. Sometimes, every inch of the sky is bathed in blue energy, followed by total silence. At other times we hear deafening thunder. The rains will slow down to almost nothing, then quickly return to a steady fervor. The character of this storm is one of mocking contempt, mixed with controlled rage and resentment. The land underneath is threatened day and night, with unfulfilled promises of unleashed fury and catastrophic devastation.

The storm seems to have a mind of its own.

"Are you two gonna be alright?" Vera says. "Chris, are you sure you don't want to come with us?"

"We'll be fine."

The power had gone out well before breakfast was cooked. We had made do with beverages, finishing every drop of my precious orange juice.

"Don't eat a big lunch, 'cause we're going out to dinner tonight," Vera says. "We'll be back late this afternoon, around six o'clock. So be ready. Chris you know where the Town and Country is don't you?"

"Out on the highway, towards the high school."

"That's where were gonna eat." She hugs and kisses us both. I feel like I am on the edge of tears.

"Chris," says John. "we'll pick up that generator tonight, okay?"

"Okay."

"We'll see you two this evening," Vera says. She hugs me again, and whispers something in my ear.

"Let's go, John."

The rain fell heavy and fast. Small puddles are everywhere. We can all hear the water streaming from the roof, spattering the ground all around the house. The unseasonable cold is remarkable. Were it not for the green that covers the trees, the day would be indistinguishable from late autumn. Through the screen door, I watch the elegant stranger and her husband go down the steps. I watch them splash through the water and get into their silver luxury car.

The car feels cozy inside. Plush and wonderful.

Vera is quiet as they back out, watching me stand pitifully at the screen door. In my behavior, she wonders if she has seen the innocence of faith, and the manner of the truly converted.

The dirt road is a strip of mud. Plenty of it has already reached up and clung to the bottom of their car.

"Alright," John says. "What's this so-called business?"

She breathes a deep sigh.

"I've got something to tell you," she says. "But let me warn you before I even start. You're *not* going to believe me. But I swear before God in Heaven, every single word of it is the truth."

He notices her grave expression.

"I'm listening."

As they drive slowly through the mud, Vera relates to him a glimpse from the gray world. How the images reached across time itself, to become part of her reality.

I am still at the door of my little house. Peering through the rain. Watching the red tail lights fade away.

"She was acting strange," Chris says. "I wonder what the problem was."

When the car is out of sight, I finally close the door.

"She's nice. I like her. But Mr. Evans looks at me funny. Just like when I was growing up. People always looked at me funny."

"He looks at everybody that way. He studies people."

"Oh."

I wander over to the window, where I lean against the wall. Staring out into the rain.

"I wish I had a piano."

"I'd love to hear you play."

"I don't think so," I say, laughing a little. "I don't know how."

He glances at my music collection, as he sits down on the little couch.

"I don't think that's gon' be a problem for much longer."

Chris watches me, while I stare out the window. I blow my breath onto the glass, and write a fancy letter R in the pane, before the haze vanishes. I seem to him like the accursed Armageddon Flower. Flourishing in a swamp.

"When I was in the room last year, I dreamt that I played a concerto. No. 23 by Mozart. A few days later, one came to me in the same key. But it sounds just like Rossini. It's the best one I ever wrote. I don't know what I would have done all these years without music."

I go over to the couch, and sit down beside him.

"I'm glad you're here. I wish you could stay here with me every day."

"John offered me a good job. He wants to put me in charge."

"Do you like farming enough for that?"

"I like *John* enough," he says. "I think Vera really likes you."

"I feel like I know her. I've never felt so comfortable around anyone before. I just love her to death, Chris."

"I've liked her ever since we met. She wasn't full of crap, like everybody else. Even John is full of it sometimes."

"She's a strong woman. And she dresses nice. Did you notice the pretty dress she had on?"

"It was nice."

"It was gorgeous. And she's beautiful. Don't you think she's beautiful?"

I guess so, he says, remembering every inch of her smooth face and lips, brushed with the lightest makeup, her blonde hair stylishly pinned, the sweet smell of her perfume, and the shape of her legs when she crossed them at the kitchen table.

"I was embarrassed when they came in here. I thought I was gonna *die*."

"I'll be glad when we finally get outta here," he says.

"Will you be making more money?"

"A lot more. We'll be able to rent a nice place."

"Do you think…"

"What?" he says.

"Do you think she suspects anything?"

Chris lowers his head.

"I hope not," I say. "I don't want her to know what happened in this house."

We're silent for a moment. Praying our history will remain a secret forever.

"I had a strange dream last night. I dreamt that I woke up beside you, and you were still asleep. And the room got so cold it was like a freezer. I could see my breath. I was holding your hand, when I saw your whole body get very dark. And then…I saw something like a dark mist, flow up from your skin. It took shape right in front of me, and started to stare at me. It tried to get back in your body, but it couldn't. And then, it tried to get me."

"What happened?"

"The storm went away, then it was daylight. And it went into the wall, like a shadow."

My mind is suddenly aflight. Moving swiftly through the rain, searching for even the slightest glimpse of the silver luxury car.

"*Momma* said they were coming back at six o'clock, right?"

He looks at me. Bewilderedly.

"I'll be glad when its six o'clock."

The sky had been the same gray color the entire day. Keeping the sun's location a guarded secret.

The rich farmer and his wife are finally done with the day's business, and are at the edge of town, about to drive back into the country.

"It's never gon' let up, is it?"

"I like it," she sighs. "The rain is peaceful. People mind their own business when it's raining."

"A farmer's rain," he says proudly. "We've been needin' this one for a long time."

Within herself, she rolls her eyes in contempt.

They're at the last stoplight in town, heading south toward the farmlands. They listen to the whining and scraping of the windshield wipers, watching the red traffic light shimmering through the windshield. A minute later, the shimmering red light becomes a green one.

But John's mind is elsewhere.

"John, the light's green."

At that moment, an 18-wheeler barrels through the intersection, crossing monstrously in front of them.

"Did you see that?" he says. "That som-na-bitch ran right through the light."

Vera clutches the armrest with one hand, and her heart with the other.

"It's a good thing I was daydreamin'," he says. "What if I had gone through?"

A car horn blares from behind them, scaring Vera's poor heart again. John drives on through the intersection and heads out of town. The old, box shaped Plymouth behind them is soon speeding past, in a big hurry to get nowhere special.

"You alright?"

"Do I look alright?" she says, still holding her chest.

"Somebody's been lookin' out for us lately."

They drive on in the rain, thinking of how close they'd come to being splattered. John thinks of the farm, and his precious fields.

 Vera thinks only of me.

"When you said you had business to tend to, you weren't kiddin," he says.

She just stares quietly through the windshield, at the headlights of the oncoming cars.

"I hope we did the right thing," he says.

"It had to be done. And I feel a lot better."

"*I* don't."

"You know better than that," she says. "I *know* you do."

They cruise Highway 17 South, which could lead them all the way to Florida. But they'll only need a tiny fraction to get home. At the moment, Vera is impressed by the lighted sign of the restaurant they're going to.

"The Town and Country," she says, smiling to herself.

"Yep. You can smell it from here."

"It's been too long, hasn't it?"

"*Way* too long. But I'll make up for it tonight, believe me. We haven't been since Brenda and Conrad took us there, when Catherine got engaged."

"What are you gonna order?" she says.

"Did you call Brenda yet?"

Vera sighs. Helplessly.

"Conrad told me he hopes Catherine breaks this one too. Then he won't have a weddin' to pay for."

"Kate dumped that medical student," snaps Vera. "She's dating again already."

"*Boy* she gets around. Say, didn't you tell me she was goin' to Paris this summer?"

"I'm gonna order fried chicken," Vera says. Pitifully.

"They invited us to dinner again. Somethin' simple, at their house. Brenda'll tell you if you ever call her back. She says you've been avoidin' her."

Brenda Lynn Harrison.

Masters degree. Former vice president of an insurance company. Leadership in half a dozen clubs and organizations. A trove of community awards. Assistant to every important local office there is. And finally, after years of trying, a cushy job in county hospital administration. She knows the mayor's wife. The former governor's wife. A senator's wife. And a few years ago, she had nearly whistled Mr. Harrison, old Conrad himself, into a big local office.

A phone call from Mrs. Brenda Harrison is *power*. If she can't get it done, it don't need doing.

And everybody knows her daughter. The famous Catherine Grace Harrison...

Who had finished third in her high school class, who was most likely to succeed, who had been a foreign exchange student, who made the *varsity* cheerleading squad as a sophomore, but quit because she didn't like the other girls, and because she had worked 30 hours a week, and because her mother had sneaked her to Virginia for an abortion because she had gotten pregnant from one of the black football players...

Who is in graduate school to become a professor, who had dumped a young medical student and is now dating a lawyer, who is learning the piano, and who is planning to study French at the University of Paris.

Miss Amazing Grace, how sweet the sound...

That made Vera sick to her stomach.

"Brenda said you left in a hurry when—"

"I don't want to talk about Brenda and Kate Harrison," she says. Fuming.

"You sure been actin' weird lately. Maybe we should get dinner and take it to their house instead."

"And eat by candlelight? In that house? You've got to be kidding me. That place makes my skin crawl. I don't know how they can stand it."

"It is kinda run down."

"It's depressing," she says. "It's evil."

"You see a rat in the bathroom this morning?"

"I wish."

"A ghost?"

"Stop being silly," she says. "But you can feel it. It's in the walls."

A brief pause...

"Did you notice how cold it was?" she asks. "I wanted to wear my coat in there. And that bathroom. It smelled like a sewer. You can tell she tries to clean, but it's like trying to wash the inside of a wood stove. Every wall is stained with soot. And it stinks of pure kerosene."

"I get the picture. I wonder what's wrong with her?"

"What's that supposed to mean?" A nearly vicious tone. Her gray eyes glisten.

"She's so quiet and skiddish, Viv. She set me to wonderin', that's all."

"Well you can stop your *wunderin'*. I've spoken to her plenty. She's just very shy, that's all. And she's as sweet as pie."

Vera watches the wiper blades, splashing the water back and forth.

"I wonder how they came to be in such a fix," she says to herself. "They could do anything they wanted. But they're two of the loneliest, saddest people I b'lieve I've ever seen. And they've been there for so long, and they don't have any children. Don't you think that's a little strange?"

"I s'pose it is."

"She is *so…*" Vera sighs, shaking her head. "Her father was Italian, you know. Her maiden name is Carmen Angelina *Elizabeth* Coletti, can you believe it? Her mother must have been incredible."

Soon, they turn off the highway into another world, where tall, dark pines rule a kingdom of crop fields. The tobacco mocked all the lower crops with derision, secure in its hold and dominion. But the corn grew with unwavering intrepidity. Complacent in its own lyrical beauty. Casting a long shadow of economic viability. They drove past the fields of enmity with neither a glance nor passing thought. Somewhere beyond these lost roads awaits their true purpose. The new focus of their time and affection.

"Let's go home first," she says. "Then, we'll pick them up."

"You know what? Lizbeth's gon' be a problem tonight."

Vera endures a chill…

"As sure as its rainin' 'til mornin'," he says.

28

By the time they make it back to the mud road, the sky is colored in a dreary, gray twilight. The cloud cover is thick and dark, and the approaching dusk already looks like early nightfall. As the car rocks and splashes slowly through the mud, Vera looks at the dark clouds flicker and glow.

"You wouldn't know it was the middle of summer. It got dark so fast."

The sky flashes brightly, framing the gigantic silhouette of the pecan tree.

"There it is," John says.

"The tree?"

"Charlie told me they've been after him for years for this land. He said they can have it when he's in the ground."

"I don't like it out here," she says. "It's creepy."

"It's just the storm. But speakin' of creepy, Charlie told me somethin' about that house."

"Somethin' bad?"

" D'pends on how you look at it. Some people like *ghost* stories."

"I don't want to hear it."

"It's no big deal," he says, ready for mischief. "He just told me about what he saw one night when he first…"

"I said I don't want to *hear* it."

"Alright, then," he mumbles, smiling to himself.

She peers through the dark twilight, at the shadow that rests where their house is supposed to be. Through the window she sees the dim, flickering glow from their kerosene lamp. John turns into the yard, and the headlights cut through the rain, flashing across the gray wood.

"Blow the horn, John."

When he does, Vera sees a dark, lonely figure appear at the window.

"Should we go in?"

"Absolutely not," she insists. "They'll be out in a second."

The flame disappears from inside the house. She sees me open the door.

"She looks like she's going to a funeral," John whispers.

Vera pinches his arm hard enough to bruise it.

"Ow!"

"Get out," she snaps, "And open the back door."

"You better watch yourself, Vera."

"I apologize," she says. Angrily. "Now, please, get out and open the door for them."

He mumbles something to himself, while he steps into the rain to greet us. Vera can see me leaning around, trying to catch a glimpse of her. Chris finally comes out of the dark house, then we both step onto the wet ground. John ushers us into the back seat.

"Well, hey you two," she says, nearly laughing. She reaches back and grabs my cold hand, and pulls as I slide over towards her.

In the brief glow of the car light, Vera's mind slows time to a crawl. I am in full gothic, with a long black coat covering a dress that is either black or navy, complete with black leg stockings, black shoes, and a black scarf covering my black hair. *Witch,* is the word that pops in Vera's head, and she wishes with all her heart that it hadn't.

Chris' eyes glow like blue ice in the dim light. He wears a long beige raincoat, like what cowboys wear in old westerns, and Vera's heart skips a beat when he grins a quiet smile of understanding. Truly, he is better looking than what a man needs to be, and in that brief moment, she was unsettled by him.

All of this floods her emotions in the tiniest fraction of a second, which seems to last much longer...

And she suddenly knows, as surely as anything, that all of this strangeness is meant to be.

"You okay, back there?" John says, over his left shoulder, away from his wife.

"Great," Chris says.

"I'm sorry we're late," Vera sighs. "It took longer than we expected."

"That's alright," says Chris. "It made us good and hungry."

"I hope you're as hungry as I am," she says. "We'll order *everything* when we get there."

Vera watches my expression go darker.

"Chris, have you ever been there?"

"I've been by there a lot, but I never went in."

"It's nice inside. We know the family that owns it. They're lovely people. And they've got the best food you've ever tasted."

Vera turns forward in her seat. She breathes deeply, and pretends she hadn't seen it.

The look in my eyes.

As we drive through the rain, Vera gladly breathes in the faint smell of smoke, and she ponders what she sensed about me.

Misery...

A deep reservoir of secret pain. A lifetime of suffering.

Hidden...

Lost under a layer of ash and dust.

Fear...

A great struggle against terror. Frightened of the outside world.

The Lady wonders to herself, how long it's been since I left that house. How long.

I stare out the window at the legion of headlights, all flying by at high speed on the dark, wet streets. Seeming to come from nowhere, and to be going there just the same.

The car slows down into the turning lane, waiting for an opening. I see the bright lights of the restaurant, and the lot full of cars and people. John pulls across the highway into the lot, looking for a place to park. The lot is packed, and we have to park a good distance away from the door.

Elizabeth Peele.

A little anxious?

My heart is already pounding under this goth exterior. The people may as well be ghosts and dragons, demons flowing in and out of a dark valley. I watch the devils drive to and fro in their chariots, moving mysteriously towards and away from the light.

Please don't let me cause trouble…

I don't want to cause problems. Really. But I know above all things, that I am *not* going in that restaurant.

Chris feels my body twitch once, as if I've been stuck with a pin.

God help us.

"You okay?" he whispers. Vera heard him clearly, but pretends not to. I don't answer. I just stare.

Laughter. Quiet, sinister laughter. A woman's voice…

Laughing.

29

"It's more crowded than I thought it would be," the Lady says, disappointedly.

John finds a place to park, too far away from the door. Vera thinks there are too many cars and too many people.

"I hope you two don't mind fightin' a crowd," she says.

"I'll go see what it looks like in there," says John. "If we can get a table, I'll wave you in from the door."

"Alright. Take the umbrella."

John opens the door, stepping into the rain like it isn't even there. He does manage to pull the hood of his raincoat over his head, just so he won't be in public with dripping wet hair.

Chris feels me twitch again when John closes the door. I am staring at the restaurant as if it were burning with green fire.

"Look at him," Vera says. "Like a turtle in the mud."

Vera and Chris glance at each other again.

Nervously.

"I can see him at the door," Chris says.

"Okay," the Lady says with enthusiasm."Let's eat."

She opens the door and her umbrella, gliding into the rain. Chris is alone in the car with his wife, who is holding her head down, dejected and embarrassed.

"You're not going in, are you?" he asks.

I shake my head.

"I wish you had told me before we got here," he says. "But it's my fault. I knew better."

Vera appears at the back door. Chris opens it a little, and breaks the bad news.

"Is she coming in?"

"No. I didn't mean for this to happen, Vera."

"It's alright. I'll talk to her. You go in with John, and tell him to go ahead and order. Tell him to get a little of everything, okay? I'll let you know if we'll be eatin' here or not."

Chris hurries towards the restaurant, while Vera gets in the back seat, and takes his place.

It is quiet and peaceful inside.

Safe.

"What's the matter?"

"I can't go in."

"Why not?" she asks tenderly. "Is it the people?"

I glance through the rain at the shimmering crowd of devils, pushing and clawing their way in and out of the restaurant door.

"All of these people are nice and friendly."

"I knew I was gonna ruin it. I always do."

"Sweetie, you didn't ruin anything. If we don't go in, we'll just take the food home with us. But there really is nothing to be afraid of. I even know a lot of these people."

Vera looks at my eyes. Not in my eyes, but at them. As though hypnotized.

"I wanted us all do something together," she says. "Away from those lonely houses. It's been so long since I've sat down in a restaurant to enjoy a good meal and good company."

She watches me, to see if it has any affect.

It doesn't.

"Will you go in with me, and keep me company?"

I look at Vera from underneath my black scarf, like a fearful little girl trying to be coaxed into a haunted house. Trying to believe that the demons and doughfaces aren't real.

"People shouldn't be alone and afraid," she says. "They should enjoy each other's company, and help each other when they need it."

If only.

"You can hold my arm the whole time. Even at the table if you want."

Quiet.

"We'll just sit here for a few minutes. Then we'll go in. I'll bet they've already got a table for us."

This girl doesn't even know me…

"Elizabeth?"

I look up.

"Are you afraid of me?"

"No."

"Are you sure?"

I nod my head.

Veranda May had only just met me today. Strangers. But Vera decides to put that to rest forever. She makes strong, serious eye contact with her dream daughter. I don't know whether to look away or stare. But I'm more afraid to *not* look.

"I don't know what's been done to you," she says. "But you'll never have to be afraid of anything. Ever again. I *swear* it."

Vera moves closer to me, and I rest my head on her chest.

"Elizabeth?"

"Yes, Momma?"

"I love you."

The rain attacks the umbrella without mercy, desperate to drown us while we walk. But there is something I had known as soon as the car door had opened, and I had stepped into the storm.

I am *not* going in that restaurant.

The people inside are concerned only with their food, and each other. But my mind shows me images of pure malice. I see the collected mob, cornering me, calling me a pasty faced little *bitch*, who is too ugly and stupid to be seen in public, making them sick to their stomachs. They'll grab me away from Vera and begin to beat me and the women will snatch at my clothes and my hair and dig their nails into my face until it is a bloody mess...

"Are you okay?"

"I can't go in." My breath quickens, and my eyes are wide.

"Just hold on to me."

"Momma, I can't do it, please let's go back." I am about to pull away and run back to the car. Vera is amazed.

"Okay, Sweetie. Let's go."

The raindrops pound us as we hurry back. Vera opens the car door, and I jump in as if there are snakes chasing after me. Vera gets in with me, closing the door.

"Honey, I apologize," she says, as though devastated. "If I had known, I *never* would have tried to make you go in."

"It's not your fault," I say, panting. "Everywhere I go, people stare. They look at me like they can't stand me."

"They stare at you because... beauty like yours, Elizabeth, with that pitiful expression. It's something they've never seen before."

Silence.

"Will you be alright here, while I go tell them we'll eat at home?"

"Yes."

The edge of a major panic had come and gone. Vera knows that my heart is playing a jungle rhythm under this black coat.

"I'll be right back, okay?"

The Lady gets out of the car, and hurries toward the restaurant.

Answered prayers. Blessings. Luck. I am thankful beyond words. Appreciative to the depths of my soul. There are things I would like to tell my new protector. Things I would like to confess.

Secret things.

We sit together in the back seat for another twenty minutes before our husbands come out, with their arms loaded with containers and bags of food. Chris is a little surprised when he sees us cozy and comfortable. And he is even alarmed, when I seem not to care whether he is in the car or not.

"John let's get out of here, Honey. Let's go."

He nearly backs into another car on the way out. I am busy wondering what is in all those bags. The smell is magnificent.

Chris glances into the back seat, worriedly, and sees us huddled close together. Vera's right arm is locked around my waist. She has removed my scarf, and is stroking my long, soft hair.

"Lizabeth Honey," John says. "I owe you a debt. I don't like eatin' in restaurants either."

The two women exchange a secret glance.

The car drove on through the dark twilight, into the evening day, past the crop rows of alien plant beings, that chose not to move when people were nearby. The distant woods seem like black, ominous worlds of foreboding and mystery. The tall, darkened trees that line the roads hang menacingly over them, threatening to close in upon the passing cars.

Stopping them, chewing away the glass and metal, pulling the people high up into the storm. Dropping them to their deaths.

My body begins to ache, and I feel very tired. I lean against Vera, resting in her arms.

Soon, the gift catches fire of its own accord. The sounds take physical form and color, and I lose touch with where I am. I commune with the spirits of pure melody, listening closely as they fill my memory with music from another world.

Three listen in fascination, as one begins to hum softly to herself.

30

"Okay, everybody," Vera says. "Let's all grab something and let's *go.*"

We all quickly oblige. Rushing to get away from the car and into the house. I am entranced, nearly lightheaded with the strangeness of it all.

The house is twice as long as a large rancher would be, covered to every corner with beautiful, light colored bricks. The walkway is lined on one side with rosebushes, all healthy and blooming with white and pink flowers. I don't glance towards the dark cornfield. I keep my eyes towards the house, as I walk with Vera underneath the umbrella shield.

The walkway leads directly to a set of brick steps. We go up the steps together, open the door, and leave the cold rain behind.

For the first time in over a decade, I have crossed the threshold into another place. The house seems to me like a darkened palace. As Vera holds the storm door open for Chris and John, I feel useless, conspicuous and inadequate.

The lights reveal an upper middle class world, which is common enough to be sure. But I am a country cricket. Born and raised in the dirt. Even as I gaze around the big kitchen, at all of the beautiful new fixtures and decorations, the stench of poverty is fresh in my nostrils, and the filth of it is imprinted upon my memory.

The appliances are pristine. As beautiful as such things can be, a world away from the broken down relics in my little kitchen. The walls are off white by choice, and are clean from top to bottom—unburdened by smoke and soot. The soapy lemon scent is that of household cleanliness, cleaning fluids and solutions that cut through the smells that make my own house inhospitable.

They have all gone to the table, and are getting the food ready to eat. Through the endless chatter about the merits of southern cuisine, Vera keeps her eyes on her visitor in black, watching me as I look around the huge kitchen. I step lightly in my black, one inch heeled shoes, noticing the doorway to my left. I peek inside, and see a glossy dining room table made of oakwood, with six cushioned, high back chairs. The large, matching display cabinet makes me stop and stare. Through its glass door I see many cups, dishes and curious porcelain things of all kinds. Little pieces of idiosyncratic style and beauty, each of which calls to different people for different reasons. I want to go into the dining room and stare into the cabinet, at the painted patterns of each knick knack, until I have memorized every flower, and every individual shape and color.

And all the while, Vera keeps a close eye on me, monitoring my strange behavior.

"You gonna join us, Elizabeth?"

"Oh," I answer, as if I've done something wrong.

Vera takes the umbrella from me, and my coat and scarf, and carries the smelly things down the front hall, neatly placing them in the living room closet. The men's coats had been completely forgotten. *Like smoke,* she thinks, as she puts away the black coat and scarf.

When Vera left the room, I suddenly heard nothing but the sound of my own heartbeat. I can still see Chris and John, but can't hear a word they're saying. The house quickly grows around me, becoming as a vast cave, with danger hiding in every unfamiliar corner. I then make the mistake of glancing towards the long, dark hallway to the bedrooms…

The hall lengthens, distending into a portal, capable of pulling me into another world—a dimension of loneliness and terror.

A hand suddenly reaches out to me, touching me on the shoulder. Vera looks quietly at me, escorting me to a place at the table.

"This is incredible," Chris says, after taking a huge bite of food. "All these years, I've been driving by that place, and I never stopped."

"I told you," Vera says.

The table was spread over, with everything from southern fried chicken and ham seasoned collard greens, to blueberry and peach pie slices. All of it is the product of concentrated, deliberate focus on simplicity. The hardest thing to develop and perfect.

I sit quietly beside my hostess, stuffing macaroni and cheese into my mouth by the spoonful. The chicken they had raved so much about lays in my plate off to the side, completely untouched.

We all hear the thunder rolling gently.

"This storm's been botherin' me since it started."

"Why?" says Vera. Cynically. "If it could drown your whole crop, you wouldn't even miss it."

"You see?" John says. It's that kind of ignorance that gets people in trouble. You never stop worryin'. Never stop plannin'.

"Nema dop woryin', nema nop blannin'", Vera mocks, almost under her breath. I snicker loudly, then cover my mouth. If I could have reversed time, I would have.

"She turned you against me, too, huh, Lizbeth?"

"No, sir."

"Don't mind him, Elizabeth," Vera says. "Don't pay any attention to Kernel Korn Evans, and his big grain empire."

"You should pay more 'tention to it yourself," he says, "If you had to run it, you'd run it into the ground."

"I'd be smart, and hire Chris to run it for me," she says, winking smartly at Chris.

"That might be the biggest mistake you ever made," Chris says.

"I doubt that. Right, John?"

"You'd do alright," John agrees, ignoring the jealous wave.

"John, you never did tell me how you were able to make it so big around here," Chris says.

"Carolina grain farmers are usually coming outta tobacco fields," says John, "and they start droppin' seeds in the ground like it's the same thing. Take a look at the cornfields around here, and you see it over and over again—rows spaced so far apart you can drive a truck through 'em. It looks good, but come harvest time, it's not pretty anymore. It's about *yield*. Bushels per acre. Have you noticed how hard it is to walk through my fields when they're grown in?"

"Yeah."

"That's 'cause I've got 'em packed so tight, a cat's gotta get on his tiptoes to squeeze through. And I keep the fields watered, and the ground *loaded* with fertilizer. Last year, we pulled in the biggest crop we've ever had. And with this rain, and that new fertilizer, I bet you I'll clear a record this year."

Vera shook her head and wrinkled her mouth. She had loved and cared for him all these years, even through a hussy hurricane named Ola Bradford, and had helped and supported him while he built this big farm.

But truthfully, it left her *cold*, and highly disinterested.

"And farmers around here are obsessed with animals," he says. "They can't decide whether they're into crops or livestock. They borrow too much money, and after one or two bad years, they're either finished, or so deep in debt they have to carry it for the rest of their lives."

"You've got debt, don't you?" Chris asks.

"None I couldn't clear t'morrow."

Chris shakes his head, and takes a bite of his well paid for chicken.

He's even pretty when he's eating, Vera thought.

"A lot of these t'bacco farmers are pullin' days right here. The same ones that warned me not to plant corn in the first place. Ben Gregory was one of the main ones. Now he and Odell spend more time out here than the rest of 'em."

"You never know what's gon' happen, do you?" Chris says.

"Now *there's* somethin' to talk about."

"Here we go," says Vera.

"*Fifteen* years ago, I was taking in some wet tobacco in my own little field, and found out the hard way how dangerous wet tobacco can be. I got so sick I almost died."

"It's true," Vera says. "He's lucky to be alive."

"Before that, I was all set. I was gonna grow tobacco for the rest of my life. And it came to me when I was sick, I mean, it *literally* came to me, that I was wastin' my time competin' with everybody for the same dollar. If I had never gotten sick, I might still be strugglin' right along with the rest of 'em. Tobacco's dead here, Chris. They just don't know it yet. *Grapes*'ll be more more important here than tobacco soon. Look at us. Smack dab in the middle of tobacco country, with one of the biggest grain farms they've ever seen. And you'll be learnin' every trick of the trade. There's more to farmin' than a field hand can even start to think about."

Vera looks at Chris, and feels his exhaustion. She actually feels sorry for him.

"And speaking of Fate," Vera says. "If you hadn't been there that afternoon, Chris, in that bin…"

"I'll never be able to repay you for that, son," says John.

"I'm just glad I was there."

Vera glances at my plate, noticing that I have finished the last spoonful of macaroni and cheese. Without a word, she picks up the container, and puts it near my plate.

The thunder rumbles louder.

"It's too bad you've gotta go back out in this weather," Chris says.

"Believe me honey," she answers, "it's not a problem."

"Chris, when are you two plannin' to move?"

"John—"

"Well, we hadn't really thought about it," says Chris.

"There's a little story that comes with that land," John says, in spite of Vera. "Especially that house."

"What is it?"

John looks at me....

And then he sees the icy fire in Vera's gray eyes.

"I'll tell you about it sometime," he says. Defeatedly.

"Maybe I can talk you two into going to church with me soon," says Vera, changing the subject.

"That church is full of lyin', backstabbin' hypocrites," says John. "It's like a snakepit."

"Is that why you've only been twice in three years?" Vera says.

"Vera, if God has anything to do with the people in that church, I don't want no part of it."

She thought about Brenda and Catherine Grace Harrison.

"Chris, did you know that a few of those "good Christians" set fire to one of my cornfields a while back?"

Vera laughs out loud. A cruel, hearty laugh.

"What's so funny?"

"That fire was so small you stomped it out with a horse blanket."

I have to pinch my own thigh, to keep from laughing hard enough to choke.

"I'm sorry, John", Vera laughs, "I'm sorry, honey. But I just remember you in the field with that blanket. I'm sorry, but you were screaming at me to call the fire department..." She put her head down, and her body shook with quiet laughter.

"Alright," he says. "You think it's funny."

"John you're not even sure if it was them."

"Who else was it then?"

"That was so long ago," she says. "What about forgiveness?"

"What about it?"

"How do you expect to be forgiven, if you don't forgive other people?"

"People can't forgive nothin.' What they say and how they feel are two different things."

"I don't believe that," Vera says. "Some people *can* forgive others, for the evil that's been done to them."

31

Every room in the house is touched by color, as the muses were so inclined, inspiring Vera to the notion that a white wall is the enemy of décor. I am arm in arm with my hostess, while we drift slowly down the long, softly lit hallway, past the tasteful little paintings and the oak wood clock on the wall, into each of the king sized guestrooms and bathrooms, and to John's spacious office-den hybrid.

Suddenly, we both hear the clock chime softly. Once. Then it chimes eight times more.

Some believe that clocks chime both joy and sorrow. Gladly announcing the death of the last hour, and mournfully, the birth of a new one.

Who's to say?

"When are we gonna tell 'em?"

"In a few minutes. But now I've got to show you my favorite room."

We cross over from the long hallway, into the huge main bedroom. The Queen's chambers.

A Gray Palace.

It is far and away, the largest bedroom in the house. The walls are a soothing, delicate gray, with well chosen watercolor portraits, made perfect by the gray mattings and thin blackwood frames. Hanging from the black curtain rods are long, sheer white window coverings, that seem to flow from the top of this gray world, all the way to the light gray carpet below.

The mammoth bed is framed in dark burnished pine wood. The carved headboard and tall, rounded bedposts rule a court of dressers and chests, all carved and finished in like manner. I notice on each drawer a shiny brass pull handle, with a shape that reminds me of the face of a mischievous demon. The King-sized bed is guarded on either side by a large night table, holding big, shell colored lamps, topped with white shades. The lamps are wide at the top, and tapered down in rounded fashion, like a piece of pottery. So subtle is the pale colouring and texture, that it is hard to fully appreciate their exquisite design and appearance.

All of this is adequately spaced. Skillfully positioned around a room of tremendous size and depth, topped by a ceiling high enough to complete the grand illusion.

The room is beautiful, and touched with melancholy.

I love it.

The large, mirrored dresser suddenly calls to me. The mirror is set deep into a carved wood display, with little shelves on both sides. Each shelf shows off a little porcelain or clear glass figurine, reminding me of the crystal flower my mother had taken from me when I was twelve. I see an old photograph of a beautiful young woman, holding hands with a simple, plain looking young man. On the main part of the dresser rests a large crystal vase, with a bouquet of white roses that are so fresh and perfect that I have to ask if they are real. I can't resist leaning forward, and breathing in their sweet, subtle perfume.

Elegant...

Reluctantly, I glance into the mirror. At once, I feel a powerful sensation of being outside my own body. In the mirror, I see a woman with perfect features and long, black hair. A woman of extraordinary beauty. A stranger.

"Let's go to the living room," Vera says.

We stroll comfortably down the long hall, back through the big kitchen. I had enjoyed washing the dishes in here. It is a domestic type's dream. Large sinks, lots of counter space and huge cabinets, packed with every manner of pretty trinket known. I paid close attention to the subtle patterns in all of the kitchen towels, dishcloths and potholders, along with the porcelain napkin holders and salt and pepper shakers, noticing that its decorator must have been very fond of strawberries. As we walk, I remember the bag of chocolate covered peanut clusters I had seen open inside the refrigerator.

In the dining room, I start to gaze again at the giant cabinet, tracing all of the tiny patterns with my eyes. Vera waits a moment, then ushers me gently, until we arrive at our final stop.

When we step into the big, contemporary-neoclassic cavern of a living room, I don't notice the plush, cushioned gray sofa and chairs, with their glossed wood trim at the bottom. I don't see the classic wood coffee table or the gray lamps. I don't notice the ash colored bricks around the fireplace, or the beautiful end tables that match the glossed wood trim on the sofa and chairs. I don't see any of the pretty green plants, or the little desk in front of the big window, or the fancy vase with the pink roses. I don't see the oval shaped, carved wood frame mirror, or the tall, wood and glass display cabinet in the corner.

I see something that makes my reality slip away.

Vera begins to disappear, among a whirlwind of schizophrenic sights and sounds. One object calls with force and power. Certain keys glow with bright, pure tones, all of the chords appearing and reappearing in sequence, corresponding to their respective colors.

Vera only stands quietly, watching my eyes twitch as I stare at the piano.

"...and when I woke up from that dream, I knew," says John. "The man told me tobacco is finished here, and said I couldn't change what was meant to be. Vera thinks I'm a dufus who just got lucky, but I've always known what I'm s'posed to do. She knew I dreamed about a cornfield, but I didn't tell her everything. There's power in secrecy, you know."

"You *were* lucky," Chris sighs. "Some people go their whole lives and never figure out what their supposed to do."

"Like you, huh?"

Chris smiles. They are together on the back porch, sheltered from the rain, treated to a summer light show in the clouds, over the big cornfield.

"You don't seem like the drifter type."But you've been nothin' but a farmhand for a long time, now. And, 'scuse me for sayin' so, but when I saw the inside of that house…"

"I know," Chris says.

"How long you two been livin' like that?"

"About ten years now."

"You've been in that house for *ten years?*"

"'Round about."

"What about poor Lizbeth? Didn't she ever try to get you to move?"

"We talked about it. But truth is, I don't know what happened, John. One day we woke up, and realized that we just didn't care anymore."

"Well, sometimes we need people to motivate us. That's what I'm here for. And b'lieve me, Vera has seen to that."

Chris laughs quietly. "She *has* hasn't she?"

"Oh, yeah."

"I really like her," Chris says honestly. "She's a special woman."

"A handful is what she is. And she's caused more problems than I feel like rememberin' tonight. But Lizbeth… now she just might be the one. I *know* she's special, and she deserves the best you can give her."

"You're right," Chris replies, shaking his head.

"Her and Vera are like family already. I think it's the start of somethin' we ain't got nothin' else to do with."

They watch the dark clouds flicker with light.

"What was that story you heard, John? About that house?"

"Oh, it's nothing. Just some stupid ghost story old Charlie Spurgeon told me when he sold me that field. He's near eighty and half gone, anyway. Course, you know that. You see him every month. He said he heard that a man killed his wife in that house, a long time ago. And he claims that sometimes at night, you can still hear her screaming."

Chris listens closely.

"He told me he was workin' the field out back one day past sunset— now this was way back in '71— he was out there 'til close to dark, and he swears he heard a scream comin' right from the house."

Then John puts his head down, and starts laughing.

"What's so funny?"

"He said he dropped a load in his pants when saw a dark light comin' from the window. And then he heard somethin' growl like an animal. *An animal that sounded like a woman,* he said."

Chris isn't laughing.

"A *dark greenish* light," he mumbles.

"What's that?" John asks, still smiling.

"Nothing."

"You were in another world," the Lady says.

I draw in a breath, staring in mild confusion.

"I'm sorry. Sometimes I see and hear things."

"Like what?"

I keep gazing at the instrument.

"You want a closer look?"

Together, we move to where the tiny grand rests in its corner. Alone and neglected.

"Do you play?" I ask, never taking my eyes from it.

"Good Lord, no. I love music so much that I tried to learn once, but it was useless. One of the reasons I like to go to church is to listen to the piano. Have you ever played?"

Not since I was in the fifth grade. When Mrs. Ida Brooks played a long passage of single notes for me, and I repeated them, without missing a single one.

"No."

"Maybe you'd like to learn, someday."

No answer.

"Well, it's getting late," Vera says. "I guess we'd better go ahead and tell 'em."

"Okay, *Momma.*"

We are spending the night. Something Vera had made her mind up about hours before. I had been quietly chatty about the beautiful house, while we sat together on the couch. I could have stayed up all night. Earlier, when I had gone to the bathroom to change into the nightgown Vera gave me, I amused myself for over a minute by just turning the lights on and off.

Vera is in her plain, rosy pink and white cotton, with the pink silken robe. She had decorated me in royal blue satin, with matching full length wrap coat, with dark blue lace around the collars, and at the tip of the sleeves.

I believe that the sleeves are long enough.

They are not.

"What time are we going back tomorrow?"

"Sometime after breakfast, I guess."

We stand at the door of the guestroom, dreading to say goodnight.

"But probably not 'til the afternoon," she says. "Chris and John might decide to get some work done. So you'll probably be here all day before we take you back home."

We both think about the shadowy house. Wishing it could just vanish away and be forgotten.

"I'm glad you're here with me," Vera says.

"It's strange, but I feel like we've met before. Like we've known each other for a long time."

Vera is silent.

"You don't mind it when I call you Momma, do you?"

We hug quietly.

"You're a beautiful person. So kind and loving. You don't make me feel bad for being ugly."

"Ugly?" Vera says, astonished. "Honey you're not even close to—"

"Yes, I *am*. And I'm clumsy and stupid, too. And I'm scared to death of everybody."

"Why do you think that way about yourself?"

"Because it's *true*."

Vera laughs to herself, at the very thought of it.

"That's what makes you so special," she says. "Because you don't even know."

We hug a while longer. Afraid to let go.

"I *love* you."

In the guest room, my husband and I sit together on our soft, queen sized bed.

"You seem a lot more relaxed." Chris says. "Different."

"I feel different. I really like it here."

Briefly I think of our own little house. The memory is a portrait in gray—framed in misery, loneliness, pain and suffering.

"Don't you like it here?"

"I don't know," he says.

"Why not?"

"Does she know?"

"What?"

"The rope bruises," he says. "I can see them."

"Of course she doesn't know. I would never say anything about that."

"What if she finds out? It's bound to happen, and then what? What'll happen to us?"

"She *won't* find out. I've already thought of that anyway."

I pause...

"I'll tell her that I bruise easily, and that I fall a lot. She knows I'm clumsy."

"Vera's not that stupid, honey."

"And I'll tell her about my mother."

"What about her?"

"I'll tell her that she used to do things."

"Did she?"

I look down, as if the memories have embarrassed me.

"I've never told you. Because I didn't want to think about it anymore. My mother hit me or beat me almost every day until she left. From the time I was a little girl. That's about all I can remember about her, is that she hurt me all the time. You remember the scars you noticed, when we first got married?"

"You said they were birthmarks."

"She would hit me with switches, sticks, her fists, just about anything she could get her hands on. And she would whip me sometimes until I was bleeding. She whipped me more than she did anything else."

"Why?"

"My mother hated me. She despised me."

Chris puts his head down.

"I'm sorry," he says. "Maybe if you had told me, I never would've..."

"It doesn't matter anymore. None of that matters."

"But if Vera sees your body, she won't believe it was all done by your mother. She'll get suspicious."

"She'll have to believe what I tell her."

There is a long pause.

"Are you gonna leave me?"

I slide close to him, and look him in the eyes.

"I love you too much for my own good. If you asked me to, I would take off this nightgown, and put that disgusting, smoky dress back on, and walk back home in the rain with you. I would do it *right now*."

A twinge of fear flashes through me, at the thought of trudging home in the middle of the storm, getting in the black truck, and driving off to some other dark, lonely place. But I love him too much. And in sorrow, I would have done it.

I would endure. As I am accustomed to.

32

*P**lease let me stay.*

I can't take the pain anymore. The shadows in that house want me to die. They want me to suffer. If I go back, they'll make me wish I was dead. The cold. The dark. I don't want to live like that anymore. The air was too thick. It was like trying to breathe underwater. Where am I? My Mother's beautiful home... she won't let them hurt me again. Here, I can't feel myself. There's no pain here. I can breathe. There're no shadows in these walls.

But I know that I can't stay.

They won't let me get away this time. They're outside in the rain. I can feel them. They know where I am. But they can't get to me. They can't make him torture me here. But they're waiting for me. Momma, please don't let them take me.

Please let me stay.

Vera had opened her mouth one time too many. Politely suggesting we stay another night. After breakfast, Chris had gathered his nerve, claiming we were causing too much trouble, and that it was time for us to go.

As Vera drives, she grips the steering wheel a little tighter than usual. She glances over at me. I am quietly looking at the rain slide across my window.

Then, the Lady cuts a glance to the rear view mirror.

Grayish blue, staring into icy blue.

Coldly.

While we make slow tracks over the mud road, a fog of tension begins to suffocate him. He has the misfortune of being trapped in an enclosed space, with two angry women.

There is no rest for the weary.

Or the wicked.

"I appreciate everything, Vera," he says. "You've been too good to us."

"Just a night's dinner and lodgin'. No trouble. But I am sorry you won't be staying longer."

"We've caused enough problems. It's bad enough you had to come all the way out here in this rain."

Ten miles or a hundred miles…

What's the difference?

Quietly, the silver car pulls into the front yard. Chris knows he'd better get while the gettin' is good.

"I'd better start unloadin' that stuff. Thanks again, Vera."

"Wait a second," she says. "Here's your pills. But be careful, 'cause they're strong. You just take these when you have trouble sleeping, okay?"

"Okay, and thank you."

Chris gathers up the two white lamps, moving with purpose through the cold rain, returning quickly for the small power generator in the trunk. Vera listens without compassion, as he struggles with the heavy equipment.

"I don't want you to leave," I say, without looking up. I sound like I'm going to cry.

"Believe me, neither do I."

"Why are you *leaving* then?"

"If he thinks you should be in your own house, what can I do? You heard me try as hard as I could to get him to stay. It might even be my fault. I might have pushed too hard. I don't have the right to come between you."

"Well, when are you coming back?"

"I can't come back today or tomorrow."

"Why not?" I say, in a choked voice.

"I just… I've already caused enough problems as it is. I don't want him to think I'm trying to turn you against him."

I glance fearfully at the house. There are traces of the same terror I had shown at the restaurant.

"I can't wear out my welcome so soon," she says. "I have to give him his space. It's the right thing to do. Don't you think so?"

The trunk was soon unloaded. Chris is on the back porch, setting up the generator.

I stare hard at Vera, who can't look back at me.

"Won't you please come inside for a minute?"

"It would just make it harder."

"Well, when will I see you again?"

"I'll come back on Saturday morn—"

"*Saturday?*" A tear runs out of my eye, and I wipe my face without a thought. I am hurt, and a little angry.

"Honey, don't make this any harder for me. I just have to give it a little more time, that's all. He'll be going back to work soon, and then I'll be here almost every day."

"He's not like that, Momma, really. He won't mind if you come inside for a few minutes."

"He would never say anything. But—"

"Please don't *go.* "

"Come here," she says.

I slide over, laying my head on Vera's bosom.

"We act like we're never going to see each other again," Vera says, voice nearly trembling.

"That's what it *feels* like."

"Maybe Saturday is a little too long to wait. How about I come by on Friday? I know a lot of nice little places we can go. Places where there aren't so many people. We can go shopping, and buy a lot of things for the house. And then maybe, next week you and me can go looking for another place for you to live. That sounds good, doesn't it?"

I don't answer.

"Maybe you and Chris can go somewhere today. It's raining so hard, no one will even notice you."

I am quiet.

"Things'll get better," I feel her say. "Someday soon, we'll both be happy."

A few minutes later, I get out of the car. Vera watches me glide through the rain. A figure in black, under my new black umbrella. Around the front of the car I drift, then onto the porch. I turn and wave, disappearing into the house.

Vera cries silently as she drives down the mud road. Her heart is crushed, and her spirit is torn to pieces.

Inside, the house is cold and dark. I've been thrown back into the fear, and the dread of shadows.

Here, my nostrils burn from kerosene and soot.

I sit still and quiet in the dark. Memories, images of the tortures begin to fall on me, building upon one another. Along with the memories come the sadness. The longing. And I start to wonder again, why there can be no end to suffering.

When the back door opens and closes, I tremble. Every footstep makes me breathe faster.

In the cold rain. From the shadows of my past—

A dark and fearful spirit.

33

*V*era was alone.

Completely.

Her life was full of people, money, and the love of a husband. But she is still the victim of an all consuming desolation of spirit. For most her life, she thought she knew what it was to be lonely. It had been an incessant aching of emptiness, a need for something. For some*one*. A lifetime of dedication to John and the farm had not cured it. Neither had the social busy bodying, nor the endless hours of volunteerism and do-gooding.

The dreams had helped. If they meant she was insane, she didn't care. But in her sleep, she had been comforted often.

The dream was made flesh and blood. *Her* flesh. *Her* blood. And now, she is apart from it. A piece of her, ripped away.

She drives on in the rain, constantly wiping the tears from her face. Before long, her silver car is moving up the concrete driveway.

There is a car at the end of it, close to the house.

Big, beige Lexus power.

Oh my dear God

No matter how confident, brave, or commanding the personality, there is always at least one other person that can cause fear.

Vera's entire day was spent at Brenda Lynn Harrison's house. Sorting out boxes and piles of donated food and clothing. There had been no choice. A polite lie on the telephone wasn't possible this time.

"Don't make me have to come after you tomorrow, Vera. I want you here early. We're going to finish these clothes and drop 'em off, and then we'll stop by the shelter until after lunchtime..."

She wanted to slap Brenda in the face hard enough to knock her to the floor. And then stuff one of those outdated dresses in her mouth until she gagged. And she had nearly done it, when a certain "*Amazing*" name was mentioned in her presence. But then, she thought about her Elizabeth.

So she endured it, as she was accustomed to.

They say that women have evils inside them. Vicious, sinister evils, that men have never dared imagine. Some believe that a woman is more secretive, and will quietly glare, then whisper and manipulate, until they have destroyed the woman they see as a threat. They can get inside another woman's soul, and discover her weaknesses, and slowly cut her to pieces from the inside. All of it done with premeditation. And precision.

"Vera, honey, can I see you for a moment?"

Inexplicably, she takes her upstairs into Kate's old room. A hideous shrine… shamelessly dedicated to a past filled with the strivings of a teenager, driven mad with the need to please her mother.

In private.

"I come in here to think," Brenda says. "To work out my problems."

"Oh," Vera says. Helplessly.

"Why are you getting so *lazy*, Vera?"

Vera doesn't know why, but she is suddenly scared to death.

"I can never get in touch with you anymore," Brenda says. "You'd think that you actually had a job to go to. I work, and I still find time to help as many people as I can."

"The truth is, Brenda, I…"

"I don't want to hear any more excuses. That's all you've been good for lately. Now are you a part of this team or aren't you? We've got a lot to do, every single day, and we can't have someone lagging behind not doing her part. I've covered for you more than I think you're prepared to realize and understand, Vera."

"Brenda, you know I haven't been feeling well. "

"I thought you had gotten *help* for that," she hisses, spitting the words. Like a cobra.

"Well, I did, but I still feel kinda down somet—" Vera's voice chokes in her throat. Her eyes water.

"That's because you like to feel sorry for yourself. You've got to work at it, Vera. Work, work, work. No one's going to hand you anything. You've got to go out and get it for yourself. That includes happiness and peace of mind. If you're depressed, then get the doctor to give you something for it. I'm not ashamed to say that I've taken anti-depressants, and they've done me a world of good. *Kate* and I were talking about you just the other day. It's gonna take more than a few sleeping pills to fix what's wrong with you, believe me."

Kate.

Sometimes, the claws come out on their own. Independent of a person's will. Vera's are out. And they are glistening.

"You were discussing my personal problems with your daughter?"

"Well, we were just…"

"Exactly what did Miss Amazing Grace have to say?"

"Miss amaz… what did you call her?"

"I asked you, what did Miss Amazing Grace Harrison have to say about my depression?"

"My daughter's name is Cather…"

"Your daughter is a pissy, spoiled, conceited, busy bodying *slut!"*

Brenda's mouth fell open. To question her daughter's moral purity is to question Perpetuity.

"I always knew you were just an *ignorant* farm girl," Brenda says, "who got lucky because her husband had a ridiculous dream."

And then, Brenda laughed.

"And I always knew you were just a phony, bottle-blonded *bitch,* who gets off on sticking her nose-job in other people's business."

The two women stand close together. Insults about corn shucking and bankruptcy, huge bosoms, dark roots and bad haircuts, cheating husbands and ugly dresses, dark circles and gray bottom teeth, barren wombs and ad nauseam are on the tip of witches' tongues. Until Brenda sensed something in Vera's eyes. That look that says a person is tired of getting beat up.

"That's it," Brenda says, "I'm not carrying your lazy ass anymore. I want you out of my house."

She grabs Vera's arm, and tries to pull her along, to parade her past the three other women in the living room and toss her out the front door.

But Vera allows the tempest to swirl. The energy flows from her spirit, into her arms, and with hardly an effort she wrenches away from Brenda's grip, and pushes her backwards into her daughter's tall bookshelf. Brenda nearly falls in a noisy clamour of broken glass, fallen plaques, pictures, books and trophies.

Vera then steps close in front of her, calmly pressing her body hard against Brenda's. Breathing into her face.

"I had no right to discuss your private issues with a third party. For that, I do apologize."

Vera backs off, tired of Brenda's coffee breath in her nostrils.

"Brenda, if you ever need…"

The farmer's wife blows a deep sigh. She just shakes her head, and calmly walks out of Catherine Grace Harrison's old bedroom.

Vera was so angry, it didn't matter that she had humiliated herself. She could probably never look them in the eye again. So she doesn't bother to try, as she marches down the stairs, back into the living room to gather her purse. Without a word, she glides across their line of sight to the front closet and slips on her coat, ignoring their bewildered looks. The umbrella is stubborn, opening while she hurries through the rain to her silver luxury car. Her Klein crystal timepiece tells the late afternoon hour.

Vera just sits inside, listening to the rain fall around her. Sorrow and guilt are coiled around her. Like two invisible serpents.

Brenda means well. She helps a lot of people. But she treats me like a dog. Yet she calls me all the time, begging me to visit and work with her. And then, she acts like she doesn't really want me around. She'll twist every little thing I do and say, and use it to make me feel bad about myself.

Maybe it's my fault.

Maybe I'm being over sensitive.

She wants to go inside and apologize. And she almost does…

Until the door opens, and she sees Brenda stick her yellow-colored, seventy five dollar hair cutted head out the door, smiling goodbye to one of her pearl-necklaced, prissy slaves.

Vera boldly starts her car right in front of them. In no particular hurry, she cruises out of the huge, black asphalt driveway. Leaving Grand Harwich Acres to itself.

Fake bitch.

As she drives home, she knows it will take a long, private session of deep apologies if she wants inside their circle again. But Vera knows it is bigger than that. She just can't do it anymore. Any of it.

The mindless, phony chattering. The local status seeking and social climbing. The sight and smell of hypocrisy—covered in expensive makeup, perfume and so called Christian charity and goodwill. She can't do it anymore. The endless flow of catty undercurrents, churning beneath cultured civility. Ebbing and flowing in a river of jealousies, bitterness and resentment. She just can't do it anymore! Eyes glistening with the lust and pride of life and living! Blaring trumpets of alms, driving deep into her mind! Watching and listening to smiles and praises to God in the name of Christ, with razor sharp tongues dipped in poison! All in all, with a pathetic lack of understanding, blissful ignorance of fallen natures, and the inability to escape the damnation of souls!

Then she remembers a certain Light. One that reveals itself through human frailty. Touching the hearts and minds of men.

Vera drives on slowly. Letting the tears flow as they desire. For all her years of pride and southern church hypocrisy…

She asks to be forgiven.

34

Vera awoke to the music of G minor and E minor tones, the music of the doorbell. Bewildered, she puts on her elegant silken robe, and hurries down the long dark hallway into the kitchen. A loud clap of thunder startles her, and she becomes annoyed at the storm, and the late night visitor.

Who could possibly be out in this weather, at this time of night?
"Who is it?"

"Momma?"

"Oh my God," she says, frantically opening the door. There is Elizabeth, standing barefoot in the rain, soaked and shivering, wearing

only a dripping wet gray dress, carrying a small bouquet of white roses. Vera could have sworn that one of the roses was ashen gray.

"Honey, come in here," she says, in her highest pitched, most compassionate tone. She takes the roses and places them on the counter. "What's the matter, baby, where's Chris?"

"Momma, why'd you leave me?"

"Honey, I didn't leave you," she says, while hugging her. "I told you I was coming back." Vera glances at the back door. "Where's your husband? Is he alright? Sweetie, you didn't walk over here, did you?"

"Why'd you leave me, Momma? I don't want to be there anymore. It's so cold and dark, and I don't want to die."

"But you're not going to die, Elizabeth. Oh, dear Lord, please tell me you didn't walk over here. Dear God I can't believe this."

She closes the door, and ushers her soaking wet visitor closer to the long hallway. The water seems to be pouring off her, from her hair, down through her dress, to her bare feet and all over the floor.

"Everything's all right, now. Now Elizabeth, just talk to me, and tell me exactly what you're doing here, and why you're dressed this way. My God you're not even wearing any shoes."

"I feel sick, Momma, like I'm going to die. And my skin hurts a lot, especially on my back."

"Your back?" She rubs it firmly. Elizabeth sucks in her breath through her teeth, recoiling in pain.

"Oh, I'm sorry. I didn't know."

"It hurts really bad."

"Well, turn around, honey let me look at it. My Lord, I still can't believe this is happening."

Elizabeth turns around, so that Vera can take a look at her back.

"You must have scraped yourself on a bush or something, I can see little scratches here, at the top of your dress. I'm going to unzip your dress, now. We've got to get you out of these wet clothes anyway."

She begins to slowly unzip her dress.

"I've got dresses that'll look better on you than they do on me. Tomorrow we can…"

Vera is suddenly immobilized by an unseen force, which she feels enter her body, and spread out into her flesh. She is instantly a prisoner of undiluted terror, which is given life and substance by what she sees when she unzips the dress…

On her back is a network of deep, bleeding cuts and gashes, which run down and across her entire back, in a mass of torn, bloody flesh. Her skin is ripped away from the muscle in more than one place, and gives visual reference to the description "skin hanging in ribbons." And among all of this is a hideous looking burn, where there is no skin at all, but only a large red area surrounded by blackened flesh. Imbedded within many of the bloody wounds are what looked like tiny pieces of wood.

Elizabeth at once seems beyond her reach—the plight of her existence too deep, too layered with secret pain and suffering for her to either affect or understand.

She is going to die…there's nothing I can do…

The fear in her body contracts rapidly, scraping her insides, forming into a single, cold energy mass, flowing like liquid ice along her spine. It moves into her lungs, and begins to expel itself through her mouth. Vera can hear the breath leaving her lungs, and then she hears the mass of fear, which slowly fills the nightmare world with something that sounds like a high pitched death scream…

The gray world dissolves. Vera finds herself in her own bed, trying to release the rest of the fear through a terrifying scream. Her screaming wakes John, who finds her lying immobile on her back, as if she were being held down and tormented. He grabs her and pulls her up, as she begins to thrash like a wild woman.

"Vera! Vera!"

He keeps calling her. Shaking her, until she calms down enough for him to hug her.

"Viv, it was just a dream. See honey? Everything's alright. It was just a nightmare."

"John help me, please! I can't leave her, I can't leave her!"

"Leave who? Vera look at me!"

"My daughter'll die without me!"

"Your daught… what're you talkin' about?"

"I'm going to get my daughter!" She starts to pull hard away from him, approaching hysterics again. "I'm taking her out of there *now*, right this minute!"

"What're you talkin' about? Elizabeth?"

"Yes! Let me go, I'm going to get her right this second!"

"Vera, we can't…"

"I said, let me *go!*" She becomes violent. John is amazed at how strong she is.

"Vera, stop it!"

"*NO!*"

John has to wrestle her to the bed, and barely has the strength to hold her down.

"I said, *stop it!*"

"NOO! NOO!"

After tremendous effort, he is able to get his hand over her mouth, and keep her from biting through it, or clawing him to death. After at least a half a minute, she finally begins to come to her senses. He takes his hand away, pulling her up again.

"I'm going to get her *tonight!*" she sobs. "With or without you I'm taking my daughter out of that filthy pig pen right this minute!"

She starts pulling away again. Slowly.

"Vera we can't go over there and kidnap her out of bed because you had a nightmare."

"I don't care anymore," she whimpers. "I don't care what you say, or what you think. And you can't hold me forever. I'm going to get her, and there's nothing you can do about it."

"Vera, listen to me…"

"I don't want to *hear* it! Now let me go!" She moves again, but he quickly grabs her shoulders, and shakes her like a someone might shake a bald headed foster child they had never really wanted in the first place.

"Vera, calm down and *shut up!*"

He pauses for a moment. Briefly.

"Sometimes I blame myself, for having not been there for you when you needed me. If I had, then maybe you wouldn't've been so lonely. Maybe you wouldn't've started lockin' yourself up in this room and sleepin' for days at a time. Maybe you wouldn't have started making up dream daughters and…"

"I told you those dreams were real, and that she…"

"Vera *BE QUIET!*"

She stares defeatedly.

"It doesn't matter whether or not they were real," he says. "Maybe the dreams meant you were *going* to meet her, I don't know. But this daughter business, Vera, its... its *crazy*. You're actin' like you've lost your mind, Honey. You've only known this girl for two days, and you're talkin' about love, and her bein' your daughter. Viv, you're *obsessed*. First it was her husband, and now it's her. I'm startin' to wonder if either one of 'em is any good for you."

"John, I can't help the way I feel. I can't help it if I love her."

"I'm crazy about her too. She's a beautiful girl, and she's special, but—"

"No, you don't understand. I love her for *real,* with all my heart. This isn't like it was with Chris. She's my daughter..."

"Vera she is *not* your daughter. You don't even know her."

"But I *do* know her. I told you about the..."

"I don't want to hear anything else about those damned dreams. I want you to *shut your mouth* about those stupid dreams!"

Vera looks down, and cries silently.

"Vera, promise me that you'll try to get a hold of this nonsense. I don't like what its doin' to you. This thing with you and them... its not normal. Its weird and its strange. The whole thing is startin' to give me the creeps and I'm gettin' a little tired of it. Okay, so you had a few dreams about a young woman, and now you've met the person who looks like her. I'm not blind honey, I can see that your feelin' for Chris led you right to her. And now its done, okay? You've found her. And let's just leave it at that. They're good people who just seem a little sad. They'll be glad to have someone like you in their lives...

218

"But Vera, she is *not* your daughter. You're not even old enough to have a daughter her age. So how can you even feel that way about her? The way you're actin' over her doesn't make any sense. Viv, I don't want you to let this come between us."

Vera looks at him with pity. As if she were looking at a person who gazes across human history, who watches the sun disappear below the horizon, then looks at the thousands of natural lights in the dark sky, and says there is no plan, no purpose and no power that guided all of it into being. The poor man just didn't understand. It was so far beyond him it was almost funny. But it didn't matter. In this, *he* no longer mattered.

Vera pulls a tissue from the grand night table, and calmly dries her tears away.

35

*T*hey had not slept again. For the rest of the night, there was quiet talking. Coming to terms with the inevitable.

It's seven o'clock in the morning.

And Vera had waited long enough.

"You see that?"

"What?"

"Look up there," he says. "The wire leadin' to their house. The storm ripped it right out."

"Oh, yeah. I *do* see it... John, I'm still scared. I need you to be strong for me."

A few minutes later, we hear a knock. We'd been awake for an hour already. Tucked away in our bedroom, talking about Vera, and listening to the radio. The two lamps and the radio are plugged into a thick orange extension chord.

"Do you think that's her?"

Chris turns the radio down. The only sounds are the noisy rain and the hum of the generator. Then came the knock again, as loudly and determined as before.

"I'll get it. I know it's *Momma.* "

I slip my new satin robe over my old cotton nightgown, gliding boldly to the front door.

"Who is it?"

"It's me, honey. It's me and John."

When deep, mournful longing is realized suddenly, it can produce mild shock in the body. Vera's voice causes my farm girl ears to ring, and my vision hazes for just a second. Then I open the door...

The entire scene feels like slow motion as I open the screen. The two of us reach across a chasm, a depth of loneliness, falling into each other's arms. We hug tightly, slipping forward from a dark past. To a present of hope and light.

"Momma," I whisper. "Momma."

"I'm here," she says. "I'm here."

Neither of us notice John behind us, knocked awkward by confusion. He can hardly believe it. It gives him the creeps.

"Oh, hi Mr. Evans. Thank you for the lamps and the generator."

"You're welcomed honey."

About that time, he is more than glad to see a familiar face in this weird wilderness.

"Hey, John," Chris says, "Glad to see you."

"Hey, Chris."

"'Mornin'," says Vera.

Coldly.

The Farm Prince and the Lady hug, unsurprised by what they feel. There is still some deep feeling. He is still her perfect angel, and she will always be his Lady.

But the fire was *out.*

"Chris, grab us a couple of chairs out of the kitchen," says John. "You and Lizbeth have a seat on the couch." Chris quickly obliges. He and I sit down, feeling like a couple of kids in front of parents who are done with trivialities. John looks at Vera, and she nods her head.

"We've got somethin' real important to talk to you kids about," John says. "I think it's a pretty big deal, so hear me out before you say anything…

"I think you both know how we feel about you. And here recently, Vera and me can't seem to go five minutes without talkin' about you. The two of you are special people, and we're glad to have you in our lives. Chris, you saved my life, son. And you kept Vera from gettin' hurt that day in the kitchen. And the truth is, you're as good at handlin' the work as anybody I've ever seen…

"We appreciate all of it. And we'll never be able to repay you. But this isn't about that, about what we owe. I think this is about *family.* I'm still not sure exactly how it happened, but you two have become like family to us. A real family. We care a lot about you, and about what happens to you from now on…

"We… that is , Vera and me, would consider it an *honor,* to have you come and live with us. Permanently."

Vera watches my eyes, and sees me begin to bite my nails and gaze fearfully at Chris.

Then, Vera's eyes meet Chris.'

Arctic.

"Of course, it'll be as much your home as it is ours," John says. "It'll take some gettin' used to, but we'll all be comfortable soon enough. And like I said, we hope that it'll be permanent."

Chris looks at his wife, who has retreated. He knows I have cocooned my emotions. Protecting them from the shards of another dream being smashed at my feet.

And then, he sees Vera's expression go *hard.*

"Um…I… we'd be glad to."

The Lady watches the Italian Girl close her eyes in relief. The weight of tension lifts rapidly, flowing upward, through the bare wood ceiling and the tin roof, out into the gray. The four of us are suddenly lost. Somewhere outside of time, where there is no past to regret, nor future to fear. There are neither words nor emotion, nor can we fully know the importance of crossroads, and the cosmic implications of choices made. From four points of origin, through an infinity of paths chosen, we have all come together. Surviving our own journeys through loneliness and despair.

Happiness.

It threatens to creep in… and tickle my soul.

✝

The rain had slowed to an invisible mist, inspiring John and Chris to walk out back, to look over the summer field.

The evil ground had been flattened, and covered well…

But his soul still torments him with guilt, and memories of days long gone.

For several seconds, Vera and I stand quietly.

The whole world is suddenly like a dark void, where we had wandered alone and afraid. But by the mercy of Fate, we are both in this Valley of Shadows, where we found one another. And we share a bond, at once more precious than blood, and more intense than we can easily endure.

Without words, I hurry over to her, and fall into her arms. Vera nearly loses her breath, but struggles to breathe deeply, breathing my scent, enjoying the feel of my body. We stand close together, holding each other tightly, with our eyes closed. Vera firmly rubs every inch of my back, remembering the dream images of a tormented soul. We are bound together by pure emotion, and by memories of a lifetime of pain.

I had enjoyed how the shadows fled before my guardian. We are sitting together in the bedroom. I've changed out of my nightclothes, wearing a longsleeved, full length gray dress. Though it is the very image of simple living, Vera insists that I radiate a powerful, irresistible beauty.

Vera had wanted to watch me change. To see what was on my skin. But she couldn't bring herself to ask. She was afraid of what she might have seen.

"Elizabeth honey, I've got something to tell you. I don't know if you'll believe me, but I can't keep it a secret any longer."

"I'll believe you. I swear to God and Jesus I will."

Vera takes a deep breath.

"I had a daughter right after John and I got married. But she died when she was a baby. I don't know if I ever really got over it. We tried to have more children, but they were all miscarriages. John begged me to adopt a little girl. But I just couldn't bring myself to do it. I was afraid that I might even hate the child, because I couldn't have any of my own. But I got better, and I focused on John and the farm..."

"Well, a while back it started to hit me again. I'd get so miserable that I'd sleep for days. I'd take pills, and just sleep as long as I wanted. And one night I had a dream about a woman. A young, beautiful woman, with smooth skin, and long black hair. In the dreams, she always called me Momma, and was the sweetest, most beautiful woman I'd ever seen...

"The dreams came so often that I started to depend on them. I needed her. I couldn't live without her. But after a while she went away, and I was angry and sad, and poor John had no idea what was wrong with me. I couldn't tell anybody because they would have locked me away for sure."

"Around the time your husband came to work for us, I started dreaming again. And they were *strong*. I would walk and talk with her, and we would sit together and look at the sky and the pretty white clouds. She always brought me roses, in every color you can imagine. She said that every rose sings its own melody..."

"Sometimes I couldn't find her, especially if a storm was coming. But if we were together, we weren't afraid. And when the rains would come, we would go and hide together, under a beautiful shelter made of white marble. The very first time we went under that shelter, she told me her name…

"She told me her name was *Carmen.*"

I get a sudden chill. Vera's voice chokes a little.

"And then when I met Chris, I…" She pauses… "It wasn't just because he was handsome, I swear it."

"I know."

"I know I shouldn't say it, but the people in this town... sometimes I don't want to come out of my bedroom. He had such a sweetness... and I knew something was bothering him. So I finally got up the nerve and came here, to see what I could do to help him and his wife…

"And when I saw you. When you walked out of that bedroom—"

Vera draws a quick breath, as though she had been jabbed with a needle. Then she lets out a quick, loud sob. I grab her and hold her tightly, whispering reassurances in her ear.

"I'm here now, *Momma.* Its alright…"

Vera controls herself the best she can. But there is no resisting the quiet, pitiful howling. After a minute, she could finally speak.

"I told you wouldn't believe me."

"But I do."

"Don't you understand? It was *you.* You were the girl I had been dreaming about all these years. My God, what you must be thinking of me right this minute."

"I'm thinking of how much I love you."

I kiss Vera all over her face. Soft, gentle kisses. She relaxes, and enjoys being comforted by her dream daughter...

But there are things that I have to tell. Things I had tried to forget for the rest of my life. About what can happen to a daughter who is raised in isolation, by a woman driven mad with grief.

I was raised by my Mother alone.

36

*V*era had listened quietly to everything. Her body felt numb. There was a drained, distant expression on her face.

Veranda May Evans knew that when there's too much to say, it's best to keep silent. From the depth of sorrow and compassion, she understood that there was nothing.

Nothing for her to say.

We sit together on the bed, for a very long time. I rest in my new mother's arms, nearly falling asleep while Vera strokes my soft, shiny hair. Vera listens to the hum of the power generator, struggling to come to terms with what she has just heard.

In all of her years, she had never imagined that such a thing were possible.

After a while, we hear our husbands clunking through the back door. They had come in once already, but had gone back out. Apparently, they are here to stay this time.

John knocks timidly on the bedroom door.

"I'd better go and see what he wants. I'll be right back okay?"

A fresh tension hangs over the living room. John and Chris have the strangest, most sheepish looks she believes she's ever seen.

"What is it, John?"

"Honey," he says, nearly under his breath. "Chris was afraid to say anything, but…"

"Well, what is it?"

"He wanted me to ask you if, well, if you wouldn't mind if he could spend some time alone with Elizabeth. To kinda say a last goodbye to this old place."

A last goodbye?

The look on her face, the quiet shock and disbelief, is a masterpiece of non-verbal communication.

"Vera, they *have* been together here for ten years. And this thing with us came up right sudden. He wants them to pack it up together. You can understand that, can't you?"

Her expression darkens, coloured by blatant suspicion and quiet, determined defiance.

"Vera this is all happenin' pretty fast. You can understand can't you?"

"I *understand*... that God only knows what'll happen if I leave her here."

"Huh?"

"I'm talking about a girl with problems worse than anything you have *ever* imagined, being forced to live like an animal in this filthy, stinking *shack* that's not even fit to be a wood shed."

Chris had sneaked out of the living room to the kitchen, safely out of view.

"When I think about her living in this woodpile, sleeping and eating here night after night, year after year..." she looks around—and shudders with revulsion. "These walls and floors are so disgusting they might as well be living *outside*. It stinks so bad that it makes me sick to my stomach. It's so dark and small in here that it scares me. I feel like I can't breathe!"

"Now you *listen to me,*" he snaps, grabbing her arm.

"*Take your hands off me!*" she screams. "Don't you *touch* me!"

In the bedroom, I listen. Comfortably.

"Vera, Honey, they're married. Why don't we give 'em a few hours alone."

She folds her arms over her power bosom, glaring at the filthy walls and floor.

John steps closer. Cautiously.

"Let's not make 'em think we're tryin' to pull 'em apart, Viv."

"What about Elizabeth? What if she doesn't want me to leave her?"

"But we're not leaving anymore. Its just a few hours this time. We'll go take care of our own business…"

"She *is* my business. For the rest of my life."

"We'll leave 'til late this afternoon," he says. "Til six, maybe."

"*Six?*"

That'll give 'em one more whole day alone here. They'll have everything in the house packed up by then, and we'll come back with the truck. Then we'll all leave here together."

"We should all leave right this minute and burn this thing to the ground," she says.

When she opens the bedroom door, she sees me on the edge of the bed, biting my fingernail again. Her expression softens.

"Chris wants to spend the day here alone with you."

"I know."

"How do you feel about that?"

"Fine."

"Are you gonna be alright?"

"Yes."

"Elizabeth, if you don't want me to leave…"

"It's okay, Momma. We'll be alright. I understand him. He just needs to talk to me."

"About *what* I wonder?"

Vera had almost let it slip. She almost told, right this minute, that she isn't a complete fool, that my long sleeve gray peasant dress isn't hiding anything from her. When she opens the door again, she catches a glimpse of her farmer husband, gazing mournfully out the window.

"John, wait for me in the car, okay?"

He obliges her, closing the door softly behind him.

"Honey, send Chris in here."

"Yes, Maam." Obediently, I go to the kitchen. Vera clearly hears me say *"she wants to see you in the bedroom."*

Chris wastes no time.

"Close the door," she says.

She met his fearful stare. When he looks away, a cold shiver passes through her, making her draw a breath, putting her hand over her mouth.

"Tell me you didn't," she begs.

He looks down. Ashamedly.

"Oh God oh my dear God"...

Her words came out in a quiet, ghostly sound. Like the voice of an apparition.

But she gathers her strength.

For me.

"Look at me," she orders. "I don't know what happened here. And God knows its none of my business. But I want you to look at me and I want you to listen...don't you *ever* touch her again," she hisses. "If you do, I swear to *God and Jesus* I'll make you regret it until the day you die. Did you hear what I said!"

"Yes Maam. Yes Maam, I did."

Suddenly, his body discerns the fear of Retribution.

"What kind of evil must it have been, to have made you *do* such a thing?"

If he could have answered, he would have.

"Someday, I'll listen to every word," she says. "But not now. I can't handle it now. Dear Lord, the pain she must have been in. The way she must have suffered in this miserable house."

Vera wanders over to the window. Looking into the gray weather, at the small woods by the yard.

"Why do people cause each other so much *PAIN!* We're not supposed to make other people *suffer."*

For a long time, she stares plaintively out the window, as though looking a great distance away.

"Come here, Chris."

He hurries to her, and they hug tightly at the window.

"I love you, Vera."

"I'll never stop loving you, Chris. If it hadn't been for you I never would have found her. I'll be grateful to you for the rest of my life."

"I won't get in the way," he says. "I promise."

She breathes deeply, closing her eyes.

"Come outside with me."

"I want to do this now," she says, "before it starts raining again. John, back the car into the road and wait for me."

"How come?"

"Just do it, Honey."

From her coat pocket, Vera discreetly pulls her little camera. When the car was out of the way, she proceeded.

"Chris, come down here and stand beside Elizabeth. Yes, that's it, right in front of the house. Okay, now, walk towards me, until I tell you to stop. Alright."

My husband and I look at each other nervously.

"Look at me," Vera says.

We don't smile. We don't frown. We only look lost. Staring like two frightened orphans. Vera clicks the shutter, capturing ghostly images for all time.

"Okay," she sighs. "I need one more with just Elizabeth. Chris move over here."

Vera looks through her little camera…and finds the daughter of her dreams. It is a picture in twilight and darkness.

A gray portrait.

A picture of a woman with scars, who had been under a curse. A cloud of inexhaustible misery. The woman stood still, holding her hands together in front of her. Obedient. Compliant. In her eyes shines the light of life. A spirit of gentleness and faith. And in her expression is a distant longing. A profound, indefinable sadness.

A breeze rustles Vera's long gray coat. She moves over to her daughter, gazing into her eyes.

"I'm gonna go now."

She gives me a hug. A long, tight hug.

"I'll be back for you," she whispers.

She kisses us both goodbye, then hurries away. The Peeles stand in their front yard, until the Evans' are all the way down the road and out of sight.

In the house behind them lay the ruins of their past. Barren, fruitless ground. Where the seeds of love and happiness were planted, but had not taken root… and had died. But in their *hearts*, the love had grown… and was nurtured.

Holding hands, the two of us turn, and walk timidly into our little house.

37

John and Vera spent the day at home. One of the longest, loneliest days Vera could remember. The seconds and minutes made fun of them, dragging like hours, while the hours crept along like days. But the clock chimes were about to ring six times…

It was time to go.

"I should be happy or excited. But I'm just scared."

"It'll all work out, Viv."

They are at the big kitchen table. Listening to the storm.

"John, I can't thank you enough for what you're doin'. You don't know how much this means to me."

"It'll be nice havin' 'em around. I think we're doin' the right thing."

"It's the *only* thing," she says. "I guess we'll be goin' in a few minutes, huh?"

"Its about that time I reckon. We'll leave their stuff in the house til tomorrow, or whenever this storm blows over."

"It's rainin' so hard again. I bet they're wonderin' where we are by now."

"It's their last day," he says. "Let 'em get good and ready for us."

Outside, the sky was darkening again. Vera listens to the soft thunder-- and thinks only of me. She imagines me in the house with her all day, while Chris and John are working. Just being together, talking about everything and nothing, enjoying every single moment of it.

Admiring me. Buying me new clothes and shoes, dressing me up like a mannequin doll. Buying things for my hair and my skin. Listening to me chatter about how much I love the house and about how glad I am to be there. Even listening to every terrible, secret thing I have to tell. Hoping to someday bring me out of the reclusiveness and fear. Helping me to cope with the pain of memories. Hoping I'll be happy.

The thunder boomed. Resounding loudly.

"John, I think its time to—"

In the next instant, the back door opens...

A phantom.

John jumps up from his chair. The last time he was this angry was when he had thrown him off his farm.

"Little, what the *Hell* do you think you're doin'? Get out of my house!"

"John, don't. *Please*. Is... is there somethin' we can do for you Joe?"

Joe doesn't answer. He only closes the door.

And he raises the Winchester.

"Have you gone *crazy?*" John says, without fear. "I said *get out of here!*" John throws his chair violently to the side, taking a step towards him.

Joe then cocks the barrel like a veteran.

"One more step," he says.

"John, please! *Please,* John!" She is begging, in a hoarse, trembly voice. Her eyes are wide, glistening with fear.

"You see?" John says. "I told you that son-of-a-bitch was no good. I knew he'd never 'mount to nothin' but trouble."

John please

"I told you he was *nothin' ,*" John hisses, shaking his head.

Joe's expression changes. From satisfaction to scalding contempt.

"And you wonder why I fired your lazy, stupid—I'm callin' Sheriff Williams, so you can finally get what you deserve, you ignorant bastard—"

John moves towards the phone. Joe points the gun, aiming it at John's chest. Vera screams.

"John if you love me, *please stop!*"

The words calm him down just enough. He stops dead in his tracks, casting a reassuring glance back at his wife. Then he looks back at Joe.

John opens his mouth to speak...

Then the room is filled with an explosion of *gunpowder...* the shot sends John Evans sprawling backwards, halfway across the kitchen and landing flat on his back.

Vera screams, bent halfway over in disbelief. She quickly covers her mouth and looks at her husband laying spread out on the floor. The bloody wound is hidden by the kitchen table. Her ears are ringing from the noise, and the smell of the gunshot is already strong in her nostrils.

Joe watches her while he walks over to John's body. He cocks the gun again and puts it at point blank range to his chest.

Then…he pulls the trigger.

The second, thunderous shot digs into Vera's body and rips a death scream from her throat.

He points the gun at Vera's head.

"Shut your mouth."

She covers her mouth again and tries hard to keep silent. Joe hurries over to the window. Not a living soul is outside.

Vera can't look around the table. At the burned, bloody wound.

Joe walks slowly toward her.

"Are you gonna shoot me, Joe?"

He only looks her up and down. From top to bottom.

"Walk me to your bedroom."

"Joseph, honey, I have a daughter…"

He slaps a flash of light from her face to her brain. He then grabs her hard by the hair and pulls her up straight.

"I don't give a god-*damn* about your daughter! If she was here, she'd be dead, too! Now… walk me to your bedroom."

"Joseph—"

He puts the gun to her face.

She closes her mouth, and obeys him.

She drifts through a dense fog of thoughts and feelings. Everything that she knew, everything she believed in had been ripped away. But as she opens the bedroom door, she uses her faith. The evidence of the unseen…

And as they step into her Gray Palace, she thinks of all she has lost. Her husband. Her new daughter. Her hopes.

Her *life*.

"Let's just go. Why are we still here?"

"They'll come get us when they want us."

Darkness has descended. The rains have returned with fury, accompanied by the lightning and the thunder.

The generator is off. There is no light in our house, except for the flame in the old lamp on the mantle. Our few belongings are loaded safely under the tarp on the truck. Except for lonely spirits, and the sounding rain…

The house is empty.

I remember Vera. Why hasn't she come back?

"Chris, I think something might be wrong."

My voice is so calm that it gets his attention.

"Let's get our coats."

I gaze through the windshield as we drive, watching the raindrops fall through the beams of light.

She hasn't forgotten about me. And there's nothing wrong.

They're probably on the way right now.

I turn to look out my side window. But there is nothing to see.

Except darkness.

Inside the beautiful farmhouse, the clock chimes softly.

Once…

Then it chimes seven times more.

The truck glides in the darkened rain, down the black, slippery roads. Chris has driven them thousands of times before, but tonight, they seem treacherous. Unfamiliar. The rain and night bear down on him and his wife, causing a sense of powerful dread and foreboding.

Some think of Fate as a river.

If so, then to where will it finally travel? Into what place, into what world?

If Fate is a river, then it flows to an eternal sea…

A Sea of Destiny.

We are two travelers on this river. Swept hopelessly along by its whim, upon its own course and direction. We don't speak. We don't look at one another. We only look forward, struggling to see past the veil of darkness, to perhaps catch a glimpse of our future, whether it be good or evil...

But we can only see the headlights, illuminating the raindrops directly ahead.

We drive onward, until we're at the Evans palatial home. The loaded truck turns in, rolling up the driveway until it comes to a stop—a good distance behind the silver Oldsmobile.

They're here... But the lights are off in the house.

What's wrong?

"The car's here," he says. "And there's John's truck. But it looks like they're not home."

We sit quietly for a moment.

"I'll bet they had to leave with somebody else," he says. "An emergency or something."

"Oh." A rare smile appears on my face. And a sigh. "That's what happened. They had to leave with somebody else."

"Vera knows tons of people. Somebody probably rushed over here with a problem. They just haven't come back yet."

"What should we do?"

"Well, if the door's unlocked, maybe they wouldn't mind if we went in," he says. "If they stop at our house first, they'll see that we left."

"Momma won't let anybody drive her to that house."

"You're right."

"Let's go in." I start to get out of the truck.

"No Honey, you wait here. If the doors are unlocked, I'll come get you."

"What if they're locked?"

"Then we'll go grab something to eat."

"Okay."

Chris steps into the rain, pulling his coat over his head, splashing quickly up the walkway to the back door. I notice how lost and pitiful he looks in the dark rain, sneaking around someone else's house, hoping their door is unlocked so we can get in.

But then, I remember something.

It's our house, too.

Forever.

The thought relaxes my nerves. Enough so that I lean back and rest my eyes. I dream of what I'm going to do when we get inside. I dream of all of the big rooms and beautiful decorations.

Chris finally makes it to the back door.

The house is pitch black inside. He wonders to himself where in the world they could be.

He places his hand on the doorknob, not knowing what to expect.

The knob turns slowly. The door opens.

He steps inside the dark house.

He turns on the lights…

It's finally over.

When I get inside, I'm going to eat. I'm gon' eat like a pig. I'll blow these things up until my bra breaks. Then, I'm going into that pink bathroom and I'll sit in that tub for two hours. I'll sit there until these scars wash off. Then I'll go into Momma's room, and I'll look through all of those pretty nightgowns. I remember a burgundy one with black lace, and a matching robe. I can't wait to slip into that burgundy gown and that robe. Then I'll sit at the dining room table and take a good look into the cabinet. Every plate. Every figurine.

And before I go to bed, I'm going to the piano.

Just to look.

I drift again. Entranced by that synesthesian world of color and sound.

Life is charged with the energy of broken dreams

I hear a simple, flowing melody. I can *see* the melody. After half a minute, the piano is joined by the rich, full sound of a huge string orchestra.

Oh my

My ability has undergone a metamorphosis. A transformation. Very powerful.

Magnificent.

What am I gonna tell her?

Chris hurries away from the grisly, bloody scene. The rain feels colder than before.

He gets into the truck, dripping wet. I am leaning back with my eyes closed, as though I hadn't noticed him get in. I hum softly.

I can hear Chris' voice. But I can't move. The music will stop if I do.

Who's dead? What is he talking about?

John and Vera?

What does he mean? Not my Momma, Vera.

She's not dead...

I am pulled from the vision, and find myself back in the truck. I look over at Chris, blinking my eyes, with a dim, bewildered expression.

"Are the doors unlocked?"

The look on his face makes me remember. Something I heard him say.

The fear in his eyes.

They're dead

My mind renews its hold on reality.

They're dead

I begin to shake my head, slowly back and forth.

"Wh...what did you say?"

"They're *dead*, Elizabeth."

"Who's dead? Chris what are you talking about? Who's dead?"

"Somebody must have broke into the house..."

"Who's been killed? Was somebody killed in their house? Who was it? Who was killed in their house?"

He can't say another word. He just grips the steering wheel and leans his head forward.

I slowly unlock my door...

It flies open. Chris looks up in time to see a dark figure, running fast around the front of the truck, towards the walkway.

I can't move fast enough. I'm hardly moving at all. The air is too thick. The rain, too heavy. My feet are weighted down and sticking to the ground. The harder I try to get to the house, the slower I run.

I have to get to her. If I touch her, she won't die…

Chris is stunned by how fast I had run from the truck. Lightning quickens my step. He leaps out and runs as fast as he can to catch me, grabbing me with both arms and lifting me off my feet.

I scream bloody murder into the rain, far over the countryside.

"Let me go! Let me go!"

I am a frenzy of savage strength and movement. I scream and thrash as wildly as ever, kicking his legs and clawing his face. I hit him in the mouth with my fist hard enough to rattle his teeth. He has to grab my arms and try to pin them to my body.

I try to bite him in the face. I come at him with my teeth. He has to jerk backwards, just in time to prevent a terrible bite on his jaw. He picks me up high, throwing me over his shoulder like a package. His long coat protects his back from my fists, which pound him with a strength he cannot believe. He hurries over to the truck and puts me down, roughly pressing me against it, grabbing my head in both hands.

A flash of memory makes me calm down.

"Get in the truck."

In a daze of confusion, I obey. He slides in behind me, then closes the door.

"What about *Momma*, Chris? Is she…"

He nods his head.

I wince in pain, moaning loudly.

He suddenly tastes blood. His own blood, from when I walloped him in the mouth. An overwhelming dread grips him.

"Where are we going, Chris?"

Silence.

"Chris, we have to go in and call the police."

"We've got to get out of here. With my luck…"

"We don't have anything to worry about. We'll just tell 'em we found 'em." Pain and grief contort my expression.

"I don't want to be anywhere near it," he says. "With my luck they'll put me in jail for it."

"No they won't."

"I'm not takin' any chances."

The truck turns out of the driveway. We're headed down the dark road again.

"What about Momma, Chris? You can't leave her there all night. We have to go back and call the police."

No answer.

"Chris, *please.*"

But he doesn't respond. So I slide over and give his arm a gentle squeeze. Then I touch his face, and press my lips to his cheek.

The kiss goes through him like a bolt of lightning. From the point of origin, through his entire body.

His new cross to bear. Until the day he dies.

"We have to go back."

"Let me call from the pay phone."

"No."

"Elizabeth, don't make us go back. I don't want to be anywhere near it."

"I don't know…"

"Let me call from the pay phone. Please."

"Okay, but let's hurry," I say, wiping my eyes. "I don't want her to stay there in the dark."

Through the summer rain. And into the night we travel.

The dark wind and water moved over our country forest. Descending, enshrouding us where we stood. The summer rain had died to a mist, and there was no energy in the clouds. My husband and I languish in the southern breezes. Words are captive, suppressed by a lifetime's weight of pain. We had gathered what courage there was left, enough to fulfill the promise of our lives, a curse bestowed to us from generations long gone. Mournfully we step together into the black truck, beginning our circular odyssey, which would take us away from our tomb towards the light, and return us quickly once again.

In total silence we drive onward, drowning in the darkened rain. The gray of futures dims the light in our eyes, until there is nothing left for us to see. We push forward in our chariot, braving the mists of what lay before us. Soon, we flow into where the lights are. The bright, artificial light of earthly progression. We disembark our rolling sanctuary into the windy haze, which glows with dissimulation, disguising itself in unnatural luster. Holding hands, we walk together into the amaranthine station.

The two of us step into this bright world, the strange and distant shore, the farmhand and his raven-haired companion. The Old West man holds hands with the exotic Earth Flower, leading her through the maze of light.

The attending woman looks up from her romance pages, to see what detestable thing has emerged at this ungodly hour to buy whatever evil, for whatever reason. What she sees makes her cease with the gum in her thin-lipped mouth, losing concentration on her fantasy story, a tale with all requisites in place—the impossibly handsome man and woman, the twisted psychologies, and wanton violence and immoralities.

Before her, in the lighted place, is the manifestation of fancy. There is a man of well over six feet, draped in long, beige trench weather coat, but wearing no hat above azure eyes, or upon the head of brown wavy hair. Underneath his velvet crown is a face of such masculine beauty as to defy description, with a sad, gentle look about the eyes, which are pale blue and piercing, like the eyes of an angel.

And drifting, floating beside this man is a woman, the likes of which cannot be imagined, but only observed in truth. The hood of her rain cloak is down, revealing a head of the blackest hair, locks pitched in ravenwood, that gives the impression of flowing beneath the cloak and down the length of her back. Her dark, hypnotic eyes are in allegiance with her hair, framing and enhancing a smooth, creamy complexion. Her nose is so sculpted as to deter attention, skillfully diverting one's gaze to her other features, including a mouth of sensuous, reddish lips. Lips soft with unrequited desire for life, perfectly full and pleasant to behold.

They gather their final elixir, their sweet orange nectar. As they approach the attending lady, she takes full measure the appearance of these two, to see if they are aware of the power they possess. They are not. What she senses, what she thinks she sees in them affects her deeply. In their eyes, on every part of their expressions is the presence of *extreme* shyness, and in their manner is the deepest humility. The man exudes strength, with all encompassing meekness. The woman labours to conceal her profound fear, her dreadful uncertainty.

The counter lady puts her book aside, watching them move towards her, finding herself unintimidated, nor wary of their demeanor. Seeing clearly that they are relics, lost at the fringes of modernity—lowly and unassuming, lacking all signs of vanity or conceitedness. Anachronisms. Out of time. And she thinks that perhaps, she perceives upon them a Light, that she hopes will guide them through their valley of shadow.

She smiles a kind greeting to the lonely, seeing that their expressions are friendly. The wife gazes anxiously, as they buy a single container of nectar, her favorite sweet orange elixir.

Then she watches them silently vanish the bright land, fading into darkness and mist. And to her bewilderment, she is compelled to say a prayer for the two of them, that they might be protected in their darkest hour. The attending lady returns to the protagonists of her romance story, seeing to all of their grand, larger than life ills and woes.

Without a word, they travel away from the delusive light, the accursed, towards the pitch blackness, the isolation of their dark dwelling, the isolation of their grave and tomb. There, the pills await…the poison of their fairest day, the salvation in their gloomiest twilight.

To this Land of Freedom, they travel through their darkest night.

39

We returned to the little house.

To the only place we knew.

For many days we've been hiding away. Kept apart from the world by fear and depression. There is no light, and no comfort for either of us. Chris has found the strength inside to cope, at least a little bit. But he is worried about me. My mood is as dark as the rainy days, which have covered the world in twilight and misery.

"I want to go outside."

I've hardly spoken in such a long time.

"We should go put food in the henhouse."

"You want to go out in this storm?" he says. "I'm sure they've scratched up plenty."

"I want to feed 'em anyway."

I slide into my long black coat, while he puts on his long beige one. In that coat, he delivers the classic image of a man with plenty to offer by way of romance, and fantasy. With the new black umbrella, we go outside in the pouring rain. Harsh, sharp lightning fills the skies.

For as far as we can see, the land is covered in a mist of gray.

"I told you we shouldn't be out here."

"I don't care. I'm gonna feed 'em."

I fill the feed bucket, open the fence and slosh into the black mud. The chickens are all active under the shelter, which is just big enough for me and Chris to kneel under without getting wet. I kneel down among the little flock of chickens, feeding them from my hand, while stroking the feathers of the speckled one. The rain pounds the little tin shelter above us—while water splashes down around us like a waterfall.

"Do you want to stay out here a while?" he asks.

"No. Let's leave 'em alone."

The rest of the feed goes in their trays, inside the henhouse. We leave the chickens to their feast, splashing through the black mud again.

"Wait." I stop in the middle of the yard.

"We should go inside."

"No."

The lightning sparks continuously, from every part of the sky.

My eyes glare from under the long, silken black hair. I seem so different to him. As if my heart is hardened.

"We have to look."

Taking his hand, I lead him past the tree, down toward the field, to where the grave had been dug. Under the umbrella, in the harsh downpour, I stare at the place where I might have been buried. I allow myself the memory—the fearful recollection of nightmares long gone. As I mourn quietly, respectfully before my grave, the storm becomes the substance of my emotions. The full expression of my inner suffering. All around me—in the clouds and in the pouring rain—I perceive the power of my soul's burden, one I have endured since I was a child.

Momma...

For several minutes, we stand. Reverently.

"Elizabeth, let's go inside."

The winds swirl again, driving the rain hard in our faces. But I do not move. I rest comfortably in my spot, at one with the strange weather. Touching a moment where fear cannot prosper. Seemingly oblivious to what is happening around me. To the rising. The rekindling of my storm's fury.

Suddenly, out past the field, a deadly streak of blue lightning arcs from the top of the sky all the way to the bottom. Chris flinches and recoils from the ear splitting thunder.

"We've got to go. Come on," he says.

He gently, firmly ushers me away from the gravesite. I act as though I don't hear the thunder. I am as calm as he's ever seen me. He wonders how long I would have stood there. He wonders.

As we get closer to the house, I stop.

"Let's go to the truck."

"What?"

"I'm not going in there."

We both stare at the old house. An empty, ghostly shell.

"Okay," he says. "Let's go."

As we walk around, Chris notices something lying dead in the mud road. Then he looks again, but doesn't say a word about it...

Every one of its diseased *feathers* is black. As black as pitch under a new moon.

Inside the truck, we are safe. Sheltered from the wind and the rain.

But there is no protection from the storm's heavy, oppressive mood.

"I *hate* that house."

Her mother's voice, he thought.

"Slide closer, Honey," he says.

"Chris?"

"Hmm?"

"Are you going to hurt me anymore?"

The question rips him to shreds.

"Never again."

We hide in the truck for many hours. Watching the rain cover the windows. Talking about ourselves, about a lifetime of broken dreams. We are bold in every recollection. Every torture and every horror.

And we talk about Vera.

"I could tell she cared so much about me. About us. Chris, I loved her. I don't know what I'm going to do."

He is at a loss.

"Nothing ever goes right for us. We can never seem to be happy."

"I don't think about bein' happy anymore," he says. "I don't deserve happiness."

"What we deserve has nothing to do with it. I think maybe we're just cursed. What's *wrong* with us?"

We both know this misery. Sitting there, afraid to get out and go inside our own house. We are free to do as we please. Free to live together without the fear of violence and pain.

But there is *nothing*.

We are descended, to a place beyond tears or rage. Suddenly gone are our expectations for the future. There is no joy, or pleasure for us under the sun.

"Who did we think we were, to think we could have had something good in life. They're probably dead because of us."

Chris notices my anguish. He feels it.

"Chris do you ever think about dying?"

"I used to. Every day."

He can't bear the thought. All he wants now is for us to be together.

"I can't do it. I can't take anymore pain."

"We have each other, Elizabeth..."

"It's not *enough* anymore. Its not enough. I'm sick of pain. I want it to end, forever. And don't you *look* at me like you don't know what I'm talking about."

"I don't think we should..."

"Well, *I* do. We've known it from the beginning. We always knew we were meant for it. We don't belong here, Chris. We never have. We're both cursed people and we should have never been born."

"I need you." he says. "How can I live if you're not here?"

"You won't have to. 'Cause you're gonna do it with me."

"I can't do it," he says. Pitifully.

"Yes you *can*. You don't have any choice."

He senses a force, perhaps more powerful than either of us can resist. Something he had felt before. A pulling. A calling from the gray world.

"Please don't think about that," he says. "As long as we're together, we'll make it."

"So I'll have to go alone, then?"

"Where? Elizabeth, what are you—"

"You *know* what I'm talking about!"

My angry glare pierces his mind. Deep in my gaze, past the controlled, determined expression, is the hint of a major breakdown. The leading edge of a hurricane.

"Elizabeth…"

He tries to touch my face. But to his surprise, his horror, I move my head away, sliding across the seat from him.

"Elizabeth, come here…"

He reaches out to me again—and I *recoil*.

For a second, his mind goes blank. It simply didn't register. It was so foreign, so brutal that his brain didn't easily process it—like when a person is knocked from his feet by a moving car, sent tumbling hard into the pavement.

Chris had been slammed. Twisted. And broken.

I get out of the truck, leaving my door wide open, trudging slowly through the rain without my umbrella. Soon, I'm up the front steps, crossing the little porch into the house.

After a minute or so, he follows me in and sees me coming out of the bathroom. I go up to him, putting my arms around him under his coat. He returns the hug, soon realizing it isn't a hug at all. I am fiddling around in his pockets.

I pull out his pristine, black pocket knife, which he had intended to throw away. I leer at him with a sinister, feline satisfaction he has never seen on my face.

Without a word, I lead him into the bedroom, closing the door behind us.

"You're all I've got," he says. "*Please*."

I have my arms around him. Lovingly. My eyes are strange and vacant.

"If you love me, you'll do it. Its what you *owe* me."

I open the knife and hand it to him.

"If you really love me, then you'll do it. You've threatened to do it a hundred times. You've cut me with it once already. And now, its what I want."

Cautiously, he takes the knife from me.

"You don't really think I'm gonna do this, do you?"

"Then you don't love me. And you never have."

"Don't," he says.

"Do you?"

"You know I do."

"Then prove it. Give me what I want. Give us what we both—"

"Elizabeth, I can't…"

"Don't you *stand* there like you can't do it, after all the things you've done to me! I need you to put it to my throat and cut the life out of me! And then you can put me back in my coffin where I *belong!"*

I back against him, pulling the knife to my throat. He stands still, holding it to my neck, trying to remember how he could have ever wanted to hurt me. How he could have ever wanted to kill me. The thought is devastating. Painful enough to bother him. He grabs my head, causing me to draw a loud, sensuous breath…

Then he folds the knife and puts it away. My anger is apparent.

"Would you have cut my throat that night?"

"Elizabeth, I…"

"Just shut up and answer me, would you have done it?"

"*Yes!*" he says. "God help me, yes I would have. But you *know* I can't think about doing that anymore."

"Why not?"

"I don't want to hurt you. Its not in me anymore."

"Because you don't *want* to hurt me?"

With serpentine cruelty, I laugh. Then I glower disgustedly. With the fires of Hell, I burn a gaze right into his soul. And from the depths, from a decade of suffering, I find an uncompromising anger.

"I *hate* you."

Then, I spit in his face.

I watch him fearlessly, as he wipes my spit from his face. Then, I *slap* him with the force of thunder. He stares at the floor. I slap him hard again in the same spot, nearly yelling with the effort. But when I see the pain flow down his face in tears, I can't hurt him anymore.

I drift to the bed and sit down. The fire, the angry look is already gone. Replaced by my characteristic expression.

It is as much malice as I've ever shown. And it makes me sorry. It only adds to my woes, further breaking me down under the weight of years. All of my anguish, all of my misery is still inside. Eating me away.

"Like I said before," he says. "You're all I've got. I guess it *was* too much to expect that you'd forgiven me."

He rests at the foot of the bed. We sit in silence, wondering how we can live another day.

"It's all my fault. My mother told me that everything bad that happened was my fault. Everyone suffers because of me. She knew I was a curse. She could see it on me. My daddy wouldn't've died if I hadn't been born. People wouldn't've talked and laughed about my Momma if it hadn't been for me…"

I pause…

"But I tried, Momma. I tried to do everything just right. I tried so hard. I tried to do my work the way I was supposed to. I tried not to break things. I never meant to oversleep, or daydream, or ask too many stupid questions. I didn't know I was playing the radio too loud, Momma. I won't fix my hair like a tramp anymore. I won't ask about the piano anymore, Momma I promise…"

Chris hears it approaching. As clear as day.

"I don't deserve to die, do I? I tried to do it all right. I tried to do everything the way I was supposed to, but I couldn't. Momma, please help me to do it the way I'm suppose to. Please don't hurt me anymore. Please tell me what I did wrong so I can fix it. Just tell me what I did. Momma please tell me. Please don't do it... Momma please don't do it anymore...Momma please..."

And on that last syllable is built a crescendo, filling the room with the sounds of violent weeping, moaning and sobbing.

The emotion tears through my voice as I sit bent over. Chris tries to touch me, to comfort me...

But I scream like he touched me with a hot iron.

"*Please don't whip me!* Please don't whip me. Please don't whip me anymore..."

I stare wide eyed, pulling away, cowering at the head of the bed, still begging, still saying that I didn't mean it.

"*What did I do! What did I do! Please, tell me!...*"

The woman begs him to tell her what she has done wrong, pleading with him not to hurt her anymore.

He tries to grab me, but my reactions are too loud and violent. Every time he touches me, I shriek like it's the most painful thing I've ever felt. He backs off, but I keep moaning and screaming, breaking into loud fits of pleading for mercy, while begging to be told why I'm being punished so brutally.

He stands horrified, watching me look as though I am trying to climb the walls, thrashing, kicking and screaming like I—

Like I am being whipped.

He walks out of the room and closes the door. After several minutes, the noises subside. He stands at the door and listens, barely breathing, terrified that I might hear him and start again.

"*No… no, I didn't mean it…,*" he hears. "*I didn't mean it… I didn't mean to… I didn't mean to… "*

And then, the violent screaming and thrashing returns. I sound like I'm being thrown around the bed, up against the wall. He cringes, when he thinks that he is hearing exactly what it sounded like, when he would close the door and whip me until he was exhausted.

He sits down and takes his madman pose. Pulling on his hair. Thinking about how much I am suffering.

Triazolam—

The pills Vera gave him! They await faithfully, out in the truck.

Then he dismisses the thought.

Promptly.

40

Deliver us from the torment of misery
From this hour of grief and mourning
Let her see the end of suffering
Grant rest for her weary soul

Forgive me for sins and trespasses
For causing her pain and sorrow
Save us from the powers of darkness
Send us Peace, and your Grace and Mercy

Amen

The storm had nearly exhausted its power, covering the land with a steady, gentle mist. Chris had ignored the thing in the road again, and was back on the porch. Every now and then, he heard me crying and wailing from the house. It was as though I were too exhausted to scream anymore.

A short time later, the house became very still and quiet. He gathered enough courage to go inside, to see what had become of me. Carefully, he opened the bedroom door and found me clutching the pillow, curled in a ball, fast asleep.

For the next two hours, he kept watch over me. He stood and paced and leaned, until he was overcome with exhaustion. Finally, he sat down in the comfortable chair and lowered his head, just to rest his eyes.

He hopes that I want to live. He really does. But if I still want to die, then we will do it together. Surely, we'll be forgiven.

As he drifts away, he feels the shadows around him. But he is not afraid.

What will happen to us now, Chris? Are we going to die?

I don't know.

Don't cry, Chris. Please don't cry—

I love you.

Chris awakens suddenly. In his sleep, he had been talking to me. We had been standing in the bedroom in the dark, hugging one another. Then came a reassuring knock. We had looked at each other hopefully, walking together to the front door. But no one was there.

He is unrested. The desire to awaken me is strong. But he leaves me to precious sleep, wandering back into the living room, looking out the window at the road.

It is still there. Lying in the mud.

He steps out the back, grabbing the shovel from the old shed, moving through the drizzling mist, toward the carcass in the road. There is nothing mysterious or supernatural about it. It looks like a common raven, but its body is enormous. The rain had not even ruffled the smooth, shiny black feathers. The beak is large and curved, and is as black as the rest of its body. The black legs and feet are bare, with curved, sharp talons on each of its toes. Whatever it is, it should have been stuffed and mounted in a museum.

But as fearful as it tries to appear, it bears little in resemblance to the ones he remembers. For six, Hellish nights in a row...

They had been prehistoric sized. Demonic creatures with terrifying, unearthly voices. Voices pitched high and low. He would never forget that sound. It had bored into his brain, along with the scalding, blistering sensation, like caustic acid was poured all over his leg when they touched him. From a single touch.

And their eyes...

They glowed a dark energy. Displaying a predator's lack of pity, mercy or fear. Pure evil, tempered with knowledge and purpose.

Because he had hurt Elizabeth.

Its dead, black eye is wide open. It seems calmly aware of its fate.

With the shovel, he picks the grotesque, oversized thing up and tosses it into the grass.

But he knows better.

The next minute of his life is spent trudging through the marshy ground, searching for the dead creature. To his disgust, there it is, just where he had thrown it. Looking bigger and more alive than ever.

He hurries on with his foolishness, taking the carcass down to the gravesite. He quickly digs a hole and dumps the sickening thing inside. Then, he unceremoniously covers it up and walks away.

He's not sure what it means. And he doesn't care. But he has to admit that he feels better. Relieved. He leans the shovel against the giant tree, and goes around to the front yard.

To him, it's like we had been ground into powder, and could both still be washed away.

She may be right, he thinks. There may only be one thing left to do.

"Chris! Chris, where are you? Chris please come back!"

In the next moment, I open the door. He sees the fear of abandonment on my face. The terror in my expression. I finally see him, then I fling the screen door open and run outside. Chris moves quickly toward the house, while I run down the steps, splashing into the front yard.

In the flowing mist, we come together, falling into each other's arms. I am lifted from my feet, while we embrace with desperate longing… and passion.

"I thought I had lost you," he says.

"I was so scared. The house was empty. Please don't leave me. Please don't."

"Never," he says. "Never."

266

He wraps his arms tightly around me, raising me up. I hold on to him as he takes me to the porch shelter, out of the misty rain.

We hold each other in a warm, loving embrace. Our minds are in ecstasy, and the feeling we have is replenished forever.

The rest of this day is spent in the gloom of the tiny house. We sit together in the empty bedroom, sometimes on the bed, sometimes together in the chair. We feel trapped, like we can't break free from the misery.

We were both born into hopelessness, and were raised and nurtured in fear—

And what we know of the world now consumes us.

The house is closed in around us, mocking us with Hellish derision, with promises of despair.

And death.

Outside, the gray turns to darkness, which envelops us. Pressing down, until there is only nothingness.

These dark hours move swiftly forward. We're pulled helplessly along, until time itself takes substance. Feverishly, inevitably we tumble along the dark path, until we're at the dead end.

Beyond that is only an abyss—

And we are now pushed well past the dead end of this life.

"Chris I don't want to live anymore. Please don't make us have to live another day."

In the oppressive dark of the little house, he looks into my expression. There is more pain than I can bear.

And my pain is now his.

Together, we move into the dark wind. The cool, summer breeze had banished the rain, and the wind began to have power over the clouds. We both splash our way mournfully through the front yard. I wait calmly beside him as he leans inside the black truck, and retrieves the big, white bottle.

Slowly, we drift back towards the house. He stops suddenly, reaching into his back pocket. He pulls the fancy pocket knife for the last time, and flings it into the nighttime woods.

As we approach the house, the wind seems to lose its chill. Like a breath of renewal, moving over the saturated ground. Chris seeks strength from a break in the clouds, from the waning light of a crescent moon. But there is none. We climb the porch steps, stopping for a moment to rest in the cool breeze. I lay my head on his shoulder.

We turn away from the outside world, withdrawing into ourselves. Inside the dark dwelling, we surrender to the shadows. We walk together into the pitch black, closing the bedroom door. Then we hug, asking for forgiveness for what we have to do. We sit down on the bed, staring at the pills in the dark. There is already a carton of our precious juice and two cups nearby. I envision him feeding me one of the pills and then taking one himself, repeating it until we have swallowed enough to die in our sleep.

My body presses next to his. My hand touches his face. He trembles when my lips touch his ear, breathing the words into his mind.

He places the pills on the floor, giving me juice to drink. I am exhausted. Helpless. Rest calls to us, and we lay on the bed. Then we fall into a deep, dreamless sleep.

The sleep of the dead.

41

here it is…

The knock at the door.

Who can it be? What could anybody in the world want with us?

What if there's nobody there?

Elizabeth…come with me.

I'm afraid to go alone.

"Chris…Chris wake up…"

He wakes up with a start, seeing the bright world through blurry, confused eyes. A loud, strong knocking pounds the front door. I sit wide awake, shaking him, staring at the bedroom door as though the Devil himself is on the other side of it.

"Who is that?"

"Is anybody home? Its Sheriff Williams!"

"Chris, run away. Hide in the field. I'll tell them you're out of town. Please just go."

The loud knocking. It resounds through the little house.

"Just a minute! I have to get dressed! I'll be there in a minute!"

"Okay Maam. I'll be waitin' right out here."

"Alright, Chris. I'll wait long enough for you to sneak away. And when they leave, we'll take the pills like we planned, okay?"

I picture him being beaten and dragged away in handcuffs, broken and bloody.

"I knew we shoulda took 'em. I *knew* we shoulda took 'em."

But Chris remembers that in his dream, there was no foreboding. Besides, if they had come for him, what did it matter? Perhaps, it is what he deserves.

"Maam, you still there?"

"Uh...yes sir, it'll just be another minute. I'm still getting dressed."

"I'm gonna answer it, Honey."

"Chris, no..."

"I have to. But I want you to come with me."

"Are you sure?"

"I'm sure. And I'm sure of one more thing."

"What's that?"

"The next time we're alone, we'll take 'em. I promise."

He breathes a deep sigh, while we look with fear and dread into our future. Together, we go into the living room and answer the door.

When Sheriff Morgan Williams sees the two of us, he takes off his sunglasses. His expression softens immediately. He sees an extremely handsome man with eyes the color of blue ice, which are kind and gentle, but full of sadness. And close beside him is a woman whose manner and appearance is unlike anything he has ever seen.

"Are you Christopher and Elizabeth Peele?"

"Yes sir."

"I need to ask you a few questions about a crime that occurred on the Evans farm a few days ago. Would you mind if I came inside?"

"Please, come in Sheriff."

The Sheriff opens the screen door, and steps respectfully into our little house. He takes off his hat and greets us both. He inadvertently touches his nose, in response to the strong smell of kerosene and burned wood. The cramped filthiness and our shy manner work together, overwhelming him with compassion. I had watched him from the start, noticing the passive, soft spoken demeanor. I studied the understanding look in his eyes. And the humble way he carries himself.

Sheriff Williams glances down at his hat, then looks up at the two of us.

"I hardly know where to begin," he says. "I came over here this morning, not knowing what to expect, and was prepared to ask about a dozen questions. But there's really only three things I need to ask you. But before I do, I'd like you to promise me something. Please, promise me that you'll tell the truth."

Chris looks at me, and I nod my head.

"I promise," Chris says.

"Exactly how did your wife react when you discovered the bodies?"

He studies us, and knows he asked the right question.

"It's alright, son. Just tell me the truth."

"She went wild, Sheriff. She started screaming."

"Where was she screaming, in the kitchen or the bedroom?"

"She didn't go inside," Chris says. "I wouldn't let her. We were outside in the rain."

"And what time did you call the police?"

"It was just after eight o'clock."

The Sheriff nods his head. He then hits his hat against his leg.

"That's what she told me," he says. "That's what time she said she heard the scream."

Who heard the scream?

"She told me she thought she was dreaming. She heard the clock chime eight times, and after that, a loud, long scream."

My eyes widen, and I put my hand over my mouth. I don't dare think it. I want the crazy thought to go away. To stop tormenting me.

"That's right honey. Vera's *alive*."

The words seem to echo around the room, until they flow into my body, where they have enough power to absorb my energy. In shock, they escort me to the chair.

"I'm sorry," he says. "I didn't mean to scare her."

"Did you say that Vera's *alive?*" Chris asks. Anguishedly.

"She is, and recovering in the hospital."

Chris sits down beside me.

"Chris, what did he say?"

"He said Vera's alive."

I just rest my head, face first, onto Chris' shirt.

"I'm so sorry," the Sheriff says.

"It's alright," says Chris, hugging me, staring into his memory. To that night.

"Sheriff how did she survive? I saw so much blood. I could have sworn…"

"That's 'cause she was hurt pretty badly. And he left her, thinking he'd done enough damage to kill her."

"I shouldn't've left her. My God—"

I begin to sob. In a hushed tone.

"Who was it Sheriff?"

"One of the farmhands. His name's Joseph Little."

Chris sighs, nodding his head.

"The police were at his house b'fore Vera even finished talkin' to me. His grandma knew where he was, and they had him before daylight. I know it broke Ms. Little's heart. But part of her must have known it was comin.'"

"John was a good man," says Chris. "A great farmer."

"Yes, he was," the Sheriff answers. "It killed me when I found out about this. Vera wouldn't talk to anybody else until they called me. You know, it's a good thing you got there when you did, son. They said she was about as close to—"

The Sheriff glances at me. I rest quietly. Biting my thumbnail.

"Well, I guess I've said all that needs be. She's worried about how she'll look to you, but believe me, she's beautiful. I'm sure you'll get over there as soon as you can. I'd best be on my way."

Chris stands up, to escort the Sheriff out the door.

"Sheriff I don't know how to thank you."

"I was glad to do it son. You take care, Mrs. Peele."

"Thank you."

Sheriff Williams is about to walk out the door, when he stops. There is more he thinks we should hear. Something he needs to say.

"She wanted me to tell you somethin' else, too. I was gonna let her tell you herself, but, maybe I'd better do like she told me. This might not matter too much now, because she survived, but do you remember the first day she came here? The first day she met Elizabeth?"

"Yes, sir."

"Well, she kinda rushed off that morning, didn't she? Said she remembered some important business?"

"Mmm hmm."

"Vera told me she'd been having premonitions. She said trouble had been hangin' over them for a long time. Well, that important business was about John's estate. The day she met you, Mrs. Peele, she went downtown and had a will made."

"What does that mean, Sheriff?" Chris says.

"Son, it means you've got more land than you ever *thought* you could have. I'm sure you know John had fields stretched over five counties. But that's not all there is to it."

The Sheriff steps over to me.

Reverently.

"Mrs. Peele...farmin' is dangerous work. And big farmers like John Evans are heavily insured."

I stare up at him with a pitiful, fearful expression.

"Vera will be collecting every penny of it soon. And she's gon' put it all in your name, Honey—

"Upwards of seven and a half *million* dollars."

Chris covers his mouth, horrified. But my expression doesn't change, which makes the Sheriff shake his head in disbelief.

"I'll send somebody out tomorrow mornin' to explain the details. Chris, Vera said you're in charge of the whole farm, and she trusts you'll know exactly what to do."

Sheriff Williams puts on his hat, and starts out the door. Chris is still in a daze.

"She wanted you to know that she loves you. Make sure you go to her as soon as you can, now. And good luck to you both."

"Th... thank you, Sheriff," Chris stutters.

"Thank you, Sheriff."

"You're welcome." Chris stands at the door, watching the Sheriff drive onto the muddy road.

Chris doesn't look at me. He just closes the door and walks over to the window. Thoughtfully he gazes at the sky. Towards the many patches of blue.

"I never asked for money," he says through introspection, shaking his head. "I just wanted to be kind to you. I wanted to be a good person."

But even as he spoke, he wonders when, and how he would pay for all the evil he had done.

I stand up from the chair and go over to him. But he looks away from me until I touch his cheek, turning his face to mine.

"Do you still love me?" he asks.

"Yes, I do."

"Then, maybe I can stand the pain of living. But only if you say so, will I ever be happy."

"Come outside with me."

He follows me outside, and together, we step into the Light of Day.

"We'll both live. And we'll both be happy."

Elizabeth?

Yes?

Can we leave this place?

Yes, Love. We can.

Where can we go?

Far away. To a place we've never been. To a place we can call Home.

he End

Isolated—

Guarded by the Great Flowering Tree,

Is the ruin of a dark and tortured past.

Dissolved by the years of wind and rain,

Is a house abandoned by Love—

A place now obsolete.

Empty—

And desolate for all time.

Afterward:

And we know that all things work together for good—
To them who love God.

Romans 8:28

The Arrival

When Elizabeth and her husband first arrived at my home, I had expected her to feel cradled in blissful safety and contentment. John's passing left me free to devote myself to her, and I endeavored to be her rest and reward, even while I needed rescuing from my own grief and mourning. But there were infinite, endless days when she was as nervous as a mouse. Walking to and fro. Following behind her husband like a puppy, terrified of her new paradise. I think she was afraid that I was hiding sinister intentions behind a veil of motherhood and civility. For several long weeks I endured at least one broken dish every single day, dropped from her nervous, fearful hands.

They were Children of Silhouette. Ashes fallen from a world of shadow and sorrow. The two of them remained partners in a misery that had haunted them from ages long gone. Depression colored their days of happiness, weighing them down until there was no real joy at all, but only a placid drifting through a mist of gray.

The only two people who had ever loved her had despised her, and shown her the severest cruelty imaginable. Her spirit remembered, and her body and mind continued to suffer under this remembrance, until it was burdened by fears and false premonitions. Briefly, she was convinced that I was conspiring with her husband in secret to begin her misery anew. She imagined we had come together in private and were going to exact a sinful punishment, locking her away, binding her like an animal, slowly tormenting her for the rest of her life. For a while, she was afraid for Chris and me to be in the same room alone together, and her mind would not allow her the comfort of true sanity.

The Gift

*I*t is written, that "gifts are without recompense." I often wonder what gifts are these, because I know that for my beloved, there was a price I had to pay. My comeuppance, I suppose. My own comeuppance that was overdue.

I, Vera Evans. Keeper of *The Rose Diaries*. The writings of Carmen Elizabeth Peele.

Only a few minutes after my husband was killed, I was escorted to my bedroom by Joseph Little. When the door closed behind me, I thought my life was going to end. What came over me was a fear so grand, so epic that the only thing beyond it is Death. I would have been grateful for the mercy of fainting, but it simply would not happen. I was more alert and lucid than ever.

He leaned the gun in the corner by the door and removed his raincoat. I begged him to let me live. I pleaded the cause for my daughter. But without a word, he slapped me hard enough to make me dizzy, and pulled my hair to agony. He then took his belt off, and I knew that for the first time in my life, I was going to be whipped as badly as any woman has ever been. He spoke only once, for me to take off my clothes, and for the briefest moment while I undressed, I felt a spark of hope that I would not die. But when he motioned for me to grip the large dresser, I did it, and I saw Death in my reflection.

Without mercy, he proceeded to whip my back until I was spitting onto my own hand and trembling. Every lash was a flame of fire. When it was done, I could barely stand, and he still made me remove my underwear, both pieces of which were covered in blood. I felt as though my whole body had been burned. But still, Death would not take me. With a small length of rope, he tied my hands behind my bloody back and threw me onto the bed. It was not through a haze that I saw him removing his clothes. He climbed on top of me and laid there with his arms around me, crushing me in missionary, biting my arms and shoulders to hear me scream the name of God and Christ. He made no thrust, but skillfully rested it deep inside, to prolong the pleasure of feeling me broken, bloody and weeping for God's mercy. Over the next hour and a half, I was raped and sodomized, beaten in the stomach, the ribs and the back continuously, breaking a rib, injuring one of my kidneys, with a broken wrist and bite marks in both of my breasts until I had to beg him to forgive me for everything I had ever said, for every negative thought, for every lustful impulse I had ever caused him to have. My *Gray Palace* was Hell, and I was a prisoner there. After the hour and a half of raping and beating, he relieved his last onto my battered body. I can still remember his voice, the smell, and the feel of it dripping onto my stomach and my breasts. I was slipping away, mercifully, when I felt something cold jab into my stomach three times, and I did not realize until I saw him fold the knife away that I had been stabbed.

I did not see him leave. But what I did see was a glimpse of the future. As I lay dying, I saw a vision in the dark room. A gray book, with the letters of a promise in black, written across the bottom of the cover. After that, the clock chimed eight times, and then I heard a scream reverberate throughout all of Creation.

The Violence

Domestic Violence is common enough to be sure. Along with the broken bones, open sores, bruises and burns is the mournful, defeated expression, oftentimes hidden underneath cut lips, swollen jaws, broken noses or crushed cheekbones. I have been in trauma wards, seeing women cut with swords, listening as they screamed like tortured animals when the disinfectant was poured. Overall, the bloody faces—and even the venerable black eyes serve only to hide the women from those of us who might have compassion otherwise. The symbols have become so common that they have lost some of their power, just as the tornado, seen in too many video images, has become a thing of passing curiosity, along with the impossible devastation it causes.

We look at an abused woman's battered face, and we listen to her woes, and we grow angry with her for not having the courage to run. After all, even a dog is smart enough to leave, right? Somewhere in the back of our minds, the woman's broken body is her own doing—her reward for choosing to rest in her own stupidity.

Elizabeth Peele was one of the most severely abused women I have ever known. The abuse she experienced was demonic. Designed to cause more than physical pain. A more accurate portrayal of her personality would have shown an unbelievable timidness. Truthfully, she was afraid of her own shadow. Her nerves were fully neurasthenic, causing her to jump at every unexpected sound or sudden movement. She was prone to auditory hallucinations, many times hearing the voice of her mother, or even the sound of her husband's footsteps, though he would be many miles away. Her *agoraphobia* was severe enough to make her afraid to leave the yard, and her *socialphobia* was so extreme that it touched the edges of *anthropophobia*, or "fear of people." If there is Truth in Suffering to be found, then the most tragic was revealed on the morning that he ordered her to never again leave the bedroom. From behind an unlocked door, she heard his footsteps go clumping from the living room into the kitchen. When the footsteps returned, a *"white mist"* appeared underneath the closed bedroom door, settling like dust. When she opened the door after he was gone, the entire living room floor was covered in *"a fine powder,"* from the bedroom, to the kitchen and all the way to the front door. This *"snow white field"* marked the first two weeks of her imprisonment, being as purely effective as a locked gate would have been.

But as it is written, the curses that plague a human life are never without origin. Those that plagued her and her husband are from seeds planted a generation before. When Chris was a child, his bitter mother (whose husband had left her for another woman), abused him often. When he was only eleven, "Margaret Peele" once accused him of stealing a ring of hers, which he did not. She boiled a pot of water on the stove, and forced him to place a large knife in the water. When the knife was hot enough, she held it to his back, his bare skin, while twisting a leather belt around his throat. Over this same incident, she taunted him for days with grim promises, until it ended with his hands and feet being tied with his own shoelaces while he slept, and a lit cigarette pressed into his side while being smothered by a pillow.

The very first incident in Elizabeth's marriage occurred just after sunset on a warm summer's evening, in the back yard of their isolated house. He had twisted the skin on her sides *"until [she] saw lightning, and couldn't breathe from the pain…"*

He often stepped on her toes with his boots, or beat her with a one-by-two piece of stick wood. He would tie her hands behind her back, placing a pillow over her head, while he beat her in the stomach. He would scrape nails across her back, threatening to nail her hands to the wall, and her feet to the floor if she moved. He would bend her wrists or fingers back until she was on her knees, slobbering from the pain. He would choke her until she was spitting blood. During her first pregnancy, he beat her in the stomach until she vomited, and then starved her for days. She lost her second child as well from pure worry, after an incident in the dead of winter. On the night she was stabbed, her upper left arm was bitten so severely that perhaps it was the dress fabric alone that saved the piece of skin. In all the years, she was in the emergency room twice: a broken arm, and when her collar bone was broken, after she enraged him by locking herself in the bathroom to escape a whipping. He often stripped her nude, and whipped her with his belt until she was nearly unconscious and covered in blood. Sometimes he tied her up nude and whipped her, at times with the belt buckle, until she passed out from the trauma.

Her burning was a signal. It was as though she had been warned that the violence was going to escalate. She told me that the searing pain was so unbearable that she could hardly think, until her mind began to hallucinate. Her brain's compensation was so extraordinary, that she believes the string sonata that came to her that night is the most brilliant piece she has ever written, as if her mind had crossed over. I wish I had the motivation, the understanding to speak more of melodies. Sometimes, I forget that she has ever written a single note of music.

On the night her Fire Sonata was rendered, he had made her heat up a kitchen knife on the stove, and to his own horror, actually touched it onto her back. Afterwards she had been dragged, kicking and screaming into the bedroom, and was thrown onto the bed. He had straddled her hips and clamped her wrists together… and the hot blade had been pressed onto her back again. Like a drowning woman she had screamed, clutching and clawing against hopelessness. Praying for the saving miracle she knew would never come. But if there was any luck to be had, it was that the big knife had *cooled* while he dragged her to the bedroom. On her back was a single, very large *blister*—except for a bright red sore, where the skin had been burned away. As burns go it was a work of art. It would have been the talk of the entire hospital. But its origin would have been no mystery, attracting the wrong kind of attention. Or the *right* kind. The comet-like scar that this burn produced is truly a thing of beauty, as though Providence had bestowed on her a Divine Mark of Suffering. Her comeuppance? Maybe, for being born with such a prodigious talent, along with a face of such perfect beauty as to defy description. Throughout her marriage and even to her death, her face remained unblemished.

The year long imprisonment that followed may have actually saved her life. Perhaps in his mind, the punishment was ongoing, and helped to ease the pain that drove him to torture her. Even before the stabbing, she was pierced with safety pins in her arms, legs, and across her waist. It had felt *"like tiny fireworms, burrowing into [her] skin..."* She had seen their reflection in the bare window, acting out the scene. The blood had trickled all the way down her arms and legs to the floor.

As a prisoner she was starved for long periods, often while she was bound and locked in the closet. She spent the coldest months of the year sleeping on the floor, before the advent of fan powered space heaters, where she would often dream that she was outside in the ice and snow. But the worst of these tortures occurred early on, before he began to lock the door. When he learned that she had sneaked to the kitchen, he gathered a sharpened hatchet, along with a small tack, the kind with a large nailing head. With the back end of the hatchet, he nailed the tack at least an inch into the muscle (grazing the bone) of her right leg.

Is there anything truly unique, or remarkable here? Maybe, if one considers that in ten years of violence, he never once *intentionally* hit her in the face. Not even a slap. I once asked him how this was possible, expecting him to tell me it was out of pity or compassion, or because she was so beautiful. Instead he told me the truth, that it was from pure, nagging guilt alone. Because he didn't want to see the evidence of what he had done, staring at him from her features. So he focused all of the abuse from her shoulders to her feet, where it would be hidden by her long dresses, and underneath her black leg stockings. The fact that her face was untouched may be all the proof I need that her survival was not luck. A sign, maybe, that her situation was unique...and miraculous.

"*All things work together for good to them who love God, and who are called according to his purpose…*"

Over the years, she gave several million dollars to causes. So much of it for the one she knew so well. The "Peele Houses" (of course, this is not the actual name) are well known where we live. And well hidden.

If she had left her husband, I never would have found her.

The House

There are many things that churn beneath the surface. Strange, unbelievable incidents that could not have been included in the main writings. Had they been, our story would surely have been dismissed as a horror fantasy.

I believe that her husband was possessed by an evil spirit. A demon, which had inhabited that evil house. Tormenting him, creating in him a thirst for violence, an irrepressible urge to cause her pain and suffering. There were forces at work, powers and principalities that wanted them both to die. If places can indeed be haunted, then that house was a living example of case and point. The first time I went into their bedroom, I am convinced that I saw a dark shadow move across the wall. To this day, that decrepit old house still stands, lost somewhere in eastern North Carolina.

"Isolated... [she writes]

Guarded by the Great Flowering Tree,

Is the ruin of a dark and tortured past...

Dissolved by the years of wind and rain,

Is a house abandoned by Love—

A place now obsolete.

Empty—

And desolate for all time."

Elizabeth held fast to the claim that she did see a living spirit, a ghost, flow into reality before her eyes that dark, rainy Sunday morning. Although she believed that ghosts are demons rather than spirits of the dead, this gray "entity" was in the definite form of a woman, dressed as a pioneer wife. The spirit had no apparent will or malice, seeming to touch her without touching her, making her as cold and afraid as she had ever been. Whatever it was, she felt it to be *"a spirit of epic melancholy... a century of weariness and despair..."* So many of the moving shadows that tormented her over the years may not have come from her own fearful psychology. It was little effort for me to learn that the house was built in 1910, and its first inhabitant was a farmer and his wife. The woman was killed after years of sadistic, torturous abuse involving mutilation. Although I expected it to be so, I still found myself short of breath, when I learned that the woman's name bore a *prophecy,* but with no middle name or initial listed besides. Is it a coincidence that Chris had never considered abusing his wife until the day they rented that old house? Does evil dwell only in the hearts and minds of men?

Aside from the violence itself, the most bizarre thing I am aware of from their marriage is Chris' spiritual conversion. After he accepted his wife's Christian faith, he was suddenly overcome with the same burning and terror he had known from those guilty nightmares. Elizabeth had stood by helplessly while he coughed and gagged, eventually dropping to his knees in more pain than he thought possible. For many long seconds, he was on his knees until the inevitable came gushing from his mouth to the floor. Elizabeth wrote *"What substance could it possibly be, that is the color of grass after sunset? The room is filled with the smell of ammonia…"* I truly believe that whatever spirit that had leapt on him from the walls of that cursed house had been spewed to the floor. Perhaps, that was part of the unusual smell I encountered when I first stepped into their bedroom, like chlorine bleach and garbage.

Sickness during a genuine conversion is not at all unheard of. But there was something else that happened over their house that day. Literally. But this incident is so unusual, so incredible that I knew if it were to ever see print in these pages, it would have to be in her own words. When I read this in her diaries, I pressed the issue with her on numerous occasions, because she had never spoken of this to me. It was then, and only then, that I learned that Chris had begged her not to tell me the full story, afraid that I would have dismissed them both as insane.

Perhaps, truth *is* stranger than fiction.

"This day is replete with shadows, as so much of our lives have been. Otherworldliness—a ghostliness—is so thick in the air that I wonder if I have not died in the coffin, and am drifting as a spirit. Briefly, I think that we are already dead.

But a branch is ripped from my Great Flowering Tree, and falls on the roof above us, shocking me back to my senses that we are both alive, resting underneath a storm of a power and duration I have never seen before. As fearful as I am, Chris is like a frightened child. Unable to sit still, pacing back and forth from the window to the door, flinching at every gust of wind, jumping at every burst of thunder. Our little house has never been so frightful to me. I have said aloud many times, "Lord, please help us."

The rain is noisy on the tin roof. It is always the most noticeable thing about every rainstorm. I guess that's why it's so shocking to me, when the metal drumming grows so dramatically softer. We both think it strange, because as surely as we can see, we see the storm blowing fiercely outside our window. But there is no sound.

Together, we are speechless for what seems an eternity, holding our breaths, watching the light dance and flicker from the lantern. It's as if we have been transported out of reality, and are literally in another realm of existence. As though a roving zone, a moving vacuum, has descended on our bedroom.

But the rains came, and the winds blew hard outside our window.

Chris begins to panic like a caged animal, rushing to and fro, too frightened to look outside, too terrified to stay in the room with me. He sweats profusely, trembling like a fevered man in a cold room. His blue eyes burn. They are frozen in blue flame.

I gather what strength I've collected through the years of suffering, and I take hold of him. I allow my own courage to become a part of him, assuring him that everything is as it should be, and that he is not supposed to go flying to the doors, looking out into the miracle, the sign that has come upon our little house. Somehow I know we are both protected in this storm.

After I calm him down, we both see outside the window, in the clouds above the trees, a long streak of blue-white lightning, which is intersected by a shorter one, having a very distinctive shape like a lightning cross. And it lights up, staying bright for many seconds. The shape of what I saw, I never discussed with him.

Then I begin to tell him what I believe. I relay to him a word about the Faith that has kept us through all the years of trial, through our long journey in the valley of shadows. I speak of the Light that has led us beyond the wilderness, seeing us safely through to our Land of Freedom. I help him to understand that everything he's ever done to me is already forgiven, and that through every trial and tribulation, he must always believe that we are never alone. Chris bows his head and repeats a prayer after me. He confesses the Way of the Cross, and for the first time, he tells me that he truly believes.

But even while we speak, the rains fall, and the winds blow quietly outside our window.

We hug, and both cry tears of profound relief, even inner joy and happiness. It seems that our years of hoping, that distant longing, has finally been abated. Our cries have been heard from the deep, and we have been rescued from the place of misery, from the cold hand of pain and suffering.

Or have we?

Though there is still a deafening silence, I can see the storm blowing fiercely. The trees are lit up from the bright flashes of lightning. It is the worst storm I have ever known…".

The Memorial

I remember her husband's burial like it was yesterday. The gray clouds. The misty rain, the rolling thunder. Why does it always seem to rain at funerals? I suppose it's a part of reality, that the world mourns the passing of goodness.

We were all grieving at once in our early days as a family. We visited John's grave often. My new Love found strange comfort in the green lawn and cemetery flowers, and all the fine tombstones and markers. Early on I always stopped fearfully, hurrying to her side. But eventually I allowed her to drift among the dead and marvel at their resting places, wondering to herself what manner of person they had been.

Not long after we buried her husband, I learned that Elizabeth had the fortune, or misfortune, of *knowing* that it was going to happen. In the spring before he died, she dreamed that Chris was preparing to leave her, and that he wasn't coming back. But a part of her was reassured anyway, because I was with her.

For weeks she had clung to him like a vine, cooing and kissing on him like a newlywed, but making sure she never annoyed him, always giving him the space he needed. She listened carefully while he prattled on about what a genius John had been, and how much he enjoyed tending that big cornfield. I know Chris was very glad that she waited for him outside more often, spending less time engrossed in her music. Every now and then, she even refused to leave his side when I called, and I think that made him feel very good inside. But though they seemed very happy, even joyful, I knew that underneath it all was still an echo of sadness. A time of new grief, waiting for them.

Chris's faith had became a powerful part of who he was, until I suppose he could have been called a Man of God. He became the classic image of that proverbial "salt of the earth," a hard working soul of kindness, generosity and compassion. The year of our second harvest after John's death is entrenched in my memory, not for that infernal grain, but because Chris had allowed his hair and beard to grow that season, until he bore a striking resemblance to images of Faith the world has known. There were many times when I held him in secret, and comforted him as the tears ran quietly down his face. A river of guilt, which poured from his past, until his days and nights were tormented.

One evening, Elizabeth noticed that he was nowhere in the house. Knowing he wasn't away on an errand, she went outside to see if she could find him. And of course, he was where he always seemed to be. Walking the long gravel road alone with his thoughts, secure in his new life of spiritual freedom and success. She was glad to join him, and together they walked the long road toward happiness and peace of mind.

But her world was plunged into darkness once again, when he hugged her in the evening, underneath the Harvest Moon, and spoke the words to her *"I might not be here for this harvest, Elizabeth."* The words crept in slowly, and they settled within, and she let the fear have its way, as she was accustomed to. Chris looked at her calmly, and in the glow of that final sunset, saw her tears flow quietly.

In the middle of that same night, he woke up suddenly, and became violently ill. But his demeanor calmed us so much that I didn't think much of it. We thought it was what he ate, which worked against us all, because the same symptoms had attacked me earlier. *"Fate will hide the truth, until Destiny is fulfilled..."* After many hours, his sickness seemed to go away on its own. But just before dawn, he began complaining of a burning, scalding pain in his abdomen, that became so severe he said he'd *"rather be dead than feel this pain."* Poor Elizabeth was terrified, and she couldn't seem to think straight.

I was irritated that we'd let it go as long as we did. We got dressed and escorted him to the car, and began driving to the hospital. But halfway there, the pain sliced though his body, and he screamed pitifully, which scared me about as much as anything ever had. Elizabeth begged for me to please hurry, and I remember her hand over her mouth as I drove. There was such a strange calm over us all. We were numb with fear.

Soon after we arrived, the doctors told us his pancreas had ruptured and poisoned his body. They said he probably wasn't going make it. I remember whispering, "I can't do this again. Please don't take him from us. Please don't take him." But somehow Elizabeth was at peace. She had been spared my ignorance, and was already prepared for what was going to happen.

I am so glad that they were given one last chance to speak. On that day he was not mine, although I had never really stopped loving him. We were told to rest in the waiting room while they attended him the best they could. A hospital waiting room is a prison of helplessness and frustration. At about nine o'clock that morning, the lady doctor drifted towards us, and escorted us quietly into the corridor. Neither Elizabeth nor myself were willing to ask, but the look on the poor woman's face told us that he was gone.

The words flowed into me, and struck me like a tornado, ripping a piece of my spirit away. Elizabeth told me that she felt the briefest sensation of lightness, as if part of her essence had left her body, and drifted away. The love of our lives had been taken, and we were left alone, like phantoms in a dark, fearful void. I held her, attempting to be a tower of strength. But even while I clung to her, my own breathing got away from me, and I began to whimper loudly, as if I were being tormented from the inside out.

Activity is the mourner's best remedy. Chris' final arrangements kept me occupied for the next few days. But from my own eyes, the tears ran in a slow, steady stream, from the moment he died to the day we buried him, even for several days after. I didn't realize until he was gone how much of me was still entranced by him. I did finally tell Elizabeth, but to my relief, she told me she had always known. I kept watch while the poor girl retreated to my room, where I let her rest from this last trauma. I think a part of her was relieved that it was over, and she could finally rest. But still, her characteristic expression came over her as completely as ever, and I know it was not as much misery she felt as it was pure terror.

The rains descended. As a gentle mist that summer afternoon. A rather large service had loomed, and would have conquered, had I given in to certain people's good-natured meddling. But I stood my ground, and saw to it that the service was kept simple and private, the way Chris would have wanted it. We had a very small, intimate memorial, with only our closest friends, who were more than glad to be there to support the wealthy Widow Evans, and her newly widowed daughter. Chris' death benefit was even greater than what John's had been.

Have we been blessed, or cursed by good fortune? Was Elizabeth blessed, on the day that Christopher Adam Peele saw her walk out of that little country church? The day he stepped onto our farm? The day the lightning pricked my heart, causing me to love him as much as I had ever loved my own husband? The day Sheriff Morgan Williams rescued them from the grave, with news that I was found before I died? I did think of these things, while I stood in the rain at his gravesite, calmly watching his coffin be lowered into the ground. Elizabeth placed a single red rose on his coffin, with the calmest, most knowing expression I have ever seen on her. She told me that after he was finally lowered away, she felt a sudden peace unlike anything she can describe, that it came close to something like joy, that he was finally free from the pain of living this life.

Can Fate be denied? Where would Elizabeth be, if she had continued down the long dirt road, away from her house of fear? If she had left her husband, when he was a prisoner of the rage that sought to destroy her? What hope would she have had, if she had stopped loving him?

Even though there was a gentle rain that day, I still remember that there were birds talking in the trees. I suppose that "*birds do not always hide from the rain...*" We rode home in a spirit of relief, touched with the pain of mourning. Our beloved had been laid to rest.

Now, we are beloved.

The Music

I had listened to her play the piano over the years, and had often wept. But not because of the beauty of what I heard. It is because such sounds came from my Beloved's imagination, even though she was still a prisoner of her own mind. And though she had worked through much of her discomfort with people, her lack of self-esteem remained evident even to the day she died. In her diaries, I have read her self-hatred, calling herself *"a scared little mouse, a prisoner of ugliness and phobia, drifting through a schizophrenia of melody and colour song."* So many people told her she was beautiful. Why then, could she not believe it?

There is nothing I can say on my own about Elizabeth's music, except that some who claim to know, believe she might be the most gifted composer who has ever lived[1], as purely Mozartian as Franz Schubert, and Gioachino Rossini (whoever they are—I care nothing for any of them). The speed of writing she claimed to have, they say, is impossible. Though she had written music of all kinds, styles and periods, she recorded no more by hand the last eight years of her life (except for a symphony called *Rossini in Vienna*, a few "songs" for solo instruments and piano, and a brief "requiem" mass), though I am sure the melodies I heard her play were probably as new and original as ever. I suppose that Fate did not have a place for a "Carmen Coletti" in the world.[2] Except for me, two professors and a few interested friends, no one in the world has ever heard her music

---

[1] A claim made by Ms. Ida Brooks, lifelong friend and professor of musicology. Though her praise of Elizabeth was often biased and unrestrained, she was insistent upon her talent, believing that she is the equal of Mozart at every level of composition. She believes without apology, that 'Carmen Angelina Coletti' is the world's first female "great composer," and has created "a body of work unrivaled in the history of classical music." Elizabeth scoffs at this evaluation, calling it *"the ramblings of a dear, sweet woman, insane with compassion and pity."* She relates that *"as it is with those who convey ideas through speech, all composers have a measure of ability, conveying ideas through the language of music."*

[2] Ida's studies of the Coletti scores are extensive, enough for her to identify their most ingenious expressions. She claims that apart from the overtures and concertos, the best music is in the 66 original orchestral suites, (labeled as "operas"), to which many of her more than 100 overtures are attached. Among these is a *"comic opera in two acts"*, from the first spring after her imprisonment (age 32), entitled *"The Crown Prince of Melody"* (a title *"The Guilty Mother"* is scratched out), in 24 separate movements, written in 4 days, composed entirely for piano, violin, cello and orchestra. Brooks notes that this score is "the third in the Beaumarchais Trilogy, filled with laughter and pain." After a performance of this score on the piano, Ida's insistence on publication for Carmen's music grew to the point of contention. She claims that her opera suites "beg to be heard…they are the least antiquated of all her scores… evoking the magic of Rossini and Mozart without effort, though with heavy romantic and modern scoring, exploding with the power of Tchaikovsky's most Italian ballet, and melodic beauty such as was never imagined." Ida believes that from childhood, "the spirit spoke to Carmen more frequently than any composer in history, with unequaled ingression to a world where none other have gone so often." Ida was often disturbed over the quality of Elizabeth's music—sometimes to concerns over Fate itself—and whether or not its discovery was truly meant to be. Elizabeth writes *"my house is Melody, where I am content to live alone."*

performed, and she had refused every request to allow it to be published. A professor of musicology once told me that her overtures and concertos would "become world famous overnight."

As to her own playing, it has been described as "unearthly," and "fearful." There were times when I was awakened by a Coletti sonata, and could not convince myself that I was truly awake, as her playing and her music could be haunting and hypnotic, as if inspired by a ghost or a spirit.[3] Her favorite piece to play was a short, obscure trifle by Mozart, a melancholy adagio for glass harmonica that she transcribed for the piano, that she said always reminded her of her mother, *"sad and beautiful,"* a piece she had nicknamed *"Ice and Snow,"* but later *"with apologies to Antiquity, 'The Death of Melody.'"* I often heard this played when she believed I was not aware, likely during a gray, rainy day, or especially under gray winter skies, when a new snow had fallen. If I was lucky enough to be about when the mood struck her, I was held where I sat or stood, enraptured, while her playing took on a somber, mysterious tone— wistfully elegant, sad, full of grace and beauty, as though the piano itself was apt to sing with more *brio*, but could not, because it was on the edge of tears. One of these, I recorded in secret—which I hold precious without guilt, though I know it was meant for her ears only. Her opinion of her own

---

[3] Despite a highly developed performing technique, Elizabeth had no praise of her talent, calling herself *"a fourth rate nothing"* on the piano. Though her posture at the piano was natural and relaxed, she sat very still, and did not sway and rock her head when playing lyrical, flowing pieces. Even if blindfolded, her fingers glided up and down the keyboard smoothly, drawing all types of sound from the keys seemingly without effort. Her playing did not lack power, though it embodied all the nuance and subtlety of a seasoned, gifted virtuoso. In her early days of mastering the keyboard, her body language was often severe and aggressive, leaning forward and banging feverishly on the keys. Although she had composed for the instrument since she was a child, Elizabeth did not learn to play the piano until she was 33 years old.

music was ambivalent, calling it *"a feeble attempt at Rossinian romanticism, with predilection for Mozartian misery."*

Elizabeth had a sensory condition, or disorder, called *synesthesia* (joined senses), which allowed her to literally "see" the music she heard or composed. She claimed the first time it happened was age 13, when she heard the overture to *The Barber of Seville*[4]. She called it *"...a blue and white symphony, flared like a comet's tail..."* The fusion of melody, harmony and rhythm acted as a key of sorts, opening the door to this ability, and she had loved Rossini ever since. I suppose this was her right compensation for the pain of life she was given. She says a great concerto is *"a wall of one flowing color, streaked by a single, dancing line of another..."* As a child, she wrote down the notes as best she could (developing into a strange code, which she abandoned as an adult), but she could hardly have explained the amazing sounds she heard.[5]

---

[4] Among the collected works are an orchestral suite from *The Barber of Seville*, and several dozen *"Concerto Suites,"* representing all 39 of Rossini's operas and three of his religious masses. Of the Violin Concerto from the *Stabat Mater* she writes, *"From [Myung-Whun] Chung, his Vienna Philharmonic, the Cujus Animam ...From [Giuseppi] Patané, his opera orchestra in Vienna, the Fac ut portem where Cecilia mourns my Lord and Saviour... and then Vienna to the last, Chung's smooth hand in the Finale—the Sancta Mater: ...interpretations as I have rarely heard, divining the most beautiful violin concerto never written, with voices in the rightful places, except in my mind, and the bars of this prison on paper. I shall hear it in my cathedral forever upon the violin and orchestra. The Allegro moderato, Adagio and Allegro cantabile...it is I, The Italian Girl in Carolina... Amen."*

[5] Although the first piece Elizabeth ever recorded was a sonata for solo harp in F minor (*"A Song For A Harp"*), her first complete orchestral work was a brief concerto for Piano and Orchestra in F major, which appeared to her in sections when she was 12 years old, on the last day of her fifth grade year. Before that time, from the age of four, every composition was fragmentary, many of which she recorded later as they had originally appeared in her mind. The brief concerto, *"in the manner of the boy Mozart,"* resided in her memory for several months, until she was able to record the individual parts to her satisfaction. At the end of her fifth grade year, she was taken out of school, and isolated on her mother's farm until she was 21. If the days with her mother and husband are all considered, Elizabeth was isolated in the country and abused for 20 years.

From where these melodies appeared she never knew, nor could she force them. But if she liked it, she would remember it, and begin to hum it softly. And no matter how long or complex, the piece would form finished in her mind, allowing her to study it and commit it to memory. It all occurred in something like a mild trance, full of instruments, and many strange, three-dimensional shapes moving about. Often I had touched her or called to her, and she would return as if waking from a vivid, powerful dream. She wrote that these are not *"kaleidoscopic splashes of light,"* but are *"vivid, geometric patterns that often dazzle with their beauty, like a flake of snow."* She said only the best performances could activate it, and rarely did she ever hear anything played the way she heard it in her mind's cathedral. Apparently, the music of Vivaldi[6], Mozart, and Rossini produce the most *"impossibly inspired shapes of simple complexities that can be drawn or conceived…"*

I suppose that Rossini's overtures and operas[7] (especially *The Barber of Seville*), Schubert's *Italian Overture in C (D. 591)* and *Piano Quintet in A*

---

[6] Her studies of baroque music are sporadic at best, but intensely focused on Antonio Vivaldi, culminating during the winter of her confinement. In baroque music, she favors the so-called "baroque sound," where pitches are lower and strings more distinctly expressive. From her 'Winter's Prison' is a Concerto for Harp and Orchestra in C major *"in the style of Handel"* called *The Advent*, written in January, one of only two concertos produced during her entire imprisonment (the rest chamber music and short orchestral pieces). The harp concerto is perhaps significant in that it coincides with her earliest copy from *The Messiah*, a version of "The Trumpet Shall Sound" made from pure memory, where the oboe replaces the male voice throughout. She had since adapted several movements from Handel's oratorio, an orchestral suite she claimed was totally unintentional, but of which she writes *"begs her often."* From her imprisonment (at 31 years old), there are two arrangements for keyboard and string orchestra—*What Child is This?* and *O Little Town of Bethlehem.*

[7] Of her many transcriptions from Rossini operas, she relates that *"with no other Opera composer, not even Mozart, is this possible on such a grand scale—being that Rossini's Opera displays orchestral emphasis unrivaled, drawing power from Mozart's grandest*

major (D.667), characteristic dances of Tchaikovsky's *Swan Lake* and *The Nutcracker,* along with <u>all</u> of Mozart[8] and Beethoven represent Elizabeth's full neoclassical ability. From what I have heard on her piano, (particularly from an original overture or concerto), her rhythmic changes are inspired and effortless, her harmonies are often bizarre and mysterious, and her melodic inspiration is extremely high[9]. She writes that her ballet music

---

concerto writing, but ingeniously incorrect and fragile, so requiring ingenious performance, to explore the limits of possibility for entertainment alone…this, often to the complete disposal of the libretto…the classical beast was buried on August 3rd 1829… " In her mind, the two composers are *"polar opposites—literally, two sides of the same genius, being that Mozart's perfect orchestral scores strive for opera, while Rossini's perfect opera strives for the orchestral, forcing even the singers to express like musical instruments… "* She notes that although Mozart *"made the most serious display of ability possible, Rossini made possibly the most frivolous. But while [Mozart] is the highest acclaimed composer of all time, he died in poverty, while [Rossini] is the most criticized, dying a millionaire… "* According to her, some of the 'Rossini Transcriptions' would be *"powerful and entertaining concertos <u>never</u> written, a worthy alternative to the concert repertoire, effortless along the timeline, from where Beethoven and Mozart laboured to their deathbed. "*

[8] In her diaries, I have seen more references to Mozart's concertos than any other: she believes that his Piano Concertos 19, 20 and 21 are *"one complete trilogy, the pinnacle of his inspiration, born from a craving to write Italian comic opera. But who can know it, merciful Heaven, for have they ever been properly spoken, with thunder and lightning? Such light scratchings I hear! Who in this day and time, except in the cathedral, from the Players of Orchestra's Light? Harmonies blended to cause new colors—their heavy, smooth basses lift me to Heaven in [every key]!* She refers to her own early concertos as *"sad and otherworldly, with strange harmonies… born of Haydn and Mozart, but with sudden modulations of surprising wit. They are like the early overtures, with passing triplets and dotted eighths hopping about, even a tiny crescendo or two—all with melodies from the River Valley—oh, what a dream I was in! This is a miracle, being that they are not totally naïve, yet written by a lonely child on a dirt farm. Is there a God? "*

[9] Ida Brooks believes that as with all great composers, Carmen distinguishes herself from all others in at least one genre. Among the many hundreds of chamber pieces are 33 *"quartet[s] for strings,"* scored for the proper instruments (2 violins, viola and cello), including one labeled *"O Indian Summer",* her first in the genre. These are profoundly unique in expression (esp. *"The Armageddon Flower"),* peculiar and dramatic (some with only 3 movements), distinguished by long, melodically brilliant expositions, followed by one instrument in extended solo, displaying command over exquisite vocal line, as though it

"rises from the east, burning blue and black fire," one bearing the title *The Golden Iris.* Her piano concertos[10], of which are 32, span the years of composition ages 12 to 37 *"to chronicle the years of torment,"* her last being inspired by the death of her husband.[11] A few of the melodies she has written are probably among the most beautiful ever composed (though this is likely bias on my account). From what I gather, she adores Bach and Chopin, but cares very little for composers like Brahms, Schumann and

---

sings an aria—with the other instruments in rich, polyphonic accompaniment. Characteristic are the beautiful, songlike melodies, both classical and romantic, the trademark of her composition. In all of the Coletti quartets, the cello makes one lengthy solo appearance where there are no other instruments played, conveying the sound of a lonely, phantom cadenza.

[10] Of the 1776 original and adapted scores, about 600 are concertos, concerto transcriptions and single movements, or many labeled as *"aria for [solo instrument] and orchestra."* One of these, a concerto in G minor for Cello and Orchestra, contains an andante labeled *"The Farmer's Aria."* Carmen Coletti's last nine piano concertos (Nos. 24-32) are the peak of her imagination, defying all formal conventions, displaying melodic brilliance and rhythmic inspiration "unheard of in the known classical repertoire." Included is *"The Winter Concerto"* (No. 24 in A major, 'Elizabeth's Concerto'), written in the winter of her imprisonment. The Piano Concerto No. 31 in C major titled *"The Second Coming of Christ"*, contains four movements rather than the traditional three and, according to Ida Brooks, "would render all other piano concertos obsolete for a time." (The four parts of this book are named after the four movements of the "Christ Concerto"). The notation in her original scores is remarkably small and condensed, likely a product of her childhood fear of being discovered, or having enough new paper on which to write. Piano performances of her music reveal a mastery of either form or formlessness in her writing, with a predominance of inspired, operatic melodies—the originality of which are striking, and of which she says is the only *"truly new thing"* in her music. Very few of her scores have been transcribed to formal reading copy.

[11] Elizabeth's longest autograph score is 800 pages (a formal hand copy from the handwritten original of nearly 400pp), written in four months, labeled *"Opera in four acts"*, with various instruments as substitutes for mezzo-soprano, soprano, tenor and bass, with references to a chorus for children. This final 'opera without words' (No. 66) contains her last overture (No. 109), which includes a brief part for piano with no orchestral accompaniment. The work is titled *Maria.* Although no storyline is attached to the music, the title is taken from the name given to the child she gave birth to eight months after her husband's death. The infant girl was a still birth, and is buried near her husband's grave.

Berlioz, and considers modern atonal style *"a travesty."* Of modern music, she says *"[John] Williams plays the truest fanfares for the common man... such sublime symphonies and concertos they are, born from Tchaikovsky's pen. In the Superman Overture, as it displays the blue names in the second heaven, I hear a divine prophecy, but spoken only in this recording alone on film, and not anywhere else this overture is heard; it is the power of God, as is his lamentation for the Holocaust, where the violin mourns The Girl in Red..."* She says there is no wonder that Haydn was Rossini's favorite composer[12] as a child. *"The Symphony No. 94,"* she writes, *"is a bolt of lightning. A Divine attack on pride and hypocrisy, elitism and complacency. It is Truth. God is Truth."* Apparently, Bizet's *Carmen* was her concern in retirement, as well as arias by Verdi and Puccini. She says Cecilia Bartoli sings bel canto *"as the angels intend...in beauty of tone and expression, but with the Love of Christ...and Humility."* In Rossini's parlor song *The Legend of Marguerite,* she reflects, *"Cecilia lowers me gently beneath the Earth... then with* [Bellini's] *Go, Fortunate Rose, raises me up again."* All of this, I know only from a deep reading of her Rose Diaries. As time passes however, I hear her piano's ghostly voice less and less, and I rarely have to go looking for her in her cottage of melody and song.

---

[12] Her love for Rossini's music was profound, particularly his overtures, believing them to be *"...diamonds in a sea of rock stones, children of Figaro's Joy and Giovanni's Sorrow— twelve are enthroned at Olympus."* Among her collected works for keyboard are twelve solo piano scores, from various Rossini overtures, including *La cambiale di matrimonio (The Marriage Contract), La scala di seta (The Silken Ladder), Tancredi, Il Signor Bruschino, L'Italiana in Algieri (The Italian Girl in Algiers),Il Barbiere di Siviglia (The Barber of Seville), Il turco in Italia (The Turk in Italy), La Cenerentola, La gazza ladra (The Thieving Magpie), Semiramide, Il viaggio a Reims (The Journey to Reims)* and *Guillaume Tell.* According to her, among all great orchestral works in music history, great performances of these are the hardest to achieve, as *"performing Rossini's music is like walking barefoot over broken glass, one false step is disaster..."* She insists that unless Rossini's music is released from its operatic prison in full orchestral power, the composer will forever be known as the 'Clown,' rather than the 'Crown Prince of Melody.'

"I worship the Throne of Melody. Queen Melisma rules Bel Canto—her song drifts one syllable into many...

Mozart is the desperation of forgotten youth. The consolation of years. But the diamond of my eye, My light of golden string is the Swan of Pesaro 'til the world is passed...thirty nine treasures hath borne from thee! Would that they could glisten with truth for the world at large, played in the Great Music Hall, above the Valley of Azurean Sand!

I once wrote with Fires of Heaven. Harmonies burned me With Sun's Energy, 'til I had scratched a thousand pieces into feeble life. But as youth fades, so too does desire for newest Fruits of Jubilee. I must travel too great a distance through my ice world, my sand infinity, my wilderness of theory to find even a single phrase I should like to remember. The need diminishes with time, and I fear it may wither, 'til there be no more melodies to write...

Whole suites for Orchestra. Ballets set to the hours. Operas without words, concertos of every type known, and some unknown. Symphonies, chamber pieces for the Lion or the Bird in the Woods... sonatas for every instrument imaginable. Most of these visit me on their own, as I do not enjoy forced composition, disliking the majority of what it produces. I prefer when they call to me.

Tormenting, haunting day or night dreams until I write them down, performing so many of them in full on my piano. How Chopin and Beethoven colour the air around me. But alas, upon the keys, my dearest Rossini is among the least of these! The orchestra was his muse! Winds and strings bear the flowers of that genius, burning brighter even than Beethoven's divine orchestra more times than often!

What am I?

Ludwig's Harmony, colored by Gioachino's Rhythm and Wolfgang's Melody, some of it gathered into modernity, music soaring upon Muse's Wing, rising the heights of my desire. When I die, and only then, perhaps someone can find use for them. Carmen Coletti's overtures may delight the world someday. Or perhaps not!

What am I?

I am nothing!

The Garden

$\mathcal{I}$ve noticed that a curious thing seems to happen with money. When it reaches a certain mass and quantity, it combusts like a star, glowing and radiating its own energy. From that point, it has the power to sustain itself for an eternity.[1] I admit that I was glad to see every stalk of that monstrous cornfield harvested for the last time, and I did not oversee the dismantling and removal of those ugly grain bins from this property. Regardless of what is said about the evils of money, it brings along with it a relief, and peace of mind that cannot be readily achieved without it.

---

[1] The death of Christopher Peele left a total benefit of 20 million dollars in trust, uniquely divided among various investment firms at the turn of the 21st century. Six years after her husband was buried, by age 39, her securities fortune had tripled to 60 million, despite several philanthropic concerns for causes. At the time of her death, Elizabeth's estate was valued at nearly 100 million dollars.

The few years we spent in the old farmhouse seem like a distant memory. The land that it once sat upon now lays bare, part of the massive landscape that is her Peele Estate—an infinite, old world-like property she oddly named *Amherst Lake*, which I surnamed *St. Carmen-in-the-Fields*, that has drawn the curious from hundreds of miles away. Isolation may have once been her curse, but I think it had become a blessing. She rested comfortably in the upper room of this grand, brick mansion house. At times, she drifted down the long, castle-like hallways, visiting the many fine rooms, glancing over the elegance she created, looking at the gold and crystalline things she collected. She was at peace when standing at the open door of her balcony during a rainstorm, gazing through the mist, across the acres that once bore part of that giant field. Now, it is an ocean of beautiful green grass, with many newly planted trees far away in the distance. Her private cottage of gray brick is in the back of our Southern Palace, where she used to spend many days immersed in that strange world, like a dark figure drifting to and fro.

Her agoraphobia had diminished considerably before she died. But I am afraid that her social phobia remained, and even to her deathbed, she was still prone to bouts of panic, and even auditory hallucinations and mild schizophrenia. I had tried to coax her into psychiatric care many times, but she would hear nothing of it, and even while I speak such foolishness, I know it was not meant for her. I shudder to think of the long tedious sessions of probing and brainwashing, and the mountain of medications they would have buried her under. What would mind pills have done to her creative abilities, if not kill them completely? I am grateful that life had allowed her a natural healing, without having been subjected to the horrors of psychiatric medicine. It is my experience, that any person truly worth remembering has not mastered sanity to any great measure.

I know her mind was at peace, when she awoke in these grand surroundings, early on any warm summer's day. There are few pleasures greater than the long stroll around the infinity of these grounds. She drew inspiration from nature's serenity and the peace of solitude. The shade trees, the fountains, the marble shelter and the statues, and the feeders for the birds, and the Great Rose Garden, where it seems every kind and color of rose flourishes in harmony. All of these worked together on her mind and spirit, until I know she often wept from feelings of pure joy. I know that for whatever shortcomings she had, she had paid for in full with the sweat of misery, and the blood of pain and suffering.

In every Eden, a rain must fall.

The Passenger

I am thankful at least, that we could enjoy long drives together. How I lived for those times when we went on a trip, usually to some big city, sometimes far away. She happily carried along her old travel bag, which she would not throw away, but which I made her conceal inside something larger and less hideous. For some reason, she did not care for suitcases. But does anyone?

I think among her deepest pleasures was the stroll through the grand music stores, through the sections of classical music. There are many lovely sopranos on the disc covers, some bearing a glimpse of her in their features, most who do not. But there was one single cover photo which always captured me, bearing the title *The Very Best of Maria Callas*. This somber, arresting photograph was a full face portrait—tinted the palest violet, where the face is lit, turned slightly, with the side of the head in darkness, save a glimpse of the ear. Her eyebrows are thick, but shaped and arched; her dark eyes are lowered, as if gazing at a place in her memory. The shape of her ivory face is perfect, her nose slopes this same perfection, and her lips are the ruby red of crimson. In the beautiful woman's eyes is a distant longing. A profound, indefinable sadness.

My friends understand her a little better—now that she's gone. But I had disappointed them more than once over the years, having to tell them I would be driving with only Elizabeth and me in the car. They tolerated her admirably, though I understand if they did not care for her goth moodiness. I shudder to think what people imagined of her sometimes. She had grown into herself, and was very comfortable lurking alone. I think that if I hadn't coaxed her from time to time, she would have never left this house. Is it true? Would she really have been trapped here?

What would she have done, if I had died instead?

> *"I savor the loveliest feeling when we're speeding the highways. I cannot relate my joy as I soar into the sky with my mind. I watch every car as if it is a Golden Wheel, and sometimes I stare into a person's face from the safety of our car. I often feel brave enough to endure the reaction in a person's eyes when I stare. As long as Momma is here, their arrows have no power. Mother Vera is beautiful. Her Love is beautiful.*

What is better than watching the city limits dissolve into the countryside, until there is nothing left but grass and trees, and maybe a field of cows or horses? My brain often tries to tell me exactly how many I see, but I always ignore it. It is a part of my mind that troubles me, and I do not wish it to develop. For what purpose can it be, except to vex my fragile nerves?

If it is Autumn, the forests are my favorite thing to see. The yellow trees call to my vision. There is a place in the Piedmont that I always remember, rounding a certain curve on Highway 40 towards Winston- Salem, where the road overlooks a vast, rolling spread of trees, rising like the base of a mountain hill. Once, I stared into the center of them, and I felt my awareness heighten, and my mind began to haze into a higher state, and it began to calculate the number of trees. But I quickly shook my head and surfaced from this drowning. It was as though I could suddenly see every individual tree, where before there had only been a forest of them…"

The Photograph

*F*or a long time after her husband's death, we tried valiantly to resist the depression. It crept into our old farmhouse like a spirit. Descending a cold touch, until it found the happiness I had worked so hard to build, laying waste to every part of it. I retreated back into isolation for the better part of two years while our mansion was being built, drifting behind the walls of my Gray Palace, my fortress of misery. My dream daughter took refuge in her music, and some of what she wrote during this time is among the most hauntingly beautiful that I have ever heard. How is it possible that she was afraid to share such a gift?

But it was not Elizabeth's death, nor was it really her diaries that drove me to this insanity of mine. These words are being written now because one day, I found her sitting at the living room desk with a few old pictures scattered about. Her eyes were so full of tears. I asked her why she was crying which perhaps didn't matter, because we both seemed in perpetual weeping.

She showed me a photograph I had taken of her many years before, standing in a gray dress, in front of the little house she used to live in. The woman in the picture was like a phantom, a ghost of the suffering she had endured since she was a little girl. She said it was *"a picture in twilight and darkness."* Indeed, it was a portrait in gray. An echo of a life replete with sorrow. The expression on the woman's face was extraordinary. I saw the depth of humility and regret—colored by an epic fear and dread of the future.

I suppose Fate has its own will and purpose, and from that autumn, through the winter, the spring, and deep into the summer, I was lost in a world I thought I would never have to know again. My heart and mind were burdened with the pain of memory, and I endured months of a kind of waking dream, using her own journals privately as a guide. I took no creative liberties to speak of, emerging from death with the material that would be used to craft our story. But had it not been reassembled proper, I fear that it may have never seen the light of day, and I would have surely been cursed to dust.

The Diaries

He psychology during her imprisonment was one of fear and extreme depression, tinted with an enduring hope that someday it would end, and things would get better. Hope and despair kept equal company in her mind that entire year. Her terror often manifested in her little notebooks. Some passages she wrote, musical and otherwise, are dripping with a Hellish dread of the future. But when the fear did subside, what remained was the epic sadness, which grew, until it spilled over into a kind of poetic memoir. An epic poem she calls *The Evening Day*[1], about the woman who gave her life, and took it from her so abundantly.

---

[1] A collection of over 100 poetic, introverted chapters (or *prosetics*), subtitled *Autumn of the White Woods,* recalling her days as a youth on her mother's farm. If every passage in this unintentional 'memoir' is to be believed, it is clear that her mother suffered from many psychological disorders, including those of classic social anxiety and sexual deviance. The

Her journals are flowered with hundreds of little reflections. Poems and scenes which saw fit to occupy her mind when there were no melodies to write—musings on nature, such as *The West Wind* and *Afterlife of Green*[2], or on the nature of mankind, in those bearing such alarming titles as *A Dead Woman's Diary* or *A Good Wife On the Eve of Dying*[3]. It is a fact that

---

diaries give allusions to veiled molestations when Elizabeth was 12, one during a punishment on her bed, in which the mother pressed against her while holding her hand over Elizabeth's mouth. Passages suggest she was neglected and physically abused as an infant, along with strict and deviant (sexual) discipline in early childhood. The child's punishments were often sadistic and severe, continuing well into adulthood. After suffering a rape by her mother at age 19, Elizabeth endured a deeply incestuous and abusive relationship for the next two years, before she was suddenly and mysteriously abandoned. Barbara Jean Coletti's parents were members of a snake handling sect of mountain Pentecostals—a remote community in the Blue Ridge Mountains of Virginia.

[2] Portions of a heartsick flow of verse set to music, resulting from the untimely death of her spiritual mentor, Miss Ida Hirschman Brooks. Before Ida's death from a massive heart attack at age 62, she had planned to introduce many of the 'Coletti transcriptions' to the public (entitled 'The Rossini Project'). Ida's plans had implications far beyond Elizabeth's knowledge or intent, beginning with the transference of her entire catalogue to formal copy, including their eventual publication, and the possible premiere of a Coletti overture, symphony and concerto in a local music hall. After Ida's death, Carmen's interest in music, especially her own, seemed to have died as well. Her last composition (age 44) is labeled *"The Garden of Antiquity,"* a brief Mass in D minor based solely on verses from the book of Psalms (Ch. 37, verses 4, 5, 8, 11, 27, 29). This likely 'Requiem' is inscribed *"Mass for a Crystal Rose—my last to thee, O Lord. Beg thy mercy, accept this gift to thy Throne."* In the years before her death, Elizabeth's interest in music had diminished so severely that it could be called a retirement, often with her being unable to listen to a single note of music for many months. Her latter writing consists of reminiscences, brief attempts at poetic verse, with no commentary of them whatsoever, nor opinion of any author or literary concern. Although her reading library was extensive, the only writer she had ever spoken of with interest was Emily Dickinson. Before dying in her sleep at age 45, Elizabeth was prone to long bouts of extreme depression, sometimes not leaving the house for years at a time.

[3] Prose parts of a collection of letters revealing how she met her husband, and their descent into violence and despair. Unlike *Autumn of the White Woods*, which was composed entirely during the spring, summer and fall of her imprisonment, the letters comprising *A Portrait in Gray (The Harvest Moon, a.k.a. Call of an Angry Blackbird)* were scattered over many years, written before and long after her husband's death. Their language is often terse and direct, with many allusions to her musical and poetical abilities. The importance of

every poem, every "vision" in these books is born from her own mysterious psychology; her memory, or her creative mind. Themes of Suffering, Death and Redemption—a tapestry of our human condition. While drafting her private verses for these volumes, I learned that for some, *"unearned suffering is not always redemptive in this life, and that perhaps there is only Fate, Destiny, and the Will of God."*

Elizabeth's diaries are so different from these private letters. The language is more musical, more fluid and alive, and is decorated with poetry. Even now, I read some of the many things my Beloved wrote about her childhood, and I wonder how it is that such things were possible— where it all came from, and how any of it came into being. I must admit that thoughts of her mother strike fear in my soul, and I often feel powerless in the shadow of her memory.

She was battered, and tormented by her birth mother until she was 21. And though the pain her husband inflicted was considerable, it pales to what her mother achieved upon her flesh, and within her spirit. There was a ruthlessness, a spiteful, malicious savagery behind "Barbara Coletti's" contempt. For a long time, Elizabeth refused to acknowledge that her mother's *sanity* had been breached by clinical depression, brought on by a lifetime of unfulfilled longing and painful recollection. Though she was not an evil woman, a part of her existed separate from the good, and she often resided whole heartedly within a sadistic pleasure, causing her to make her daughter suffer without hesitation and without remorse.

Like so many people, I had endeavored to write, knowing there were seeds of a book in how I came to know Elizabeth Peele. What I didn't know is that every character, every situation, every thought, feeling and

---

these chapters is paramount to all of The Rose Diaries, having been the main inspiration for the novel *The Farm Girl's Opera* (a.k.a. *Elizabeth).*

philosophy was already recorded in her journals, written for her eyes only. But on a strange, rainy autumn day, reminiscent of days I have known, I was compelled to ask her what was in all of the beautiful volumes she had been writing in for so long.

The words that I read—the images they burned into my soul…changed my life forever.

V. E

ABOUT THE AUTHOR

Jonathan Lovejoy is a graduate of the University of North Carolina at Greensboro, with a B.A. in Religious Studies, and a graduate of Liberty University with an M.A. in Theological Studies. He currently lives in Winston Salem, North Carolina.

For more info on the author's life and career, visit jonathanlovejoy.com.

www.ingramcontent.com/pod-product-compliance
Lightning Source LLC
Chambersburg PA
CBHW060514180626
46817CB00002B/364